ELECTRIC STUFF

A NOVEL

JUSTIN ZEPPA

For Elín

CHAPTER 1
Tumbleweed

THE ARMBAND MEMORIALIZING the death of Charlie Conroy's second father was too tight.

Charlie looked down to where it was choking the left sleeve of his baseball jersey like a garter worn by 19th century riverboat gamblers. The black, elastic fabric was being strained to its limits, though this was not due to Charlie being in particularly good shape. The gaugeless blood pressure cuff of mourning was small on purpose, the result of his cagey mother instituting an arm-measurement lineup and then doing the math on the least amount of fabric needed to establish adequate bereavement.

The embroidery in white thread of the late Herbert Tinley the Third's initials was the most successful part of the tribute. Gazing down the third base line where the rest of his teammates had lined up, Charlie could not help feeling like the HTIII-band lent a certain panache to the otherwise silly uniform of the Tombstone Tumbleweeds. Adobe pink in color, the home jerseys screamed for attention. It was as if the vibrant hue could add a layer of excitement to the otherwise lackluster Single-A baseball it was representing. The armband stood out like a sorrowful racing stripe, though Charlie would be the first to admit that he was a sucker for such ornamentation. The league patches celebrating various anniversaries or deaths, along with the fine needlework of the hat logos, had always been among the most satisfying features of his extended minor league experience.

He forced himself to look up at the small dais that had been constructed just left of the pitcher's mound. It was hardly worth the time it had taken to put together, as it raised the participants of the impending pre-game ceremony a mere six inches off the ground. But, he supposed, it was slightly more formal than walking out to an arbitrary place in the middle of the field, performing the ceremony, and then walking away.

His late stepfather, whom Charlie had always thought of more as his mom's second husband, beamed from a blown-up photo placard, that was perched on an easel borrowed from the Tumbleweeds' locker room. A man of merry paunch and blinding teeth, Herbert had been a larger-than-life personality. He'd spoken loudly and spent freely, though this bravado had been built on a sinkhole of shady business practices that had earned him a lackluster reputation in the community.

This he had ignored, throwing lavish parties for the right people and serving as an easy quote for the local media regarding any goings-on that might impact his business interests. Not that his business was interesting; the HerbCo Fishing Supply outlets may have had inventories bulging with spoons, spinners, and jigs, but none could lure back the customers who had been abandoning the drowsy aquatic pastime over the past decades. It therefore seemed appropriate to send his memory off to the Valhalla of shitty businessmen in front of a partially full ballpark's worth of his former customers.

Those attending were applauding politely when prompted but did not seem remotely invested in the tribute. The truth was that Herbert had done nothing particularly memorable for the community beyond owning the team and convincing the taxpayers to fund a new ballpark he then named after himself. And Tinley Park *was* a very respectable field relative to others found across the lowest of minor leagues. But no matter how cushioned the seats were or how strong the WiFi, no amount of tax dollar infusions could make the baseball team interesting. As such, Herbert was memorable in a way that had few pleasant memories attached. Charlie himself felt almost nothing for him or his memory.

A smattering of applause rippled from the stands as the public address announcer introduced the recent-widow and current-owner of HerbCo Enterprises, Margaret Tinley. Charlie's feelings toward his mother were the exact opposite of those toward Herbert, and he sometimes wondered if he cared *too* much for her. She crossed the dais and shook the announcer's hand. She wore the requisite black suit of mourning and hid her eyes behind dramatically large sunglasses. The clapping quieted as she approached the microphone, head bowed. After taking a moment to gather herself, her voice boomed across the ballpark speakers.

"Today we remember Herbert Tinley as a man who loved owning this team and the baseball it played."

She paused, allowing Charlie a moment to process her words; they were honest in their emptiness and had been spoken in a methodical way that suggested they held more meaning than they really did. It was classic Margaret Tinley.

"My husband would have been happy to see all of you here at this, his official memorial service. He always appreciated a strong gate. And an event-based t-shirt, of which there is one for today's memorial, now available at the Tumbleweed Merchandise Outpost."

Charlie raised an eyebrow. *Subtle, Mom.*

"We will remember him as an important part of the Tumbleweed story because he paid for them and named the field after himself. Thank you."

His mother was already off the stage and halfway to the home team's dugout tunnel when the idea of applauding the abrupt speech finally took root with the spectators. Charlie's teammates began to disseminate from their station along the third base line, shrugging before falling back into their familiar routine of warming up. He understood. His mother was not always the easiest character to decode, but one couldn't deny that she said only what she meant. If there was little in the way of sentiment to her speech, that was exactly as she had intended.

He reaffixed his cap with a sharp tug and slid his hand into the second baseman's glove he'd had tucked under his arm. While he was not given to thinking too much about such things, he briefly wondered what this memorial meant to his mother.

Herbert had passed away right before the opening of the season from the types of complications that appear at age 86. Charlie couldn't help but notice that his memorial service had been scheduled only *after* it had become clear that the Tumbleweeds had played themselves right out of the playoffs. It was now late-June and the familiar feeling of waiting until next year had already descended upon the team and its fans.

Attendance had declined accordingly, inspiring some novel attempts at recapturing the public's attention. They'd hired the services of the Boot Hill Historical Reenactors to perform a re-creation of the OK Corral gunfight between the third and fourth innings, but the firing of blanks had frightened the fans and distracted the bullpen. Equally unsuccessful had been the 'Full Count of Monte Cristo' night, in which fans received half-off on fried sandwiches whenever a Tumbleweed count reached three balls and two strikes. This had been a two-pronged initiative, encouraging the Tumbleweed batters to work the pitch count, while also plowing through a surplus of sliced bread that had been the result of sloppy concession supply ordering. A slight uptick at the turnstiles had been encouraging, but the seats and bleachers were left coated in powdered sugar and raspberry jam, calling for park attendant overtime and profit losses all around.

So it was that the embroidered HTIII armbands had been ordered alongside the poster sized blow-up of Herbert's puffy face, and a press release sent out announcing the memorial tribute to the late owner. These steps complete, it was now time for the team Herbert Tinley had owned to play a game befitting his legacy.

THE EXULTANT JOY of feeling the bat make contact with the ball was tempered and extinguished almost immediately. Charlie ran down the first base line and chanced a look just in time to see the ball bloop in the grass right before the infield dirt. Even as he watched the shortstop vacuum up the grounder with ease, he felt obligated to make a push, and pressed his 39-year-old legs as hard as possible. With nine feet left to go, the ball arrived with a *snap!* in the first baseman's glove, and the double play was completed, as was the game.

The Tumbleweeds' hometown fans offered little in response. They had mostly dispersed after the seventh inning stretch, when it had become clear that an eight-run deficit was unlikely to be made up before game's end. Charlie ran through the base regardless, eventually turning to walk his way back to the dugout. There, Tumbleweeds manager, Kurf Plunkett, glowered at him from the top step.

Plunkett was a fireplug of a man, known for little other than having a terrible attitude and a surplus of coarse hair on his forearms. As Charlie trotted down the steps and removed his helmet, the team's skipper approached in his usual position: arms crossed, and brow furrowed. "I thought I told you to lean in."

Charlie's shoulders slumped. He'd been expecting this. "Come on, Skipper, I had a good bead on it. I made contact."

"Dying quails don't count, Conroy, you ignoramus." Plunkett was now in his face in a way that had become disturbingly routine. "Your job is to get on base. When I say lean in, you *lean in.*"

"Skip, I can't do it anymore."

"You can and you will."

Charlie couldn't fault him for his logic – he *could* lean into a pitch. There had been a time, some ten years earlier, when he'd done so for a healthy portion of the season. It had been a record-breaking assault-by-beanball, and his skeletal and nervous systems had never fully recovered. When Charlie swung these days, he did so in a defensive way, chopping wildly to ward off the curse of the forthcoming chin music.

"I was just trying to get a rally going, Skipper."

"You taking one in the ribs *is* the rally, you loser." Plunkett spat and shook his head. "Your dad would be ashamed of you."

The words struck Charlie with more velocity than any hit-by-pitch and he felt his face go red. He knew Plunkett was not speaking of the recently deceased Herbert Tinley. He was talking about his real dad.

Jackie Conroy had been a legendary figure up and down the minors. His had been an electric career in the making, brought to an untimely end under tragic circumstances when Charlie was only eight years old. Beloved by most, Jackie's death had cast a long shadow over Charlie's life. It was an umbra that had forever kept him scrambling for his own glimpse of the sun. And now Plunkett was twisting the knife of shame that had been permanently lodged between his ribs. He turned away to strip his batting gloves, refusing to give Plunkett the pleasure of seeing him in agony.

"You hear me, Connie?"

Charlie grimaced; he hated that nickname. He was about to consider saying as much when a third voice cut across the dugout.

"*I* certainly did."

Player and manager both turned to the voice that came from the darkened tunnel leading to the clubhouse. From the shadows of the doorway emerged Margaret Tinley, still cloaked in her mourning-wear.

Plunkett shook his head in disgust. "Aw hell. Is this what we're doing now? Open door policy on the goddamned dugout?"

"Which one of us *owns* the dugout?"

Plunkett dragged a hand down his face and began pacing the concrete. "Uh-uh. No way. There is *no goddamned way* this is gonna work." He turned and pointed at her. "I don't care what the will says, lady, this ain't a drive-through window. It's a dugout and it's Tumbleweeds only. You want a parent-teacher conference, you can make an appointment, okay? Because this is just *not gonna work.*" He crossed his arms again, apparently satisfied with how he'd laid down the law.

"Kurf, you're absolutely right, twice-over," said Margaret, stepping further into the dugout. Plunkett eyed her, his jaw grinding away on his belabored game day gum. "It's *not* going to work," she said, staring past him and out to the desert that waited beyond the chain link fence of the outfield.

Plunkett didn't respond immediately. Finally, the moment in which Margaret could have qualified her statement passed and he rushed to fill the void. "That's right," he said. "I'm glad we can see eye-to-eye on that."

She turned to face him, a slight smile adorning her otherwise placid face. "Of course."

Charlie's eyes flicked back and forth between them as his decades of experience shot flares up his spine. His mother was rarely so agreeable.

Plunkett looked equally disarmed, but his voice had lost its edge of consternation. "Okay then, I… I guess we'll be seeing you later." He shifted his stance as though clearing the way for her departure.

Margaret remained motionless, her arms neatly crossed.

He squinted at her. "Is there an issue, Mrs. Tinley?"

"Not at all," she said. "It's *exactly* like you said: the dugout is for Tumbleweeds only."

"That's right," said Plunkett. *"My* team. The Tumbleweeds are *my* team."

"Perhaps," she said, shrugging. "But not in the same way that they're *my* team."

Plunkett took a step toward her. "But I'm the manager."

"Are you?" she asked, tilting her head slightly.

Charlie, having incited many of Plunkett's fiery outbursts over the years, saw the familiar flames of rage spark behind his manager's eyes. "You don't have the guts," said Plunkett, his voice quiet, menacing.

Seemingly immune to the palpable tension clouding the air, Margaret took a breezy step toward him. She leaned in. "And *you* don't have the lawyers." She nodded toward the tunnel exit. "Tumbleweeds only."

Now, it was Plunkett's turn to go red in the face. His beady eyes narrowed, a familiar vein pulsating on the side of his forehead. Charlie was worried he was about to spontaneously combust, but finally the surly skipper grunted and spat on the concrete before storming out of the dugout.

His final words echoed from the darkness of the tunnel. *"This goddamned Black Widow…"*

Margaret raised an eyebrow and then turned to her son as though this was all to be expected. "Another vintage performance from you, I see. Why make one out when you can have two, hm?"

Charlie's jaw dropped. "Mom! Did you seriously just fire the skipper?"

"I did," she said, turning back to the empty field.

He was shocked. Plunkett had been with the team since he'd been a rookie. The grizzled manager had been scolding him for over two decades. "Well…well, can you *do* that?"

"I'm the owner of the team, I can do whatever I want," said Margaret, her voice calm. "And I've been wanting to do *that* for a long time."

He couldn't believe how easily she was administrating this execution of the Tumbleweeds' leader. Kurf Plunkett had never been an enjoyable man to be around, and he'd always seemed to loathe the young men who played for him. Yet, he'd been a force of consistency in an otherwise tempestuous business. It could never be said that he wasn't always there to tell people what to do and where they were batting in the lineup. "But who's going to replace him?"

"It doesn't matter."

"Mom, we've got a game tomorrow, a doubleheader this weekend–"

"Enough." She whipped off her massive sunglasses and turned to him, her jaw set in grim determination.

Charlie was used to her being annoyed by him, but this examining stare of hers was perplexing. It made him anxious. "Enough-what?"

"Enough of... whatever this is," she said, gesturing to his uniform. "You're done."

"I'm *what?* Wait," he said, a thought occurring to him, "you mean I'm going to Double-A?"

"I mean you're retiring from baseball. This madness has to stop."

Margaret's voice was clear and steady as she dealt the killing blow, but Charlie could not help thinking there must be some mistake. "Okay, Mom, very funny – maybe not great timing, considering that pink slip you just handed out, but, yeah, you got me." He made his best effort at laughing it off before changing the subject. "Listen, I've been studying the spray charts for the Groom Lake Grays and I think they've been reverse-engineering our defensive shifts. So, tomorrow, when we get out there–"

"Charlie," said Margaret. "It's time for some straight talk." She stepped toward him and stared up, into his eyes. Her tone was all business. "You are the worst player in minor league baseball."

It took him a moment to process this. The words were heavy. They might have buried another man. However, in the face of this blunt truth, Charlie found himself almost relieved to hear it spoken aloud. He wasn't stupid – he knew he was a poor player.

The chart of his motivations these past 22 years had begun with high hopes. He was the son of Jackie Conroy, the best player to be forever stuck in the minors. He had spent almost ten seasons waiting for his inheritance of skills to arrive, assuming one more year would be the difference. He spent another three seasons coping with the fact that they would *not* be arriving, and the rest of the seasons patching it together when Plunkett needed a warm body to throw to the hungry wolves of the opposing team. This was combined with the floating sensation that takes hold of a person when it is finally understood that the future they had envisioned for themselves would not be coming to pass.

His career had been the very definition of insanity, but there had been no other option he'd been able to conceive of for himself. He knew he was a local punchline, but he had pressed on. Pressed on to please the memory of his father and to support his mother in her declining second marriage to the team's owner. It was a purpose that allowed him enough solace to get to sleep at night when he was left to face the shadows of his failings in the same bedroom he'd grown up in.

Yet, her words incited a defensiveness he was not expecting, and he found himself taking exception with her assessment. "Don't you think that's kind of debatable, Mom?" It was the flailing of a man who has just had the rug of the only career he'd ever known pulled out from underneath him.

Margaret was unmoved. "The only thing to be debated is whether or not you're the worst player in the entire history of the league." He squinted, as though taking a punch to the gut. Margaret pressed on, now looking over his shoulder at something in the distance. "Chet Fitch from the paper is coming over for the post-game. We'll make the announcement then."

"What about Plunkett?"

"Dead men tell no tales, Charlie. That oaf can put out his own press release if anyone notices him missing." She beckoned to the newspaperman as he approached the dugout. "Chester, you're going to be speaking with Charlie today." With that, she began wandering the length of the dugout, scrolling through something on her phone.

"Wow, lucky me," he said, looking at Charlie. Chet Fitch was a good-natured seller of ad space for the local daily, *The Tombstone Trigger,* and was known for 'reporting' on most of the Tumbleweeds' season from the bar across the street. He took out a small notepad but did not bother to flip it open. "You wanna give me the blow-by-blow on that double play, champ?"

Charlie grimaced, now faced with delivering the day's second eulogy. "Well, uh… actually, I'm retiring today."

"Yeah? No kidding?" Fitch's eyebrows elevated in surprise behind his sunglasses. He flipped the cover of his pad. "That's kind of a big deal, huh?"

The notion of a post-baseball void was starting to take root in Charlie's mind, and it was feeling very much like a big deal. "Yeah, it is," he said. "But I've had a good run." Platitudes – his mother had always stressed the importance of empty words given to fill an empty space.

Fitch thought for a moment, his pen hovering over the pad as he did the math. "So, you started in the league in…"

"'98."

"Right, right, right," Fitch said, chewing on the pen. "Wow, so, that's gotta be a record for the longest spell in Single-A ball, right?"

It was, but Charlie was uncertain if this was something he should be bragging about. He sighed and kept it vague. "Most likely, yeah."

"I'd look it up if anyone cared of course, but–"

"No one cares."

"Right."

"Uh-huh."

Fitch's pen had yet to make a mark on the 30-cent pad, and Charlie began to see it as a symbol of validation; his news would not really be news until the newsman had noted it.

Fitch seemed to pick up on the mix of emotions Charlie was cycling through. "Still, 20 seasons–"

"22."

"22 seasons is not bad for a career utility guy. There could be an angle there. You're like the lousy version of Cal Ripken – a budget Iron Man."

The familiar sound of hearty scoffing erupted from behind Charlie as Margaret joined their conversation. "More like a Starch Man, if you ask me." She chuckled in approval of her burn.

Fitch was also amused. "'Starch Man.' That's a good one, Mrs. Tinley – can I use that?"

"I'd be disappointed if you didn't."

"So, what's the plan, Charlie, now that you're retiring–"

"*Retired,*" Margaret said. "He is now definitively retired."

"Right, right, right. So, what's the plan, guy?"

Charlie took a moment to roll this question over. What *was* the plan? The Tombstone fans deserved the truth and he spoke from the heart. "I have no idea."

His mother stepped forward again. "Charlie thanks all of the fans and is excited for the next phase of his career as a coach."

"Am I?" asked Charlie. The news of his future-doings was arriving at a furious pace.

Fitch turned to him. "Are you?"

Charlie shrugged. "Well, I guess so, sure."

"Where you gonna be coaching?"

Charlie turned to his mother. "Where will I be–"

"He'll be with our Triple-A club in Cape Haddock," she said directly to Fitch. She pointed to his pad. He dutifully scratched one line.

"Cape Haddock…" Fitch frowned for a moment before it hit him. "Oh, the Cola Cans, right? The Cape Haddock Cola Cans?"

"Coelacanths," said Margaret. *"See-luh-canths."*

"Right, right, right," Fitch nodded. "What's a Coelacanth?"

"It's some kind of fish."

"Isn't a haddock already a kind of fish?"

"Goddammit," said Margaret, rolling her eyes, "what do I look like, some kind of Bass Masterson? I'm just the owner – you want answers to the big questions in life, go to the goddamned aquarium."

She returned to scrolling through her phone, leaving Fitch to sheepishly turn back to his interview. "That was your dad's team, right? Your first dad?"

"That's right," Charlie nodded. "We only lived there until I was eight, so I barely remember it."

"He was a helluva player, your dad. Wow."

"That's what you all tell me."

Margaret stared at Fitch, an eyebrow raised. "You're not going to write about any of this, are you."

Fitch chuckled and flipped the notebook shut. "Nah, probably not. You know I only get two inches of column next to the classifieds for this. You'll get the score and *maybe* the memorial."

"Fine," said Margaret. "But try to mention the memorial t-shirts. We need them to start trending in 'viral' fashion so we can break even." She turned to Charlie. "Let's pack up your locker, dear. Then we'll focus on more pleasant matters."

He looked at her in disbelief. "Such as?"

She gave him a tentative pat on the arm. "Let's go to the cemetery."

CHAPTER 2
Tombstone

As was the case with much of Tombstone, the roads and paths spidering through the grounds of the city's third-most-popular cemetery were made of hard-packed, subgrade dirt. Tombstone's Tombstones was a poorly named expanse of land, but one that had found success in a field where such an unfortunate moniker mattered little to its clientele. The plots were covered with fist-sized stones and only the sporadic green of a low tree or the occasional scrags of grasses broke up the monotony of relentless desert brown.

"Herbert didn't make it into Boot Hill, huh?" Charlie asked his mother. They had spent the last ten minutes placing careful, dress shoe-clad footsteps on the path to avoid a rock-induced sprained ankle.

"I never would have thought a 140-year-old graveyard full of crooks would be so exclusive, but there you have it," she said, shaking her head.

Herbert Tinley, having grown up in the golden age of serialized Western radio adventures, had long adored the notion of gunfighters and outlaws. It had been one of his final wishes to be buried next to the infamous McLaury brothers, who had been gunned down by the Earps and Doc Holliday and were buried at what had since become a popular tourist site. In life, Herbert had lobbied the local city council for his own grave to be added, but his bribes and ambiguous threats had not swayed them.

The obvious next choice (which many would have considered to be the obvious *first* choice) was the modern Tombstone cemetery, but they had balked at the size of the monument Herbert had designed for himself. Charlie had never heard of a cemetery making a hard pass on a future internment, but having seen the preliminary sketches for the headstone, knew it was not an unreasonable action. And so, the desert-adjacent Tombstone's Tombstones had gained what was now its most famous burial.

Mother and son crested a low hill and the controversial monument appeared. Forty feet tall and carved from gleaming white marble that had been quarried and shipped from the Italian province of Carrara, the marker towered over the scrub of surrounding desert.

Taking advantage of its height, Charlie and Margaret moved into the shadow it cast. At close range, the myriad details became apparent. At the base was a smooth square detailing the pertinent life and death information of Herbert Tinley the Third, now dead at the age of 86. Atop that was what could only be described as a mound of carved fish, leaping from the stone in various contortions and eye-bulging expressions. At the very top of this narrow, conical pile sat a winged cherub, carved in Baroque style, but wearing a bucket hat and holding a fishing rod made of gold. It was quite simply the dumbest hunk of statuary that Charlie had ever seen.

He glanced over to his mother, as though to confirm the reality of the stone – to prove this was not simply some tacky desert mirage. Margaret's face was largely unreadable. Her lips were tightly pursed, though this was not unusual, and her eyes were hidden behind the massively round lenses of her sunglasses. Charlie thought he saw the twitch of a sneer touch the corner of her mouth.

"It's kind of weird to do a fishing statue in the desert, isn't it?" he asked.

"Perfectly fitting for a man with no taste who *had* to have everything his way," she replied.

It was a grim sentiment, but Charlie had long ago become used to the frostiness between his mother and stepfather. Whichever manner of love or chemistry or tax savings that had brought them together, it had long ago faded into a mutually respectful contempt.

"He liked the cowboy stuff," said Charlie. "Why didn't he just stick with a cowboy theme?"

"Because he was a gaudy jackass who wanted everything!" Margaret said. "'Bury me with the cowboys, Margaret, but make my tomb a tribute to the bounty of the lakes and seas – it's my legacy!' Disgusting."

Charlie took in the collection of effigied sportfish. The white marble made them look like ghosts of all the unfortunate creatures who had fallen prey to the lines and lures of a HerbCo fishing pole. "It's just such a lot of fish, isn't it? Like… a lot."

"Mmm," Margaret nodded. "It's based on an Austrian monument commemorating the end of the plague. Fitting, in that I feel a similar relief."

"That's kind of a silver lining, huh?"

She turned to him, an eyebrow raised. "Tell that to this poor desert," she said, gesturing to the mountain-lined flats surrounding them. "Nature has to be stuck being blighted by this obscenity."

"Maybe it's art?"

"Charlie, it's an abomination! A vulgar abomination. At $800 per cubic foot, no less. And that's *before* the shipping and sculpting."

"Whoa," said Charlie. "That's probably going to eat into your quarterly profits, huh?"

"What profits?" she scoffed.

This came as a surprise. "From the company," he said, turning to her. "The company that pays for the teams and the… the this?" He gestured to the sculpture. He would be the first to admit that he knew very little of the machinations at work within the offices of HerbCo Enterprises, the parent company of HerbCo Fishing Supplies and HTIII Sports Acquisitions, LLC. Herbert, and now his mother, had always run the show. But this seemed like a red flag.

Margaret continued staring up at the marker. "There are no profits. HerbCo Fishing Supplies is belly-up."

"Seriously?"

"Dead in the water."

Charlie began running over the details of HerbCo Enterprises as he understood them. Herbert Tinley had made his small fortune in the fishing supply business, sometime in the 1950s. It was the perfect market for such a man, one that grew every year as the post-war industrial vacation complex exploded, and one that required zero skills beyond tying a feather to a hook.

With these ingredients, Herbert had doggedly built his brand. The results of his toils were a factory and warehouse in downtown Cape Haddock, which had then led to his eventual purchase of three minor league baseball teams. Herbert had previously cared very little for baseball itself but enjoyed the feeling of owning a thing so many others enjoyed. This had been the status quo for decades, so the news of insolvency was shocking.

"But... *how?*"

"We were overextended," said Margaret with a wave of her hand. "We reached beyond the market, pumping out all kinds of idiotic products for a dying recreation."

Charlie considered this for a moment. "It was the flashlights, wasn't it."

His mother groaned. "Don't remind me. Flashlights on the nets, flashlights on the rods – Herbert was obsessed with goddamned flashlights. Always trying to chase the next big thing and stick a flashlight on it. As if it would inherently demand a beam of light." The words rolled out of her mouth in disgust. "All for a world that no longer cares. Who wants to go fishing when you can put pictures of your caprese salad on social media?"

"Isn't that a little judgy, Mom?"

"Not at all. They're absolutely right," she said with finality. "The lakes and rivers are riddled with bugs and scat and...*wildlife.*" She said the word like it was an accusation. "And who wants to be on the ocean? It's full of garbage!"

"I thought Herbert booked Duncan Roughy to be the celebrity spokesman?"

Duncan Roughy was a champion sport fisherman, now in his 90s. He'd had a popular Sunday morning public access fishing show in the Midwest for over thirty years, and still managed to put out a weekly podcast about the angler's craft. He'd been a big get for HerbCo.

Margaret rolled her eyes. "He did! And then they got into some blow-up over politics, and now Roughy's blasting HerbCo on every episode. Obsolete idiots, both of them."

Margaret turned back to the grave. Her body language was reluctant, and Charlie strongly suspected she was going through the motions expected of a widow. As though she'd read his thoughts, she glanced down at her phone to check the time and began her private eulogy.

"You were a good man, Herbert. Or a decent man, anyway." After a moment she corrected herself. "You were a man." Charlie nodded at the accuracy of this. "And while you've left us in this desolate hellscape to pick up the pieces of your so-called 'empire,' at least you've left us with almost nothing to do it with."

Charlie waited for her to speak further, but nothing more came. "So, what's the plan? What happens to the company?"

"This *is* the company," she said, nodding to the tombstone. "Good lord, the expense of this nonsense. What a waste."

Charlie had rarely seen her so abhorred. "Well, it's what he wanted, so–"

"Herbert Tinley is dead," she said firmly. "And from now on, I'll be the one who calls the shots on the family holdings. And the affiliated luxury rocks. HerbCo is as good as dead, and after this season, the Tumbleweeds are too."

"Wait, what?" Charlie had been a Tumbleweed for so long, this made him feel as though a part of him was literally withering up and tumbling away.

"I'm selling the team and we're getting out of here altogether."

"So, firing Plunkett was–"

"An impulsive assertion of my authority, yes," she said with a shrug. "It felt good, so I did it. And if he thinks he's getting a letter of recommendation, he's got another thing coming."

A thought occurred to Charlie. "What's happening with the Deadwoods?" Their Double-A affiliate was a member of the bleak Badlands circuit. It was not a division to be envied, but it had always been Charlie's hypothetical next stop, had he ever been able to play his way out of the Tumbleweeds.

"The Deadwoods will soon be kindling for the fire sale," Margaret said. There was little pity in her voice.

"So, it's Coelacanths or bust."

"Coelacanths or *busted,*" she nodded.

"Is that going to work?"

"It's going to have to work."

"What am I supposed to do with them?"

"It's time for that undergraduate degree you once completed to pay for itself. You'll be coaching, but mostly in name only – do not break the talent," she said, pointing at him.

"That's a great vote of confidence. Okay, Mom."

"Your primary responsibility will be to drag this team into the baseball world of twenty years ago. You majored in statistics, so start crunching the numbers."

Her points were well taken. For as long as he could remember, Charlie had always found the math behind the game to be the most interesting part. He had memorized the lists of seasonal stats on the back of hundreds of baseball cards, had suggested innumerable opportunities where Manager Plunkett could use their team's players in ways that made sound, logical sense. He often lamented the fact that, had he not been the worst player in minor league baseball, he might have been listened to.

"So, what's their deal? Don't they have someone who does that? Lots of teams have stat-heads."

"Gray Whalen claims he doesn't 'do' statistics."

"What's a Gray Whalen?"

"He's the manager – an old friend of your father's. Completely disagreeable, but one of the few decent men left in the game. Stick to him like glue on a junkie's top lip. Learn what you can and make him get with the program."

"He knew Dad?"

"They were briefly teammates, yes."

Charlie thought back to those days but was unable to place a face to the name.

Margaret turned to him. "This was your father's team," she said, removing the sunglasses. Her eye-contact underlined the serious nature of this giant leap he would be taking in less than 24 hours. "And now it's *our* team. Our futures depend on it. But never forget how important it was to your father."

"I'll try, Mom." It was the best he could offer, and it was the truth. All of this was unexpected – he'd never been capable of wrapping his mind around the idea of life after baseball. The game was all he knew, and this was the path the game had set out for him.

Margaret sighed and reaffixed her sunglasses. A breeze wafted through the desert, stirring the grasses as they stared up at the tortured mass of stone fins and gills. Charlie could almost hear the gears turning in his mother's head.

She crossed her arms and spoke in a distant voice. "Is there a market for resale marble?"

CHAPTER 3
Dead Air

FRANCESCA MORETTI CLUNG to the shadows as she strode the concourse of HerbCo Field. It was a typically sweltering Cape Haddock summer day and the path of shade she was following, courtesy of the upper deck, was a welcome respite from the relentless sunshine.

The sound of her shoes falling on the cement slap-echoed their way across the empty ballpark. She gazed out at the frame of green grasses and allowed herself a moment to enjoy the well-manicured confines in which she worked.

She felt this an important daily affirmation to make, for while the current circumstances of her career as a radio broadcaster were less than ideal, she was always able to find reassurance in the aesthetic beauty of HerbCo. It was one of the oldest parks in the entire Triple-A system, but local funding had kept the forest green bandbox in excellent repair, while the team remained mediocre enough to warrant a consistent level of mild interest throughout the region. The baseball wasn't great, but at least it was being played in a nice location.

Her eyes darted out to center field, drawn by the screeching of seagulls from the harbor across the street. They winged their way over a monolithic result of the bond that Herbert Tinley had glad-handed through to approval with the local government. It was a 60-foot-long fishing pole, mounted at an angle across two massive I-beams that had been sunk into the berm beyond the outfield wall, complete with a flourish of white neon that emulated a line in mid-cast and ended with a feathered lure. The pole featured additional lights, mounted where the guide rings sat and flashed their way out from the reel to the tip-top in lazy succession like the marquee of a needy roadside diner. The words 'HerbCo Fishing Supplies' blazed beneath the rod in red block letters. Francesca had found it odd that one sport should be the primary advertising platform of another, but such were the bizarre marketing methods of HerbCo Enterprises.

Turning away from the field, she made her way to an unmarked door, through which she passed into the utilitarian guts of the stadium. Making her way down a few flights of stairs, she could not help but question why it should be that such a pleasant ballpark would require her to dig up her own screwdriver.

Her phone vibrated in the pocket of her blazer and she paused to find a message from her now-former producer, Damien.

Thanks for asking. I have feelers out in AA.

She sighed.

The placid field resting nearby belied the recent chaos surrounding the Coelacanth organization. As Francesca began checking the doors lining the stadium's utility tunnel, she cycled through the chain of events as she understood it: The longtime owner and alleged-millionaire, Herbert Tinley, had recently passed away, and control over his business empire had passed to his missing-in-action widow, who was now executing a series of brutal staffing cuts that included the crew of AM 1371.

AM 1371 was a low-wattage, Class D station worth as much as the paper its license was printed on. Still, it *was* a legitimate frequency, begrudgingly acknowledged by the FCC and listened to by the small Cape Haddock population. Originally a source of 1950s pop music and local weather reporting, it had since been swept up into Herbert Tinley's purchase of the Coelacanths decades ago. It now existed as an antenna limited to the ballgame broadcasts and a Saturday morning swap meet-style call-in show called Trade Baiters. While no one outside of Francesca had the sense to check on such things, she couldn't help but feel embarrassed to note that Trade Baiters typically pulled better ratings than the team.

A twinge of guilt gnawed at Francesca's conscience; while her entire production staff, Producer Damien and Engineer/Researcher

Hiroki, had found themselves victims of the chopping block, she was an anomaly of corporate cutbacks. In a world where the maxim was 'last one in, first one out,' she had somehow survived the culling, despite having started in April of that year. To make matters more confusing, it had come down the grapevine that she had been handpicked by the very owner who had now shitcanned the team she had worked so hard to ingratiate herself with.

It had been a process. She'd begun the season as anyone beginning a new job would, treading lightly, observing how things worked. Her observations informed her that the crew of AM 1371 were a collection of well-meaning pros being held as psychological hostages by her co-host, the veteran color commentator, Dip Lockerbie.

Obnoxious, oblivious, and self-involved, Dip was of the oldest of old schools and had been the meandering voice of the Coelacanths for close to 40 years. Francesca could not fathom how he had survived the redundancies but assumed his lengthy tenure had ensured him an ironclad contract. As a fixture, he was seemingly indispensable.

She knew there was little point in wallowing in this state of affairs and had spent the past week coming to terms with reality as it was: the Coelacanth broadcast was now a two-person operation. This meant she was responsible for both play-by-play *and* the mixing board, just like her days in college radio. She had been around long enough to realize that if she didn't do it, it would not be done. Dip had been entrenched in the droning of his minor league war stories for so long, he clearly hadn't so much as looked at a fader, let alone knew how one worked.

The phone vibrated as a second message from Damien arrived.

Sorry about the chair – yikes

And there it was, the reason for her excursion.

The chair in question was nothing but an average office desk chair, and yet somehow it had become so much more. It was a symbol of the relationship she had with her broadcast partner: broken and divisive without her understanding why.

The first game of the season had been a prime example of things to come. Francesca had spent the entirety of spring training familiarizing herself with the players, their stories, their abilities. Her time calling Division-4 softball had taught her that in the broadcast booth, time was a liar. Depending on how eventful a game was, a live broadcast could either fly by in a rush of exhilarating athletics or grind itself down into a slog of bullpens and bench players. This experience, while boring, had been informative, and she had since taken great pains to load up on as many talking points as possible. Air that was alive with words was always better than air that was dead with silence.

The only thing that had been missing was Dip, who was apparently vacationing right up to the day the season kicked off. In lieu of being able to cultivate a rapport with the man, she had made the time to vet him online. The results of her research had raised no red flags. He'd played some ball in the mid-1960s, put up lousy numbers, pivoted into radio, and had spent the subsequent years putting together a career that would probably get him into one broadcasting hall of fame or another, if only because he'd stuck around for so long. She had long been aware of the good ol' boy networks that made such questionable tumblers fall into place.

Otherwise, with the Cape Haddock Coelacanths a perpetual mediocrity, there were few feathers in the Lockerbie cap – no trademark expressions or calls to his credit, no formal industry acknowledgment of excellence. His profile was simply one of a man who had spent several decades talking over baseball games while wearing a fedora. In fact, the most prominent feather in his cap was his actual cap. It was the one constant in any images she'd been able to pull up. The idea of having a visual trademark while working in an aural medium had struck her as silly, but she had accepted it, just as she had accepted the idea of him as a co-host. Perhaps he would lend her valuable insight into their trade and take her under his wing like a benevolent baseball-grandpa. This was her first serious gig and she was hellbent on making it work. Sure, their half-century age gap would be weird, but possibly not the weirdest.

Yet how quickly the weirdness began once Dip finally breezed into the booth an hour before the first pitch of opening day. His presence seemed to embody a chilling effect that was immediately felt, and Francesca had been baffled by her (until that moment) gregarious and normal crew transforming into mute automatons who now scurried with clenched jaws and avoided eye-contact. The introduction of eager, make-nice sentiments she had so carefully choreographed in her mind was coolly rebuffed by him without a welcoming handshake or anything beyond a dismissive 'Uh-huh.' This was followed by a scowl at Damien and Hiroki, as though they were to blame for this presumed prank.

She had tried to see past this awkward first impression, empathetic to the feeling of trespassing she must have been instilling in him. Familiar with navigating the pathetically thin membrane that was the male ego, she tried to defer.

"Dip, I'm looking forward to seeing the legendary 'Mr. Coelacanth' in action."

He stared at her, eyes magnified by the thick lenses of his glasses, his mouth slightly agape, as though her words had been full of outrageous slurs.

She tried again. "You just give me the ol' high sign if I'm giving it too much stretch, okay? I don't want to step on you, or the spots or anything." She felt that perhaps a bit of radio banter might thaw his attitude. They were peers and they would be depending on each other to make a good show.

His mouth remained open like that of a confounded mackerel. After an uncomfortably long silence he shook his head in apparent disbelief and turned to their shared desk overlooking the field.

Francesca exchanged a confused look with Hiroki, who shrugged. Anxious to start the broadcast, she sat at the desk to run through her copy.

"Where's my chair?" There was an awkward silence in the booth as her co-host turned to the producer. "Damien, what happened to my chair?" His eyes flicked over to Francesca, the accusation unspoken but clear.

Damien looked confused but did as all good producers do and gave the talent his full attention. "Sorry, Dipper – what's the issue?"

Dip pushed the back of the chair that was positioned in front of his microphone with one finger. "You know with my back that I need the *good* chair."

"I didn't realize there was a 'good' chair–"

"Well, there is, and I need it. Now, where is it?"

"Dip, I'm not–"

"I don't need an excuse, I need my goddamned chair!"

The randomness of the explosion was almost comical, but the reddening of Dip's face was anything but. He was pouting, staring at no one. This was the tantrum of a child who did not want to leave the toy aisle.

The atmosphere in the booth was thick with tension. Hoping to diffuse her co-host's anxiety, Francesca attempted a gesture of goodwill.

"Dip, you can try my chair, if that would help." She stood and rolled the seat toward him.

He glared at her as though she was worth less than nothing, then yanked the chair away from her. Using his foot, he brushed his own chair away from the desk and into her general direction. He then sat, fuming over his notes in silence until the red light was on.

Francesca could have brushed this outburst aside as a simple first-day faux pas. Maybe the seats had been shuffled before the pre-show prep, maybe she *had* accidentally taken the 'good chair.' Whichever the case, she had not done so purposefully, and would not be doing so again.

Yet, three months had passed, and not a show had gone by without her having to get up and trade seats with him. It didn't matter the circumstance – whether she'd labeled each chair with gaffer tape, or switched them herself before he'd entered the booth, the chair was always wrong. She had come to expect this useless exercise, but now, with Damien and Hiroki no longer present to buffer the pouting, this madness had to end.

Behind the third door she checked, she finally found a custodial closet with a large cleaning cart, and knew she was close. After another moment of rooting around, she procured a small toolbox, from which she took two screwdrivers and a ring of hex keys. She wondered if whoever had placed these in this closet still worked at the ballpark and poked her head back into the hallway to see if anyone was taking note of her scrounging.

Glancing down the corridor to the Coelacanth clubhouse, she noticed a tallish figure in street clothes pass through the door, dragging a suitcase behind him. He did not look familiar. Curious, she closed the closet door and followed him.

Entering the clubhouse, which was spacious and comfortable in a way that suggested the rejuvenating potion of taxpayer dollars, she saw the stranger at the far end of the room. He was hovering outside the manager's office next to his suitcase, a ream of printed pages under his arm.

She approached cautiously, observing as he put his ear against the door in cartoonish fashion. He seemed too old to be a new player, but not so old that he would be an acquaintance of Manager Gray Whalen.

"Excuse me? Sir?"

The man's head snapped around, his eyes betraying his mortification. "Uhhh… huh?"

"Are you lost?"

He quickly pulled himself away from the door and began smoothing his blazer as though this had been the issue. "I'm sorry?" he asked in a way that suggested he needed another moment to gather himself.

"Are you lost?" she said, slightly slower this time.

"Oh," he said, gesturing to the door. "I was just, uh… listening to that door."

"I noticed," she said, raising an eyebrow. This man was rather amusing. She eyed the carry-on suitcase beside him. "Are you looking for the check-in desk? Because the rooms aren't ready until two."

"Oh, no, no," he said, grinning. "I swear I'm supposed to be here." He pointed to the tools she was carrying. "Are *you* looking to steal a car battery? Because the parking lot's outside."

"If you knew my salary, you wouldn't blame me," she said, swinging the ring of hex keys on her index finger with flair.

He held up a slip of paper. "I'm looking for the manager's office. You know him?"

She eyed him, suspicious. "Uh-huh. This isn't, like, a contract to kill or something, is it?" she asked, half-joking.

"Ha!" he blurted. "No, scout's honor. I'm the new bench coach."

"Really?" she asked. This was surprising – a new hire in the midst of downsizing? She peered at the page he was holding. Sure enough, there was a terse message from the owner herself, Margaret Tinley, commanding him to a meeting with the Coelacanth manager, Gray Whalen. Apparently, this strange man was legit. "Wow. You have some pretty good connections, huh?" *You must come incredibly cheap,* she thought.

"Yeah, I guess so," he said. He seemed embarrassed by the question.

"Sorry," she said, trying to diffuse the awkwardness, "I'm Francesca. I do play-by-play for the game broadcast. Welcome to Cape Haddock."

He seemed to relax as they shook hands. "Charlie," he said. "Nice to meet you, ma'am."

She smiled at this odd greeting – he was clearly ten years older than her. "Just 'Francesca' is fine. 'Sir.'"

They laughed, and she ran through the ever-growing rolodex of minor league characters she'd been assembling since the spring. There was something familiar about this man's face...

"Wow, so you're on the radio, huh?" He seemed impressed.

"Yeah. Barely, but yeah."

"Barely?"

She made a prompt decision to not dump her workplace angst on the newcomer. "Well, it's my first season with the team. Still getting my feet wet and all that."

"Gotcha," he said, nodding. "The good news is you're not the new kid anymore, so I guess you don't have to worry about everyone wondering what you're doing here."

"That's a relief," she said. "I guess I just did that to you, huh?"

"It's a fair point," he said, shrugging. "I don't really know what I'm doing here. So, you must be kind of famous, huh?"

She laughed at this. "Not exactly." The idea of fame being attached to AM radio was adorable. If being steamrolled by her co-host daily and doing the occasional pre-game broadcast from a card table on the sidewalk was fame, then she was Beyoncé. "You know, I'd love to talk with you after practice, if you're up for it."

He seemed surprised by the request. "Really? You want to talk to *me?"*

She shrugged. "Yeah, I mean... it's Cape Haddock. There's not really a whole lot going on here, you know? Coelacanth Nation doesn't exactly get to fly its flag every day. This is, like, the minorest of minor league teams."

"I'll bet I've seen worse," he said.

Sadness seemed to overcome him, and something clicked in Francesca's memory. "Wait a minute, I know you. You're Starch Man, right?" She was thrilled to have been able to pull this reference, but he was clearly surprised to be recognized. "There was an email this morning," she added.

He nodded as though this made perfect sense.

"And the nickname's hilarious."

"Thanks. I'm still getting used to it," he said.

"Wow, so you played in Single-A for a long time, huh? The longest, right?"

"Probably, yeah."

"And now you're hired in the middle of a downsize. That's pretty good, Coach."

"Well, I do statistical analysis too," he said, looking almost bashful.

"Oh!" she said, excited. "You're a quant!"

"Yep," he nodded. "That's me."

"Wow," she said. "Whalen's finally getting a quant. How things change." This was unexpected – the Coelacanths had never shown any inclination toward Moneyballing. It appeared the cutbacks wouldn't be the only changes for the team.

At that moment, Dip emerged through the frosted glass door of the manager's office, closing it behind him. He was tossing a baseball to himself, his anachronistic fedora cocked back on his wrinkled forehead. He whistled an incessant, tuneless song. Everything about him grated on her. Still, they were partners…

"Hey – Dip?"

He blew right past her without a glance. "Madam, I am a happily married man," he said, dismissing her. This was a typical assumption for him to make. It was hideous, but it had become normalized over the past few months.

"Dip, don't be gross. It's me." She pointed at her face. The color commentator finally looked back at her. His face fell, and she could only imagine how disappointed her very existence must have made him feel. She most likely represented everything he disliked about the 21st century. Which made her feel a little proud.

"Oh. It's *you.*" He could barely disguise his contempt as the worlds rolled out of his mouth.

Despite his incessant rudeness, she had always made her best effort at keeping their communication professional. *Somebody* had to be professional. "Listen, I want you to meet someone."

"Is that right?" he said, rolling his eyes. "Got the ol' autograph booth up and running early today, do we?"

She gritted her teeth and did her best to power through. "Dip Lockerbie, this is Charlie. He's the new–"

As though someone had dumped a fresh battery into him, Dip's entire posture changed. His voice switched from perturbed to charming, and he was suddenly 'Mr. Coelacanth,' the goodwill ambassador of his own stories and local celebrity.

"Well, hey there, sport, it's good to meet you! Hey – catch!"

Charlie dropped his papers as Dip tossed the baseball at him with no warning. He caught it but was quickly interrupted by an earnest handshake.

Francesca sighed. "He's not a fan. He's the new coach."

The old man frowned. "You don't say..."

"It's true," said Charlie. "And sir, we've actually met before. Several times. My dad–"

"Son, I know it's going to be tough to focus while you're working with a legend like myself, but you just let *me* do the heavy lifting around here." Here, Dip put his hands together and took an off-kilter practice swing of an invisible bat. "But I'm always here with advice if you need it – off the record, of course. Gray Whalen loves picking my brain. Say, whatcha got there, a baseball?"

Charlie looked down at the ball in his hand. "Uh–"

"Say no more, of course I'll sign it! I know it can be embarrassing to ask..." Dip grabbed the ball back out of Charlie's hand and pulled a fine-tip marker from his jacket pocket. "Now, who should I make this out to?"

"Oh," Charlie said, caught off-guard. "Uh, 'Charlie Conroy.' I guess."

Francesca was disgusted by the gall of her colleague. "Dip, he's not here for–"

"Now, is that 'Charlie' with a C?"

"Yes?"

Dip began mumbling the inscription as he wrote it. "'Dear Chas…You're my biggest…fan…Signed, Dip…Locker…bie.' There ya go, champ."

Dip tossed the ball back to Charlie. He tipped his hat to them. "You kids enjoy the game, now, huh?"

Francesca sighed. "Dip, I'm going to see you for pre-game prep in, like, 20 minutes."

"And stay in school!" he added, ignoring her. He gave them a playful point and laughed as he exited the clubhouse. Charlie looked at Francesca, puzzled.

"That's my co-worker," she said.

"Are you sure? He didn't seem to know you."

"Yeah, that's Dip Lockerbie. Since I'm the new to the show, I suspect he's having a hard time sharing the broadcast.

"Really? How long have you been working together?"

"Since March."

"Whoa. It's July."

Francesca nodded. "The denial's pretty deep." She knelt to help him pick up his fallen papers. "How do you know him?"

"He was calling the games on the radio back when I was a kid. And he was good friends with my stepdad," said Charlie. "Apparently they used to party together."

"Ah," Francesca nodded. This made sense. "Word is, Dip has always liked to walk around Cape Haddock like he owns the place." They straightened as he shuffled his papers back into a stack. "So, you're getting the real welcome wagon treatment with Whalen, huh? Gray really knows how to bust out the party balloons."

"Seriously?"

She laughed. "No, I don't think that's his style. Good luck though."

He grinned. "Thanks. You too."

She waved the screwdrivers and turned back to the tunnel. "I'll need it!"

CHAPTER 4
Purpose Pitch

CHARLIE WAS MET with billows of smoke as he passed through the frosted glass door. Waving the plumes from his face, and wishing he'd had the foresight to steal an emergency oxygen mask from his plane, he peered into the room.

The office was a dingy closet of a space and carried the feel of a photograph that had been developed using tar as the primary chemical agent. A low row of beige filing cabinets lined one wall, each piled high with cardboard boxes, filled with folders, binders, and thoroughly used legal pads. The opposite wall was scattered with team photos of smiling players sporting haircuts that Charlie placed in the mid-1970s. Mixed among these were portraits of wizened baseball men, one of whom he recognized as former dugout mastermind, Casey Stengel. The legendary skipper was seated in a dugout, legs crossed, puzzling over a copy of *Baseball's Greatest Managers*.

His eyes struggling to adjust to the combination of smoke and cheap overhead fluorescents, Charlie's gaze finally settled on a battered desk at the opposite end of the room.

"Hello?" he called out.

The chair behind the desk began swiveling its way to face Charlie, squeaking in a lackadaisical way that suited the sloppy environs. As the seat completed its rotation, Charlie was faced with the wiry frame of what was, presumably, his new boss. A veil of smoke dripped lazily upward from the cigarette drooping beneath a grey mustache.

Both were attached to a craggy face and flanked by muttonchops of another era.

The old man squinted at him. "Yeah?"

"Are you, uh..." Charlie shifted the unruly stack of pages beneath his arm as he looked down at Margaret's instructions once more. "...Gray Whalen?"

The man's face fell into a thoughtful frown, his gaze surveying the office, as though for the first time. "Well, it's his desk I'm sitting at, so I'd hope so. The guy's supposed to be a real prick about such things."

With an air of reluctance, Whalen removed the cigarette from his mouth and stubbed it into an overflowing ashtray. Charlie glanced behind him to push the door closed and turned back to find the skipper leaning back in his chair and throwing his feet onto the desk. He flinched, blurting an "Aah!" as Whalen's chicken legs landed on the desktop with a *thud,* revealing him to be wearing cleats and stirrups, but no pants.

Whalen frowned at the reaction, curious. "Okay..."

Charlie exhaled, disconcerted. "I'm sorry – you're not wearing any pants. It caught me off-guard."

"Huh?" the manager asked, looking down at his exposed kneecaps. "Oh yeah... pants. Well, sometimes you gotta drive with the windows down, you know?"

Charlie's eyes narrowed as a thought occurred to him. "You are wearing underpants, aren't you?"

The skipper rolled his eyes. "Oh, for god's sake," he said, his cleats clunking back to the floor as he leaned forward in the chair. "You're not gonna make me stand up, are you?"

"No, sir," said Charlie, hoping this was the answer that would quickly de-escalate this pantsless situation.

He was relieved when Whalen nodded in approval and pushed back to place his feet atop the desk once more. "Good. No point in standing if you don't have to."

Charlie raised an eyebrow but decided against challenging this philosophy. "The sportsman's motto," he said.

"'Why stand when you can lean, why lean when you can sit, and why sit when you can recline' – that's *my* motto," Whalen said with a nod. "Now, if there are no further questions about my pants, who the hell are you, and why are you interrupting my me-time?"

"Sorry, Skipper, I didn't mean to intrude. I'm your new bench coach," Charlie said, sliding his mother's note across the desk like a juvenile delinquent checking in for detention. "Charlie Conroy."

"Ah, so you're ol' Maggie's boy, huh?" Whalen looked at him with new interest, examining Charlie's boyish face, as though waiting for something to be made clear.

"'Maggie?' Really?" Charlie had never heard this nickname before – not once. The assuredness with which Whalen said it implied this must be an actual, humanizing 'thing.' Like many things regarding his mother, it made Charlie anxious.

"Say, does your ma go by 'Maggie Conroy-Tinley,' or 'Maggie Tinley-Conroy' these days?"

Charlie was uncertain if Whalen was pulling his leg. "She's usually just 'Mom' to me."

Whalen nodded, and using the tilt tension of his chair, gave a deep lean back and catapulted himself up, onto his feet. He meandered his way around the desk, stopping in front of the team photos on the wall.

"Of course, I used to know her as Maggie Conroy when your dad was alive. Played many a game with that man." Whalen pointed to a figure in one of the photos. Charlie leaned in, allowing plenty of space between himself and the skipper's bare legs. He felt a sudden pang in his chest as he found the face of his father smiling back.

He was younger than Charlie remembered, just a new man, fresh to the rigors of life. Charlie tried to make sense of the long hair sticking out from beneath the Coelacanth hat, the strange, high-waisted cut of the '70s-era uniform. He found these elements impenetrable when asked for more depth regarding the man within them. *What is your life like?* Charlie wondered to himself as his new manager shuffled back to the safety of his desk.

"He was one of the best teammates a guy could ask for, rest his soul," Whalen said.

Charlie turned to find the old man leaning on the desktop, staring at the photograph. He seemed lost in a thought, his eyes darting back and forth between Charlie's face and that of Jackie Conroy. "You don't remember me, do you." He waved Charlie off as the younger man opened his mouth to sputter panicked excuses. "Don't even, there's no reason why you would. I left the team when you were about four." He held a hand out to shake. "Gray Whalen."

"Good to meet you again, Skipper."

He shook the old man's hand with what he hoped was a respectable grip. He did not remember this man, it was true, though he assumed him to have been one of the background figures wearing the Cape Haddock home whites in the few memories of his father he'd been able to retain.

"She back here too, your ma?" Whalen asked.

"She'll be along in a few hours," Charlie said, mostly hopeful this was true. "She was detained at the airport because of an incident with a flight attendant. And an obscenity I'm not comfortable repeating." The acrid taste of public humiliation lingered, fresh in his memory. And while the appropriate threats had been made, he hoped the attorneys hadn't been called – the deposition would be ugly.

Whalen chuckled and sat back in his chair. "That sounds like Maggie, all right."

Charlie's attention was quickly brought back to the present as he watched the manager tap out a new cigarette from his crumpled soft pack and light the end. The old man leaned back, seemingly without a care in the world, as he inhaled.

Charlie could not believe it. "Are you actually doing this? Right here?"

Whalen looked at him like he was insane. "It's my office, and I'll lean back wherever I want, you little–" He broke off as Charlie scurried to the office door and threw the lock. "Uh... what is this?"

After testing the knob, Charlie then whipped off his blazer and crouched to roll it up against the crack by the floor. Whalen watched, fascinated. "Charlie... is this something you *do,* or should I be worried?"

Charlie crossed back to the desk and grabbed the cigarette pack. He held it up with an emphatic shake, then stuck it in his shirt pocket. "Skipper, you can't smoke in here – it's the 21st Century."

"I believe I'm proving to you right now that one *can* smoke in the 21st Century," Whalen replied. He used his non-smoking hand to display the cigarette with a game show host's flourish.

"But the kids, Skip," said Charlie. "It sets a bad example."

Whalen shifted in his seat with a sigh of exhaustion. "Charlie, I'm *already* a bad example. Holy hell, did my wife send you or something?" He stared at his new underling for a moment of unblinking disbelief, then leaned toward him, his tone softening. "Listen, I never do it on the field, okay? Jeez, we're a lousy ballclub, not a bunch of burnouts at the track. That's for the off-season."

"Gambling?" Charlie's eyes bulged with newfound stress.

"Shhhh-sh-sh-sh, forget I said anything," Whalen said, waving the idea away with both hands. "Listen, I gotta be honest, Charlie," he said, staring off to the side and scratching the whiskers framing his right ear, "I know your ma's got you all set up for your first big boy job and everything, and I'm just thrilled about it, believe me. But, I'm not really sure what you're bringing to the table here. You ever play ball?"

It was a fair question. "I was with the Tumbleweeds, yeah. Single-A."

"Is that right…" Whalen nodded. Charlie suspected the motion was intended to be one of respect, but it came off as an appraisal. A sizing-up. "Must've been a while ago. You play long?" He took a long drag off his cigarette.

"22 years."

Whalen coughed, his ancient chair screeching as he leaned forward and waved the plume away. "Sorry," he said, hacking again. "I thought you said–"

"I did," Charlie nodded. His humiliation was complete. He was fine with it. It was what it was and there could be no hiding it. "I was the longest-tenured Single-A player ever."

"Really?" Whalen examined him as though he was missing something. "And I've never heard of you?"

"There was an email sent out about it."

"Ah," Whalen said, nodding as the pieces fell into place. "Must've missed it. I don't do email. Don't believe in it."

Charlie feigned understanding with a nod. Anxious to change the subject, he instead broached one that had been weighing on him since his retirement. "Listen, Skipper, just because I'm technically the owner's son, that doesn't mean we need to make a big deal out of it with the rest of the staff, okay? I'm just one of the guys."

"How generous of you, my liege," said Whalen.

Charlie checked the time on his phone. The game would be starting within the hour. "When is the staff meeting, by the way?"

"This *is* the staff meeting," Whalen said, motioning his finger between them.

At first, this didn't register. Charlie rolled the words over in his mind once more and his stomach turned. She couldn't have. "You mean–"

"I do," said Whalen, leaning forward. "Your mom – my boss – has decided to tighten the belt a couple of notches. Which means my staff have been squeezed right out of their pinstriped short pants."

"All of them?" Charlie knew his mother had considered a culling, but he didn't realize she'd be dropping the heaviest hammer possible.

"That's right." Whalen rifled through his disgusting ashtray and plucked out a half-smoked cigarette. Pleased with himself, he struck a match on his desk and was soon grumbling smoke back into Charlie's face. "Pitching coach, hitting coach, first base coach, third base coach, personal trainer, bat boy… and bench coach. Although I guess you're here to save the day on that account."

Charlie was stunned. This was a massacre, one that effectively ended almost any kind of structure or leadership. It was an administrative nightmare that was now his to enjoy in all its chaotic glory. *Thanks, Mom...*

"Can she actually do that?" Charlie asked the manager.

Whalen shrugged. "I have no idea, but she did. We took a pounding from the Amberjacks last week. The fellas came back to the locker room and found walking papers in their inboxes."

"Whoa," said Charlie. "Fired via internet. That's cold."

"And also, probably against Human Resources' protocols, but they got canned too. I might have been booted too for all I know, but, like I said–"

"You don't do email."

"Exactly."

They sat in silence. Charlie had always been one for bluer skies, but even he had to admit this was challenging.

"I've gotta say, Skip… it feels like we're a little handcuffed."

"Mmm," Whalen nodded, stubbing out the remains of his cigarette. "Handcuffed. And thrown into a streamer trunk. With a padlock. And dumped into a river. Just like Houdini."

"Mom's always enjoyed challenges," said Charlie, rubbing his chin. "Usually it's the Thursday crossword."

"Ah, but *you're* here now," said Whalen in faux awe. "I trust you've got a key you can cough up to pick our locks?"

Charlie promptly snapped out of his malaise. "Oh yeah! Here, let me show you," he said, his face lighting up with statistical enthusiasm. He *did* in fact have something to offer the grizzled manager.

"Whaddya got for me, Coach Conroy?" said Whalen, clapping his hands together. "I can't help but notice this enormous stack of paper I absolutely do not want to look at."

He nodded to the stack of pages Charlie was cradling on his lap. The manager's face morphed into a scowl as his new bench coach heaved the ream onto his desk.

Charlie began flipping through the stack, revealing page after page of columnated data. "Now, what I've done here, is collate all of our batting, fielding, and pitching data from the past three years. It's a small sample size, I know, but it can work in identifying trends and places we can improve our odds of success, and–"

Charlie broke off, double-taking at his new skipper, who stared at him, blank-faced. The old man began shaking his head with slow precision. The sentence Charlie had started, took an abrupt left turn.

"...and you're shaking your head. I'm sorry, is there a problem? Is it the sample size? Because I can always–"

Charlie was interrupted again as Whalen reached across the desk and flipped the top page facedown onto the stack with a flick of the wrist. His weathered hand rested there, as if the numbers would escape if not held down.

"Charlie, no."

Charlie was aghast at this denial of carefully orchestrated figures. "What do you mean, 'no,' Skipper? This is important information we can use to–"

"You know, kid," Whalen said, an unmistakable boredom coloring his voice, "ever since the millennium rolled over, hotshots like you have been coming to old coots like me with a stack of paper like that." Here, he pointed to the offending pages, eyeing them as though they might combust. "And you talk about percentages and averages and splits and sprays and tendencies and all this other jazz that nobody looked at for over a hundred years. And you all think you've done the formulas the *right* way and can 'solve' the equation of shitty baseball teams. Am I pretty close here?"

Charlie was caught off-balance. "Uh, well–"

"And to a person," Whalen continued, brushing past Charlie's forthcoming excuses, "you crazy buncha students completely dismiss this thing known as 'the eye test.' Which would more accurately be called 'the brain test.'"

Charlie eyed the old man as Whalen absentmindedly began poking his finger through the ashtray once more. "The... the brain test."

"That's the one," Whalen replied, jabbing his index finger at Charlie. He then reached down to remove two half-smoked remainders and held them up for examination beneath the overhead fluorescent. "You can measure everything happening on the field... except the distance between one emotion to the next – what is going on inside a player's *mind.*"

Charlie was still uncertain about what Whalen was driving at but took a shot at responding anyway. "Well, Skipper, actually the Ultimate Zone Rating–"

"Nah-nah-nah," Whalen said, waving him off with an expression of near-disbelief. He tossed the shorter of the used filters back into the tray and stuck the other between his teeth. "The true Ultimate Zone..." he began, sparking a match and inhaling the ensuing cloud, "is the space between the player's ears. For instance: do you know how your shortstop will be fielding when he's still half in the bag from the night before?"

Charlie puzzled over this as Whalen exhaled a steady stream of smoke into his face. "Uh..."

"Do you know how your left fielder will be swinging against a pitcher, any pitcher – righty, lefty, fireballer, junkballer – the day after he finds his girlfriend demonstrating her 'mound presence' to your right fielder?"

Charlie was pretty sure he was successfully reading between Whalen's lines, but not sure enough to comment with any statistical confidence. "I don't think that stat exists yet, Skip."

"And yet," Whalen said, groaning as he sank back in his chair, "it's just as important as your numbers. I know these kids, and they need some guidance from someone who's been where they're at and been where they wanna be. Not a mathematician."

Charlie nodded slowly, considering this. "So, you're saying I should be more of a father figure to them."

Whalen sat up again, coughing with surprise. "What? No!" He crushed the yellowed cigarette butt back into the ashtray. "No, the best you can hope for is to be their shitty stepdad. Or maybe the older brother who lives at home in the basement."

"My room was upstairs," Charlie offered.

"Whatever!" Whalen said, waving him off. "Point is, until you're in the hot seat here, *I'm* their dad."

"You think so, huh?"

Whalen sneered at him. "Oh hell, you've only been here for five minutes and I'm already *your* dad."

Charlie was appalled by the assumption. "Dad, that's just not true!" He slapped a hand over his mouth.

"See?" Whalen grinned knowingly, his mustache bristling in triumph. "Now, listen: all you've gotta do is make sure the guys are in their little outfits before the game starts," he said, pointing to a wall that Charlie presumed faced the field outside. "And when the radio lady comes by to see where we went wrong, you just tell her that they played hard and that you'd like to see them string some hits together and push some runs across the plate."

"You have just described the entire objective of baseball," Charlie sighed.

"Exactly," Whalen nodded. "Besides, wait 'til you get a load of our team. You'll see. In fact..." Whalen took his feet off the desk, straightening with a stretch and a groan. He looked over at the clock on the wall, "...why don't you go put your jammies on and join the fellas on the field? Game's on soon. I'll meet you out there."

Charlie felt a rush of panic at being thrown into a situation in which he knew no one but tried to roll with it. "Um, sure." He pointed to his stack of data. "Should I...?"

"Tell you what, why don't you just hold onto that for the time being, so it doesn't, uh, get lost in here, okay? That'd be a real shame."

"Okay, Skip," Charlie nodded, manhandling the pages back under his arm. He paused as he reached the frosted glass, dipping to grab his rumpled jacket from its place against the bottom of the door. Tossing it over his shoulder, he turned back to the manager. "And Skip? Thanks."

Charlie held his free hand out to shake. Whalen tilted his head to the side in disbelief.

"Did you really want me to stand up and walk over to you, looking like this? Because I'm gonna have to bend over to get these pants on, so–"

Charlie raised his hand in surrender, and promptly slid his way through the door. "I'll see you outside, huh?"

"There you go," the skipper said with a nod. Charlie felt the knob catch under his palm as the office door shut, sealing the pantsless baseball pharaoh inside his tomb once more.

CHAPTER 5
Team Chemistry

CHARLIE EMERGED FROM the poorly lit walkway tunnel and into the blinding light of late afternoon at HerbCo Field. The faint tingle of déjà vu skittered up the back of his brain as he stepped into the dugout and beheld the forest green-painted beams and light tower parapets of the park. He had been here before, probably many times. But he had been young, so it had been the feeling of the place that had remained, rather than the details.

Cabbing into town from the airport had put this dissonance under a spotlight. Everything about Cape Haddock now felt markedly smaller when compared to the slideshow of memories he'd stowed away in the attic of his mind. Where once had been a summer haven of larger-than-life, user-friendly maritime tourism, now sat little more than five sleepy blocks of fudge and taffy shops, mixed with the occasional seafood restaurant and harbor tour charter house. Still, the salt air was a visceral punch in his gut, stirring memories of being a boy and playing with his father. As the hulls and masts of 150 years' worth of docked nautical history flew by the taxi window, he'd decided it best not to wallow in such thoughts. There was little dimension to them, let alone comfort. And there had been a reason he and his mother had moved away from the sea. The sea rarely gave back what it took away.

Now, peering up and out of the dugout, the snapshots of afternoons at HerbCo Field gone by flicked through his consciousness and the exception to time's compression of space was found. After decades at Tinley Park in Tombstone, with its capacity for little more than a triple-digit fanbase, HerbCo Park still felt enormous. The massive fishing pole in the outfield was new, but not surprising considering how much Herbert Tinley had enjoyed branding places and things with his name.

Beneath the stretch of neon-lined rod, sat four low flagpoles. On each was a triangular pennant fluttering lethargically in the faint breeze that wandered across the street from the ocean. They embodied the sad glory of the Coelacanth heyday, some thirty-odd years earlier. None were divisional, league, or national championship flags. These were *playoff* flags, the saddest of all banners. They served as reminders of the few times the Cape Haddock Coelacanths, led by Jackie Conroy, had been able to claw their way out of the cellar and into an extra couple of games before being sent packing for the winter. At a distance they added an essential flair to the ballpark. But at close, readable range, they were billowing manifestations of a team that had never been talented enough to win. On the bright side, this also meant there was not much of a legacy for Charlie to screw up, though he was hopeful it would not come to that. Despite all signs pointing otherwise, he didn't *feel* like a jinx.

Mounting the dugout steps, Charlie surveyed the mild buzz of the fans taking their seats and the players warming up. He watched the grounders and long tosses absentmindedly, distracted by the fit of his new uniform. He'd found an empty stall in the locker room, but a uniform was an entirely different issue. After rummaging through two storage rooms – both of which appeared to be filled with items that had been broken and `subsequently hidden – he'd managed to dig up a set of the home whites. However, while he could live with an evening in the all-purpose Bat Boy jersey (number 0), the thing was cut for a teenager, and strained against his middle-aged frame.

"Hey, mister!"

Charlie's head snapped in the direction of the voice and beheld an unusual scenario unfolding next to the on-deck circle. He wasn't sure which was the bigger disturbance: the astonishingly unattractive foam rubber mascot that was presumably the team's namesake, or the fact that one of the Coelacanth players was posing with this mascot for a series of selfies when he should have been stretching and running drills.

The player looked to be in his early-20s, and a young early-20s at that. Charlie had seen enough rookie classes file through the Tumbleweed lineup to know that not all players who'd reached the legal drinking age were equal. Some rolled in, looking like they could be the other players' dads, while others were fresh-faced, still in their wrappers. The young man who was now wagging his phone at him was clearly of this make and model.

"Will you get a picture of me and this guy? I need both hands if I'm gonna do wild-and-crazy-face."

"Yeah?" Charlie was uncertain if he should be encouraging whatever 'wild-and-crazy-face' implied but felt like he should embrace the newness of his situation. *When in Cape Haddock...* "Okay, sure."

The young man handed him the phone. Charlie took a few steps back to frame up a shot of the player and mascot, as they contorted their faces into something hideous. The player dragged both hands down the front of his face, pulling his skin awkwardly away from his eyeballs. The mascot did an admirable job of imitating him, his bulging, cartoonish fish eyes adequately getting the craziness across as his foam rubber fins slapped his oversized, gill-lined cheeks. Charlie took the picture, inciting the tinny cough of a digitized aperture sound effect.

"Thanks, mister, I appreciate it," the player said, taking the phone back. His fingers immediately flew into a blur of typing.

Charlie looked on, fascinated. "What are you doing there?"

The young man did not look up from his typing as the phone emitted various clicks and bloop sounds.

"I am posting these pics..." and here came the longest bloop noise yet, "...on Blither."

"What's a blither?" Charlie asked, hoping this was something he wasn't supposed to already be aware of – how long had this been a thing? Should he have been 'blithering' this entire time?

The player only reinforced this impression with a skeptical look. "Seriously? It's the platform used by *all* the cool kids."

"Yeah? Huh. I've never heard of it."

The player gave him a sideways glance but continued typing. "Your words, not mine, mister."

Charlie turned his attention back to the foam fish mascot, examining it in all of its appalling glory.

"So, this is the legendary Coelacanth. He's pretty gruesome to look at, isn't he."

It was true – the goggle-eyed specimen with the downturned mouth was the stuff of night terrors.

The player shrugged. "Hey, say what you will about the species, this guy's a great listener. Mostly because there's no earholes on this thing. You okay in there, Steve?"

Charlie watched as the young man peered into the black mesh that made up the fish throat, allowing the person inside to see.

"'Steve?'" said Charlie.

"Yeah, don't you know Steve-O-Canth the Coelacanth?" The player's expression suggested Charlie was slipping even lower in his esteem. "This guy's a local legend. Isn't that right, Steve?"

The Coelacanth offered a shrug, then doubled over in silent laughter. His player-friend chuckled as well, taking another picture. "That's great – that's a lot of clicks right there, buddy."

Charlie was relieved to see Whalen approaching – pants on – sparing him the awkwardness of pretending to get the joke.

The skipper gave him a once-over, taking in the too-small uniform. "You know Charlie, there's a saying about first impressions–"

"I get it," said Charlie, adjusting the hiked waistband of his pants.

"I see you've met our mascot," said Whalen.

Charlie gave the Coelacanth a sideways look. "He's, uh... gruesome."

The mascot shook his head; Charlie found the motion jarring coming from a fish – it seemed anatomically inappropriate, if not impossible. Miming the motion of tipping his cap with his fin, the foam creature proceeded to soft-shoe himself into the outfield.

Whalen watched as the logo capered around some fly ball shagging outfielders. "Yeah, he's pretty unappetizing, no question about it," the skipper said, spitting into the dirt. "But no more so than this guy here." Whalen gestured to the young, phone-happy player. "Charlie Conroy, meet Windy Turner. This here's your new bench coach, Windy – can you contain your excitement?"

Windy looked up from his phone. "Huh?" Shooting Whalen a confused look, he gamely shook Charlie's outstretched hand.

"'Windy,'" said Charlie, trying the name out. "You've got some wheels, huh?"

Whalen grunted a laugh. "Nah, but he sure can talk if you let him. Ain't that right, Windy?"

"Classic, Skip," the young man said, rolling his eyes. "By the way, the battle of Gettysburg called – they want their 'chops back." He pointed to the skipper's sideburns.

Whalen chuckled, clearly enjoying the pushback. "Nicely done. If not a little obvious – and will you *stop that,* please?"

Whalen reached out and smacked Windy's phone away as he attempted a selfie with his manager.

"Come on, Skip! I've got fans out there who wanna know what I'm up to!"

"I really don't think that's true," Whalen said, shaking his head. "Also, didn't I tell you to leave it in the locker room after the sensitivity seminar we had? You know, the one about not direct messaging dirty pictures to people when you're representing a ballclub?"

"You did, Skipper. But I've got an obligation to both of my fans to give them an up-close look at a professional baseball player's experience!"

"Yes, because this scenario definitely oozes professionalism," said Whalen.

"First of all, they were *requested,* and second of all, they were artfully done!" Windy said, outraged. "And there's no need for the sarcasm, Skip. It's not the 90s anymore."

"So I've been told," Whalen sighed. "Say, why don't you go be a 'professional' and play some second base right now, huh? Help your buddy, J.J. out."

Windy began making his way to the field, shaking his head. "Okay, but you know he's not gonna throw it down to me."

Whalen rubbed his temples with the exhaustion of a put-upon dad. "Windy, please... no defeatism until the ballgame actually starts, you know the rules."

"All right, Skip, but I don't know why I bother."

The old man turned away with a sigh. "I don't know why I do either..."

"What's all that about?" Charlie asked.

"Ah, never you mind – Dad's taking care of it," said Whalen, waving him off.

Behind him, Charlie noted the three umpires conferring as they walked along the third base line. "What about the ump crew? Should I meet–"

"Don't worry about them," Whalen said.

"Why not, Skip? Shouldn't I–"

"*Don't* worry about them." Whalen's tone was not to be argued with. "You leave ump-time to me. Me and them have an understanding, see? There's a precarious balance of power that we do not need to upset. They're mostly calling the pitches the same for both sides these days. So, let's keep it that way."

"Okay, Skip." Charlie thought for a moment. "Do they have names?"

"Nope. As far as you're concerned, they do not. It's home plate and his two buddies. Moe and the Stooges – whatever you gotta tell yourself. Just leave 'em be. Now come here and meet our prized fireballer. Hey, Hayden!"

Charlie followed the skipper's gaze to find a pitcher and catcher who had been warming up across the field. Whalen flagged down the scowling hurler with a wave. The young man dropped his head and jogged over to them. The manager turned, gesturing to Charlie as the young man slowed to a stop before them. "Hayden Chandler, this is Charlie Conroy, your new–"

"Uh-huh," the pitcher said, offering a fraction of a glance in Charlie's direction before turning back to Whalen. "Skip, is there any way we can get somebody else to catch? This guy's a total asshole."

The three men turned to see his batterymate watching them in the distance, mask in hand. He looked bored, an expression only enhanced by the lazy chewing of his gum.

"Hayden, we've talked about this–" Whalen began.

"He doesn't even try, Skip!" Hayden said, the faintest trace of a whine entering his voice. "He doesn't listen when I shake his signs off, he never tries to gun a runner down at second–"

"And I told you, he's trying to help you learn how to control the running game," Whalen said. He spat to accentuate the point.

"By letting them run whenever they want!? It's bullshit, Skip!" The young pitcher held his arms out in disbelief, then let them flop to his side with dramatic flair.

Whalen stepped forward and placed a hand on Hayden's shoulder, guiding him in the opposite direction of his irksome catcher. "Listen, we've got a big day ahead of us, there's no need to blow all your rage out during warmup, okay? Why don't you take five and go do some drills with Windy, huh? Go throw some at Javi."

"Whatever." Hayden shook his head and walked out to the shortstop position.

Charlie watched him, frowning. "Kind of got a chip on his shoulder, huh?"

"Yeah, well, he's got a big arm and no sense, that's for sure," said Whalen. "And he's a rookie, so he sulks and pouts and alienates himself from the other guys. They're gonna pick on him until he starts winning 'em games, then he'll be the hero. Then he'll start to decline, and everyone'll be on his case again. Circle of life."

Whalen turned to the abandoned backstop and gave an aimless wave. "J.J., come on over here!" He turned to Charlie with a mischievous grin. "You're gonna love this guy. He's my buddy – my eyes and ears on the field."

"Always keep your eyes and ears covered with a mask, huh?" said Charlie.

J.J. joined them. His expression was that of a man enduring life's wretched punchline. "What's up, Gray? Was that rookie goober talking trash?"

Whalen halfheartedly pointed at Charlie, as though apologetic about his presence. "J.J. Pike, this here's Charlie."

J.J. gave Charlie's uniform the once-over. "The bat boys get older every season, huh?"

"He's a coach," said Whalen, shaking his head. "Goddamn, I should have done this in front of everybody and gotten it out of the way in one go."

J.J. nodded at Charlie. "Welcome to my nightmare."

"Thanks?" said Charlie.

"So, how's he coming along today?" Whalen asked, nodding across the field, where Hayden was starting a double play sequence.

"The kid?" J.J. asked, following the skipper's gaze. "He's a total asshole."

"Mmm..." Whalen nodded, as though this was expected. "But how's his stuff looking?"

"Oh, his stuff is electric, no doubt about it," J.J. said, shrugging through his chest protector. "It's just high-90s and all over the place. But, you know... high-90s."

"He's a little wild, huh?" said Charlie.

J.J. scoffed. "Are you kidding me? The safest place to stand would be directly over the plate."

Whalen leaned toward the backstop with an air of conspiracy. "You throwing down to second today?"

"Ah, get outta here with that shit, Gray," J.J. said, recoiling. "You know better than that."

"Come on now, buddy, do it once for me," Whalen said, struggling to maintain a straight face. "Prove to the new guy here that you can do it."

J.J. shook his head and began walking to the batter's box. "You're the worst, Gray, you know that?"

"Yeah, I know it," said Whalen, chuckling. He turned to Windy, who was busy fielding grounders at second base with varying degrees of success. "Hey Windy! Comin' down!"

Windy turned to the manager, mystified. He pointed to himself to verify there had been no mistake. Receiving Whalen's nod, he shrugged and dipped into a crouch over second base.

Behind the plate, J.J. wound up and took a forceful step, hurling the ball with a roar. "What's the *POINT?*" His angst rang throughout the ballpark,

Windy stared up, following the arc of the ball as it soared over his head and into the outfield, where it rolled to a grassy stop.

J.J. spat again and turned to Whalen. "Hope you're happy!"

Whalen chuckled and wiped a tear from his eye. "More than you know."

"So, wait," said Charlie, following the manager as he started down the first base line, "he *never* throws to second? He's the catcher!"

Whalen glanced back with a shrug of indifference. "Well, he's also a nihilist, so that keeps it interesting. Hell, J.J.'s been around the leagues almost as long as you were." Charlie winced as the teeth of Whalen's words sank into his heart. "He doesn't care one way or the other about how the frame shakes out, so long as the check clears."

"That's kind of a bleak outlook, isn't it?"

"It's one of his greatest assets," Whalen said as they meandered their way in parallel with the first base chalk. "The game's not personal with J.J. It's just playing ball and working toward that pension so you can pay off the ex and the child support and whatever else."

Charlie nodded. "The national pastime." He'd seen this attitude many times in Low-A ball.

Whalen laughed. "Ain't it the truth?"

Charlie looked back at Hayden. "Okay, so the kid's got ace-potential, that's good. What about the rest of the rotation?"

"Well, we pitched Manny Hulacox yesterday and the game took four-and-a-half hours."

Charlie bit his lower lip. "Did you win?"

"We did not," said the skipper. "You've had the good fortune of joining us in the middle of quite a skid."

"Mom mentioned," Charlie said, offering an empathetic nod. "How many is it now?"

The manager turned to him, an eyebrow arched. "Let's just say that the last time we had a 'W,' there was a reasonable chance of flurries."

"Oh wow."

Whalen sighed. "Anyway, ol' Manny's almost your age, but he's an okay number two. We've also got Reg Pretzel, but he's as stupid as his name."

"Okay," Charlie said, logging this information away. "Who else?"

Whalen shrugged. "I suppose at some point this will stop coming to you as a

surprise–"

"*Three* pitchers?" It was an absurd proposition.

"Yep," the manager nodded. "Just like in the 1890s. You know, when Buffalo Bill's Wild West Show was still a thing you could go see."

Charlie shook his head in disbelief, then slipped firmly into a state of denial. "Okay, wait… this can still work. Bill James did a thing about this a few years ago." He began nodding as the details of the article came back to him. "As long as we pull them after either 80 pitches or five innings, we're– why are you laughing again?"

"Sorry, but I'm getting a real kick out of this," Whalen said, chuckling through his mustache.

"What are you talking about? This could work, Skip! We just need to avoid fatigue pitches–"

"Charlie, open your ears; it's a three-man pitching staff."

"But the bullpen–"

"Is empty."

Charlie refused to accept this. "No."

"I promise you, it's the day after the Pamplona encierro out there. So, our guys are either gonna go the distance, or they're getting pulled and swapped with one of the other two. The one who doesn't pitch, pitches the next day."

"So, it's a *two-man* rotation."

"Well, the league doesn't have mercy rules like in sandlot ball, so sometimes it's a one-man rotation."

"Holy shit."

"I know," Whalen said, patting him on the shoulder. "We've been gutted, kid. Gutted like the dumb fish on our unis."

Charlie felt lightheaded. It was as though the stadium walls were collapsing around him. He grasped for a controllable. "You want to run down the rest of the team for me? I only know their stats."

Whalen raised an eyebrow. "Okay but understand that these are seconds of your life you can never have back." He pointed across the field and continued strolling down the first base line. "At third base you've got Malcolm Watts – well-meaning, but he's a bum. Shortstop, Greg Snemmens, also a bum. Left field, Crotch Callaghan, a bum. Center field, Johnny Yourz, bum. Right field, Turp Salazar, he's… well, he's fine. We've got Joaquin Reverón DHing, but it's really more of a title than a thing that happens. He bats ninth."

"I love the confidence."

Whalen slowed as they entered the base coach box. "And that right there is the only reason any of us have a job right now. Javier Coronado."

Charlie followed Whalen's gaze to what could possibly be best described as a giant. He wasn't really – not in a mythical sense – but as they watched the young man receive throws from his infielders, Charlie couldn't help but recognize the way the first baseman exuded presence. There was effortless power in the arm that threw the baseball back around the horn, and with that power, an air of authority. If the baseball diamond was an ecosystem, Javier Coronado was at the top of the food chain, and not another creature in the barn would question this.

"He's a man-mountain," Charlie said,

"You're goddamned right," said Whalen, offering a slow nod. "You know how some of us are lucky and get a cup of coffee in the Bigs? Well, this kid's having a cup of coffee with us right now. He's as much a sure thing as there is in this game, so just sit back and enjoy while you can."

Javier laughed as he pulled down a high throw from shortstop. He shouted encouragement in Spanish before whipping a grounder toward third.

Charlie was enthralled. "He's really that good?"

Whalen watched his first baseman haul in the throw from across the diamond. "The Big Club signed this kid when he was 16. The scouts said if he developed the way they hoped, he'd be Hank Aaron in bigger pants. Yeah, he's that good. Better, even."

The ball exploded across the field from Javier's massive paw.

Charlie turned to Whalen, stunned. "So, what's he doing here? Why not send him up?"

"Couple reasons," Whalen said, shrugging. "First, he's got some habitual issues."

"Ah," Charlie said, guessing what came next. "What's his deal? Drinking? Drugs?"

"Nah, that'd be easy enough to deal with," said Whalen. "We'd just ship him off to a nice rehab and dry his ass out."

"So, what is it?" No matter how his mother had tried to shield him from the darker aspects of adults playing a game for a living, 22 years in semi-pro ball had shown Charlie an expansive spectrum of personalities and behavioral issues. He figured there might be a very good chance that he'd seen it all.

Whalen's eyes followed the ball as it traveled, back and forth, between infielder and first baseman. "He's an eater."

"An eater?"

"Heck yeah! Look, you can see him getting hungry right now!" said Whalen, pointing at the big man. "He's from a poor village in the mountains of Venezuela, you see. But, now he's here in the endless buffet we call the States, and he is *really* digging in. He's a red-blooded binge-eater if ever I've seen one."

"It's *that* bad?"

Whalen turned to him with a smile of disbelief. "Charlie, we live in New England – every time the bus passes a billboard for Wok Lobster, the kid starts hollering for biscuits. You know two-a-days?"

Charlie frowned. "Yeah?"

"Well, for him that means 'two-lobsters-a-day.' Fresh ones too – he's got it written into his contract. Have you ever seen a 270-pound kid go through a tank of lobsters a month? It'll give you the goddamned gout just watching it."

Charlie found this difficult to believe, but Whalen did not strike him as the type to tell fish stories. Or even lobster stories.

"What's the other reason?" he asked, now unsure if he actually wanted the answer.

Whalen turned to him, an eyebrow raised. "Well, surely you know who's batting third and playing first on the Big Club, right?"

This was unexpected. Charlie ran through the roster of their major league affiliate, seeking a name that would pop out at him and explain the arrested start to this potentially-superheroic career. A moment later, his breath caught as the answer arrived.

"The Franchise..." he said, awestruck. It was the nickname bestowed upon one of the game's most prominent players, and it was as iconic as the man himself.

Whalen nodded as this sank in. "That's right, The Franchise. And The Franchise has played 150 or more games a year, not including post-season, for the past 17 years, and has a loaded contract running for another two."

"Still, wouldn't you want to get this guy some at-bats or something? Figure something out with the DH? No offense to The

Franchise – he's a first-ballot Hall of Famer, for sure – but the guy's almost as old as I am."

Whalen shrugged. "These are the milestone years. The Franchise is approaching 3,000 hits, he's at 1,800 ribbies, well on his way to 1,900, maybe more. He's an All-Star every year and he plays in almost every game. The people pay to watch him play; he knows it and the head office knows it. And if he's walking upright, he'll be there, hovering over that bag like it's his firstborn child."

Charlie watched Javier move as he considered this. There was power in the young man, but there was no doubt it was piled onto a mortal frame. "And he can't play anywhere else, huh?"

"Come on now, you know the deal – if you can hit, you're in the show."

"It's that bad, huh?"

Whalen grunted. "Well, what do you think? The kid's a giant! Asking him to field is like asking a goddamn building to breakdance."

Charlie nodded. "He is kind of a rhino out there, isn't he?"

"A brontosaurus," Whalen said with authority. "The kid's a brontosaurus. Nice, big target to throw at, but he can't play anywhere else out there. He's gotta stick to first. I mean, just because he's a hell of an athlete doesn't mean he can move well, you know?"

HIGH ABOVE THE WARMUP action sat the second deck radio booth for Cape Haddock's AM 1371 station. Within the walk-in closet-sized space, Francesca was trying her best to focus on the bullet points she'd assembled to fill the space of what would most likely be a grueling nine innings against the Coelacanths' perennial rivals, the Splake Steelheads. As usual, her efforts were being thwarted by the presence of her co-host, who was loudly cycling through a series of inane vocal exercises.

"...Dip-dip-dip-dip, ommmmmmm..." he droned, flipping through a sheaf of papers at a pace that suggested he was not taking much away from them. "The Big Dipper. The Big Dipper dips. Win one for the Dipper. If a Dipper had a flipper, would a Dipper flip dips? The bigger the Dipper dips, the more the Dip gets bigger. The *deeper* the Dipper dips, the bigger the deep dips get Dippered–"

Francesca could no longer hear her own thoughts. *"Dip!"* He paused, turning to her with a look of complete incomprehension. She tried to keep her voice measured, professional. "Please. You have to not warm up with your name. It's insanity."

Dip scowled at her. It was as though no one had ever indicated he should stop making noise of any kind. Ever.

"Say," he began, his face rebounding quickly, his tone one of charming negotiation, "you know, I'd love a bottle of water right about now. You think you could help me with that?"

Francesca was awestruck by his audacity. "You'd definitely want to ask... anybody else. Listen, Dip." She was adamant about using his first name. Despite him never properly learning hers, she felt this was an essential part of establishing herself as an equal. "I've fixed the chair, okay?" She held up a screwdriver.

He opened his mouth to speak, but she was careful to head him off. "Actually, I fixed both chairs." She turned to give her seatback a wiggle to demonstrate its firmness, then reached over to do the same with his.

His eyes traveled from one chair to another, undoubtedly looking for the hole in her logic. Finally, he spoke. "Listen..."

He looked at her expectantly.

"'Francesca,'" she sighed.

"Fine," he said, crossing his arms. "Frank, I know we're a little short-handed these days, but don't start *doing* things, okay? Leave it to the professionals."

"The chair professionals?"

"The broadcast professionals, Frank!" She found this inability to acknowledge her as a woman infuriating. "Don't you know a broadcaster is only as good as his chair?"

"What—"

"You *would,* if you were seasoned in 'the biz.' Which is what we in the field call 'the business.'"

"Speaking of, you do see what's been going on around here, right?"

He sneered at her. "You mean your little power grab? Taking over the board, cueing the ads – *fixing the furniture?"*

"Straight talk, Dip: Mrs. Tinley is making cuts across the organization. Hell, Damien and Hiroki worked with you for almost a decade and you haven't wondered what happened to them?"

He laughed. "You don't survive fifty years in the reporting business by asking questions, Frank. It's a tough game to play, show business. Clearly, those two couldn't hack it when they ran up against your lust for radio glory."

"They were fired, Dip." His eyes narrowed at her, but she pressed on. "The team's down, attendance is down, and I'm hearing rumors that HerbCo's going down too. It's happening. And now there are two of us doing a job you did by yourself for decades? How long do you expect that to last?" He did not respond. Francesca allowed herself a glimmer of hope that she might be reaching him. "Work with me, okay? Let's do the best shows we can and then we can both survive the purge."

His lip curled in disgust at this proposal. "Oh, you'd *love* that, wouldn't you. Take a ride on the Big Dipper's coattails to fame and fortune in Fish Town? Ha! Not on my watch, you assassin!"

She sighted, defeated. "That's not what–"

"I've been in this business since before your parents were born, Frank. *I* call the shots around here." He stared out at the diamond below. "I've known Margaret Tinley longer than I care to admit, and I'll tell you something, Frank: she doesn't scare me, and she doesn't know baseball." He turned back to her, his expression stony. "So, I'm going to keep doing *exactly* what I've been doing. I'm Mr. Coelacanth. And no… *widow* is going to take that away from me."

She refused to respond to this directly. If he wanted to dig his own grave, so be it. "You know, she's coming into town today."

Dip raised an eyebrow and chewed on this for a moment. Finally, he cleared his throat. "Listen, Frank. When folks tune into 1371, the region's leading AM station, with all of those classic hits from 1953 to 1963, *and* the official home of the latest news and notes about the greater-metropolitan Cape Haddock goings-on, what do you think they expect to hear?"

"Uh, operating hours for the farmer's market and something by The Moonglows?"

Dip leaned back, aghast. "No! Well, yeah, they can get that too, I suppose – but that's not what I'm talking about." Here, he waved a hand in the air as though showing off an invisible banner. "Think 'Cape Haddock Coelacanth Baseball.'"

Realizing there was no trapdoor out of this conversation, she played along. "They're tuning in to hear the Cape Haddock Coelacanth baseball games."

"No!" he cried in triumph, clearly ecstatic she was now right where he wanted her. "They're tuning in to hear Coelacanth great and former big-leaguer, *Dip Lockerbie,* tell them about the Cape Haddock Coelacanth baseball games!"

"I'm sorry, is there a gas leak in here, or–"

"See, Frank, I paint 'em a picture of what's happening on the ballfield. And the brand of paint I use is called *words.* " He spoke slowly, as though dealing with a toddler. "It's important, because with radio, you can't actually see what's going on. Are you following all of this, Frank?"

"'Francesca.'"

"I will *never get it, "* he said, his tone suggesting this was absolutely the case. "Point being, it doesn't matter what the hell we call you, because you don't amount to much more than the breath between my sentences. So, if the powers-that-be insist on... whatever this is," he continued, waving his hands through the space between them, "that's fine. But I will remind you that the rules here are simple: You do the play-by-play and stick to the play-by-play. You do not deviate from the play-by-play." His right index finger came down like a liver-spotted hammer as each point was expressed. "I don't care if a goddamned spaceship lands in the outfield and honks out 'Luck Be A Lady' with one of those La Cucaracha horns, you don't say word-one about it." His beady eyes bored into her, and while Francesca found it hard to find the old man menacing, she could tell he meant every word of this. "If anything exciting happens, *I'll* be the one who tells mom and dad at home about it, you get me?" he added, his eyebrows migrating northward as he awaited her response.

"Dip, you have to know that doesn't make for good listening," she said, attempting a plea of common sense. "That would be like you working with a robot that just verbalizes motion."

"Exactly!" he said, his eyes lighting up. "That's what I thought we'd be doing this season! But I guess the technology isn't there yet or something, because *you're* here." His face fell at the thought.

Francesca exhaled deeply, gathering herself. "Well, Dip, this all sounds completely unacceptable, if I'm honest."

"Oh, and we all want that now, don't we? Couldn't have a goddamned baseball game if Frankie Skirt-blouse can't be honest, huh?" His exasperation was palpable.

"Dip–"

"I'll tell you what, Frankie-gal, here's what you do," he began, holding his hands out as if about to describe how to build a deck. "If something happens and you absolutely cannot hold it in and you just *need* to throw your two bits in because you think anyone cares, you just shout 'Whoaaa, Dip!' And I'll fill in the rest. Understand?"

"'Whoa, Dip.'" Francesca stared at him, expressionless.

"There you go, now you're getting it!" Dip clapped his hands together in triumph, suddenly all smiles. "So, Javi Coronado hits a homer into the next time zone and *you* go 'Whoooaaa, Dip!' And I'll be there to speak your mind about it!"

Francesca's monotone matched her feelings about this plan. "Whoa, Dip."

"Yep, yep!" he replied, clearly missing the subtext.

They both turned to the window at the sound of the modest crowd applauding. Francesca watched as the Coelacanths, aglow in their home whites, took the field.

"And listen," Dip said, turning back to her, "Normally, I would be pushing back *much* harder regarding your attitude. But this game is happening right now, so, let's just table it until later, huh? Good."

Without waiting for her response, he sank into his chair and immersed himself in his notes. Francesca stared down at him as his eyes scanned the pages and his mouth moved slightly. Shaking her head, she turned back to her own notes, trying with every ounce of patience she could muster, to not be driven mad by the words he now whispered.

"Dip-dip-dip-dip, ommmmmm..."

CHAPTER 6
Pitch Count

CHARLIE WATCHED WITH great interest as the Steelhead infield reacted to Coelacanth center fielder, Johnny Yourz, digging into the batter's box. The third baseman shifted across the diamond to the right side of second base, rolling the shortstop and second baseman up and into the shallows of right field.

Beside him, Whalen shook his head. "Goddammit… Again with this Jimmy Dykes, Boudreau-bullshit!?" he roared at the visiting dugout. Receiving no response, he spat on the field and turned back to the bench.

Charlie checked his clipboard and noted Yourz's unidirectional spray chart: dead-pull hits into right field, all of them. "They're running the Williams shift–"

"I *know* what they're doing, Charlie," Whalen said, dragging his hand down his mustache. "They do it all the time. Drives me nuts." He turned back to the opposing dugout and shouted, "You're pathetic!"

"But, Skip, you can work around it–"

"I shouldn't *have* to work around it," the manager grumbled. "The third baseman should have to stick next to the thing his position is named after. It oughta be illegal!" he hollered at the field. The Steelhead pitcher turned to the dugout, his expression a mixture of curiosity and annoyance.

Charlie could understand the manager's frustration, but the reality was that this was how the game was now: play the odds, trust your pitcher, and risk the bunt or the opposite-field power alleys. The aggressive nature of his manager's glowering suggested he might not currently be open to this level of honest appraisal, so Charlie attempted a more subtle argument.

"So, what happens when our guys use more of an inside-out swing?"

It was a risky maneuver, but he was broaching the subject of the obvious solution to the skipper's shift woes – swinging with the hands in front of the barrel – in a way that assumed this had already been tried and then dismissed with good reason. Charlie knew it was important to not insult his baseball intelligence, but also highlight that which he might have missed since such shifts had become commonplace.

Whalen turned to him with a blank expression. Charlie girded himself for a tirade of Plunkett-esque proportions, but no explosion followed the manager's unblinking stare. Whalen finally unfroze himself with a scratching of his muttonchops and glanced out to the scoreboard, which showed Johnny Yourz sitting at no balls and two strikes.

He then turned to the batter's box, where the overmatched center fielder was digging in with his back foot and clapped his hands. "Atta boy, Johnny, way to hang in there!"

Yourz looked over to Whalen with such surprise that Charlie could only assume this kind of managerial outburst was rare.

"Inside-out now, Johnny! You've got this – inside-out swing!" said Whalen.

Yourz peered around the barrel of his bat once more, clearly baffled by the coaching.

Charlie looked over to the manager as well. "Subtle," he said.

In an instant the pitch arrived, touching mid-90s heat as it bored its way through the strike zone. It had cracked into the catcher's mitt before Johnny Yourz's shoulders had even made a half-rotation. The center fielder had followed his skipper's commands and lead with his hands, but the swing was unbalanced and sent him flailing out of the box.

Stepping back into the dugout, he was greeted with a sarcastic round of applause from the 25% capacity crowd, and a slap on the back from Whalen. "That's okay, Johnny, you don't need that shift bullshit. There's no honor in it." Whalen then turned to Charlie, a mischievous eyebrow raised. "Thoughts?"

Charlie gave his head a quick shake before staring down at his clipboard with renewed interest.

BY THE TIME an hour had passed, the space once occupied by the potential to snag a win had been replaced by the tedium of losing. Francesca's eyes were locked on the field as she narrated the game action.

"And there's a shot up the middle, and that's another single and two more runs on the board for the Splake Steelheads, who have been–"

"You are absolutely right, Frank." Dip's voice came across her headphones like an invasive ocean species being introduced to freshwater. "The Splake Steelheads have taken the bull that is this game by its horns and have *definitely* decided to not let it go, for fear of being gored by said game..."

This dissonance had been the result of their collaboration for months. She would do her play-by-play, the thing she was being paid a borderline amount of money to do, and Dip would step on her. It was behavior to set your clock by, a chronic inability to let anyone else have the floor. This would then be punctuated with what could not even be considered dad jokes, but rather great-granddad jokes.

"...And you'd better believe the Steelhead lineup will be receiving a strongly-worded letter of complaint from the A.S.P.C.A. for being so mean to that beloved animal known as baseball..."

What does that even mean? Francesca asked herself. She could feel years of her life being pulled from her body like reluctant water-skiers. *What does any of this mean?*

CHARLIE AND WHALEN watched from the dugout as their team went down like the Lusitania. Whalen was stoic, staring intently at the game action, his arms crossed. Charlie was more anxious, picking through pages of data on his trusty clipboard.

"This is rough, Skip," he said, wondering if, perhaps, his manager had zoned out at some point, and was unaware of the unfolding disaster.

Whalen didn't look at him. "Yup."

It occurred to Charlie that maybe Whalen was not aware of the details of this scene. "I mean, this is the second inning and Hayden's at 57 pitches already–"

"Yup."

Charlie looked at his clipboard again, shaking his head. The numbers were painting a clear picture, and not one brushstroke looked to be trending favorably for their young starting pitcher. Making his hashmark for the pitch Hayden was currently throwing outside of the zone, he chanced another try. "We've gotta pull him soon, right? At this rate–"

Without tearing his eyes from the game, Whalen reached over and gently pushed Charlie's clipboard away. "Listen, will you put the papers down and just watch the game? If you wanna do an audit, I'll give you my W2s and the kids' student loans."

"I'm paying attention, Skip," Charlie said, holding up the unacknowledged clipboard. "I'm just saying, he's thrown a lot of pitches for not a lot of innings–"

Whalen finally turned and, at a measured pace, removed both clipboard and pen from Charlie's hands.

Charlie watched as the manager scrawled out a brief note on the pitch count. "Wh-what are you doing, Skip?"

"I'm signing my name."

With a flourish, he finished writing, and took the clipboard to the side of the dugout. He was greeted with a handful of cheers from the nearest seats as his head popped up, above the dugout roof. After a quick scan of the waving crowd, he signaled to a young girl wearing a vintage 1960s-era Coelacanth hat.

"Hey, kiddo – want an autograph?"

The girl ran over, the baseball glove enormous on her hand, keeping her slightly off-balance. Her eyes went wide as he handed over the clipboard with a half-smile. "Wow! Thanks Mr. Whalen!"

"You got it – and I like that hat!" he called after her as she ran back to her Dad, holding up her secondhand office supply with pride.

Charlie watched her go, absolutely gobsmacked. "My numbers... My beautiful numbers!"

"...Are now a souvenir, yes," Whalen said, reassuming his one-leg-up position on the dugout steps. "Don't worry, I'm sure you'll be able to bid for it on eBay when you get home. Now, will you pay attention to the game with your eyes, please?" He pointed to the dreadful gameplay on the field, the bored expressions on the players' faces. "You're trying to see everything with your numbers, but it's like hiring Helen Keller to run the CIA or something – there's a very good chance you're going to miss something."

Charlie had to admit this was possibly a fair point. He sighed and nodded. "Okay, Skip."

"Okay!" Whalen turned back to the field, gesturing to the left field wall. "And if you absolutely *need* numbers, look up at the scoreboard. It tells you everything you've gotta know."

"Yeah, but–"

Whalen's tone sharpened. "It tells you the inning, it tells you how many hits the Splakies have, and it tells you how many runs they have. So, we know Hayden's getting shelled like Fallujah, right?"

As he spoke, the Steelhead batter smacked a fat pitch that had been left hanging up in the zone. Charlie looked over to see Hayden's head drop, oblivious to the scrambling that now ensued around him.

Whalen continued to stare at Charlie. *"Right?"* He pointed to the scoreboard as the new runs dropped into place for the away team.

Charlie looked at the bloated number. "Right..." It was almost funny how a figure so inflated could be so deflating. Almost.

Whalen waved his bench coach's attention back to the field. "Now, using your eyes, look at the game. What do you see?"

Charlie watched as Hayden kicked the mound, his face a storm of emotion.

"God*dammit!*" the young man shouted at no one in particular. Charlie watched as the pitcher scowled up at the sky, as though hoping for the divine to intervene and end this nightmare.

Charlie processed his player's existential rage accordingly. "Hayden looks angry."

"Yes, he does." Whalen nodded, again running an absentminded hand over his mustache. "Well, he does have, what, fifty–"

"61."

"Right, 61 pitches on the day. And they seem to have hit most of 'em." Whalen's tone was one of grim resignation.

"Then why won't you pull him, Skip?"

"Because he's gotta get his work in!" Whalen said, shaking his head. "Come on, Charlie, you know the drill here – the kid's throwing high-90s gas, so he's gonna be called up to the Big Club no matter what. And they're gonna be expecting five to six innings a start from him!"

The skipper seemed adamant about this, but Charlie wondered if perhaps the old-timer had lost a step. Scanning the dugout for options that could bail them out of this leaky inning, he spotted the dugout phone. It hung on the wall, utilitarian in design and wholly ignored by the team. *The bullpen.* He moved to it, reaching for the handset.

"Do you at least want me to call the bullpen and get Reg Pretzel loose–"

"Charlie, get your hand off the phone."

Charlie froze, mid-reach. "But–"

Whalen waved away his protests. "As far as I'm concerned that phone is for incoming calls only."

The manager's words were real, but Charlie found the sense behind them lacking. "But Hayden's already thrown 37 pitches this inning, and there's only one out–"

Whalen turned to him, exasperated. "Charlie, the kid's 19 years old. If he can't throw a baseball 37 times in a row, maybe he shouldn't be a professional baseball player."

Hayden threw another ball, outside, and Charlie winced. Hayden glared at the umpire before rounding the mound, picking up the rosin bag, and spiking it into the dirt.

Whalen watched the disaster unfold, transfixed. "This kid's like a wild puma chained to an oil drum... or a Scarsdale infant whose routine was interrupted." He lowered his voice in a way that made Charlie feel as though he was finally being taken into the older man's confidence. "There's no telling what he's capable of. You gotta tire him out of his rage – break him a bit before you can approach him."

As Whalen articulated his curious player-domestication process, Hayden threw another ball, high. Behind the plate, J.J. shook his head and whipped the ball back to the mound.

"Come on, kid, this ain't high school! There's a strike zone — *strike* it!"

In the stands, what was once a dammed trickle of mumbles and hoots, now became a faulty breakwater, with boos squirming their way into the air over the gameplay. The sounds of vocal disapproval stoked the fires of anxiety in Charlie's belly, and he began to pace anew.

Whalen didn't budge but tilted his head to the side at the discontented bench coach meandering in and out of his periphery. "Charlie..."

Charlie sidled next to Whalen, his expression pleading, as though proximity could change the manager's mind. "Skip, this crowd's gonna tear him to pieces – you've gotta get him out of there!"

Hayden threw ball three, a heater, miles outside the zone. J.J. barely moved in response, just turned, in sync with the umpire, and watched as it sailed past. Hayden stalked a circle around the pitching rubber, mumbling to himself.

Whalen turned to Charlie, who watched as the young man melted down before his very eyes. "Do *you* wanna go pull him?"

Charlie's eyes followed as Hayden received a new ball from the umpire, then turned away from the plate to scream into his glove. "Well, that's, uh... that's the manager's job, isn't it?"

Whalen's eyebrow arced upward in response. Charlie turned back to the field as Hayden threw ball four. The crowd groaned as one, peppering it with abrasive curses hollered by the inexplicably faithful. *Why do they keep showing up?* Charlie wondered. *This can't be anything other than a hate-watch.*

He was torn from his ponderings by the unexpected movements of Whalen. Charlie watched him, as surprised as an undertaker whose deceased has yawned and hoisted himself from the embalming table. He watched as the skipper moseyed a few feet away from the dugout's top step.

"Hey, Blue!" he barked. The home plate umpire turned to the Coelacanth dugout, his face imperceptible behind his mask. Whalen spat into the foul territory grass. "If you get on your knees, it'll be a lot easier to blow that call."

Without a moment's hesitation, the ump ripped his mask off and pointed at Whalen. "You're outta here, Whalen, you piece of garbage! Get off my field!" He launched his hand into the air, as though physically tossing Whalen toward the showers. He then turned back to the batter, who stood just outside the box, uncertain of how to proceed. "And you," the ump said, pointing to first, "take your base! Buncha lousy bums, all of ya!"

With a whisper of a shrug, Whalen turned and headed toward the dugout tunnel. He pulled the lineup card from his back pocket as he passed his new coach and slapped it against Charlie's chest with a grin. "Okay? Now you're the manager! You have fun now, I'll see you inside."

Whalen chuckled and ducked into the tunnel. The sound of his cleats clomping echoed from the hall as he headed toward the clubhouse.

Panic flooded Charlie's face as he watched his leader depart. He looked back to the pitching mound.

Hayden kicked up a plume of dirt. *"Fuck!"* he screamed, no longer bothering to cover his mouth.

Charlie pushed his hat up to the crown of his head and sighed. "Oh, it's a beautiful game..."

"MY, OH MY!" Dip exclaimed, leaning back in his chair. Francesca observed as he checked his watch, his face projecting a boredom absent in his voice. "And Hayden Chandler is issuing trips to first base like an official representative of the Baseball Transit Authority. And he is double-checking seat assignments and punching tickets to pay a visit to the big man, Javier Coronado."

Francesca gambled, uncertain if he was done speaking. "Wow, and it looks like Manager Whalen might have been run from this–"

Dip's head snapped in her direction, freezing her mid-sentence. He scowled and reached over to the mixing board, slapping a button. Francesca watched as the tiny LED lights over the microphone inputs started blinking, their buses now muted.

He leaned toward her, his voice a low snarl. "Uh, do you remember what I told you to say when you think you might have something interesting to share, new meat?"

Francesca's eyes narrowed. "Oh," she said, taken aback – surely he wasn't serious about this? She stared back at him, hoping this was all a joke. A subtle fury danced in his eyes, and she quickly realized it was not. "Um... 'Whoa, Dip.'"

Dip unmuted the mics without a word and pointed at hers. Francesca shook her head, baffled, as she leaned back into it.

"Whoa, Dip–"

"No hope with dope and soap-on-a-rope! Get the towels ready, clubhouse fellas – it looks like Skipper Gray Whalen is taking that looong walk down the tunnel to hit the showers early tonight!"

Francesca watched as Charlie popped out of the dugout. He gave a nod to the umpire, signaling a timeout, and made for the pitcher's mound.

Francesca cleared her throat, nodding her head toward the field. "Uh – whoa, Dip?"

Her co-host didn't even bother to look at her as he jumped back into his expansive narration. "And with the Skipper listening to the rest of this game back in his office, that means new bench coach..." Dip rifled through his mess of printouts, squinting as he tried to decipher them through the thick lenses of his glasses. "...Charlie Conway–"

"Roy!" Francesca whispered at him, ducking away from her mic.

Dip restarted without missing a beat. "Roy Conway–"

"No, Con-*roy*. Charlie Conroy!" Francesca whispered, exhaling in disbelief.

"...the strangely-named Conroy Charlie Conroy is now in charge of the team. And it looks like he might be faced with the unenviable task of removing the young fireballer from this game..."

BOOS RAINED DOWN from the few people left in the stands as Charlie trudged to the mound. He took his time, realizing that the rubber was about to meet the road. He kept his head down for the most part, stealing only the slightest glances of his pitcher, who muttered to himself as he rubbed up the ball. He appeared to be on the brink of a psychotic break, and his mood did not seem to improve upon noticing his strange, new coach approaching.

"Who the hell are you?" he asked as Charlie dared set foot on the mound. Charlie knew pitchers were territorial about their terribly specific dirt but reminded himself that he was technically (if not in spirit) in charge.

"I'm the, uh... well, I'm the manager," he said. His voice sounded unconvincing. "For right now," he added.

Hayden was not impressed. "So?"

J.J. ran up to join the confab as Charlie realized he was being asked by someone who was 20 years his junior, to plead his case.

"Well, I'm thinking – actually, *we* were thinking," he said, lamely gesturing back to the manager-less dugout, "it's time for you to, you know... probably come out of the game."

J.J. drew near just as these words left Charlie's mouth. The catcher scowled, his eyes darting to the enraged pitcher as he turned on his heel and began walking back to home plate. "Oh shit..."

Hayden didn't register any of this, simply stared at his new bench coach with an unblinking, laser intensity. "I'm sorry, *what* are you doing out here? I'm not done yet. I've got this guy."

Hayden waved his glove in the direction of the on-deck circle, where the Steelhead's designated hitter, Bart Chaney Sr. waited. He was a goon of a man, his face grizzled with age, his torso an enlarged cupboard housing seasons' worth of roadside diner meals.

Charlie straightened at the sight of the uniformed mass taking a series of violent warmup swings. He turned back quickly to his young player. "Hey, don't get me wrong, I love the confidence. It's just... you've thrown a lot of pitches–"

"I said *I'm not done yet,* grandpa!"

"Well, I'm 39, so–"

"Hey, NASA!" The home plate umpire glared at the pair from the front of the batter's box. J.J. stood beside him, shaking his head in disgust. "Let's play ball, huh?"

Charlie signaled for another moment as the boo-birds sent their calls of discontent showering down upon the field. A glance around the diamond revealed to Charlie every member of his team, standing around, arms crossed. They looked borderline catatonic. He quickly turned back to his young pitcher with a new strategy.

"You're throwing a lot of fastballs today, huh?"

"Yeah, that's kind of what I do," said Hayden. "So?"

"Well, I studied the book on Chaney Sr. last night–"

"Great, we'll go to Pizza Hut after the game – who gives a shit?"

Charlie felt the pitcher's attention slip from his already tentative grasp. "79 and 7, okay?"

Hayden's eyes bored into him, his jaw clenching. "What the *fuck* are you talking about?"

Charlie inwardly acknowledged that he probably could have been more specific. "He swings at soft-away 79% of the time, but he only makes contact 7% of the time. He won't lay off it and he can't do anything with it either." He examined his pitcher's face for any sign of understanding and found none. "79 and 7," he said again, as though this repetition might etch the figures into Hayden's mind through sheer vocal erosion.

"Uh-huh. Thanks, computer."

Charlie held his hands up, attempting to calm him. In that moment, it felt more like surrender. "Soft-away, okay? He can't hit soft-away."

Hayden glared at him like he was the summer's peskiest mosquito. "Great, now sit... *down.*"

Charlie backed away, toward the dugout. "Just think about it."

As Francesca finished the sponsored live reads that were designated for timeouts, she noticed Charlie leaving the mound and looked over at Dip. He was trying his hardest to ignore her presence by staring down at the same piece of paper he'd been engrossed in since before the game started. *I don't even think there's anything on there,* she thought, before hailing his attention. "Whoa, Dip..."

Dip turned to her, fury in his eyes. His expression morphed into bewilderment as he followed the motion of her head-nod to the action on the field.

He squinted and pushed his glasses up on the bridge of his nose as he leaned into his mic. "And it looks like Hayden Chandler is staying in this game to face Bart Chaney Sr., the Steelheads' thunder-dumping designated hitter..."

Francesca felt a throbbing in her temple and watched as Charlie scampered the last few feet to the dugout, like a farmer who'd just stuffed dynamite into a gopher hole. And with that little scamper, a question entered her mind: *I wonder if he knows what he's doing...*

CHARLIE DIDN'T KNOW what he was doing. Despite throwing around all the weight his temporary authority could afford, he watched in dismay as J.J. waved his fellow Coelacanths back before taking position behind the plate. "Everybody move back. Mooove back..."

With a sharp flexing of the bat, Chaney Sr. stepped into the box as the catcher lowered his mask. Hayden leaned in, going through the motions of reading J.J.'s signs.

The booing waned, as though this next pitch required everyone's rapt attention. It was a chore that was to be endured, and every single person in the stadium knew which pitch was coming. All except one.

Soft away, soft away, soft away, Charlie chanted in his head. It was a mantra, and he was the guru, willing his belligerent student to make the right decision.

As Chaney Sr. crushed the inevitable fastball, sending it to the warning track, the boos rained down. The Steelhead runner on first base crossed home plate, the sight of which sent Charlie staggering back and collapsing onto the bench.

Just as his wise skipper had suggested, Charlie looked up at the scoreboard for the pertinent information he needed and found it there.

Only seven more innings to go...

CHAPTER 7
The Wake Of Defeat

FOR AS AGONIZING as the four-hour drubbing had been, the Coelacanth clubhouse was alive with good-natured banter as the team dressed down for the day. This was not new to Charlie – he'd been losing for years and had long ago become accustomed to putting the beatings behind him. Some would have argued that this was the foundation of his entire career. Had the stat been invented that gauged such an ability, Charlie would have been the all-time leader – the Rickey Henderson of failing forward.

What was new was the digital recording device Francesca had shoved in his face. He had been backed up against his locker, left with no apparent exit as she tried to pin him down with talking points.

"Coach, another tough loss for the team tonight, As the newest set of eyes in the clubhouse, what're you seeing from your players?"

What was he supposed to say to that? Certainly not the truth – the truth would only reflect poorly on what was left of the organization. Charlie leaned toward the recorder. "Um, well, they're definitely playing for the, uh, money that we pay them. So."

Francesca didn't waste any time. "What do you foresee working on with the team?"

Rivets of sweat lined his forehead as panic sank in and every ill-stated pull-quote leading to a publicity disaster he'd ever read flashed through his brain. *Platitudes – don't forget the platitudes…* His eyes darted down at the recorder. The device had two microphones bent toward each other, crisscrossing like Wonder Woman's gauntlets.

Charlie faintly recalled them to be known as the 'Bracelets of Submission.'

He cringed at the thought and, seeing that she was still asking questions, forced himself back into the moment. "We definitely need to string some hits together if we want to score runs. And I've always believed that you cannot win this game unless you score at least one run."

"And what sort of plan do you and Manager Whalen have to get that going?"

"Uhhh–"

"Do you see the potential here for this team to win?"

"Uh–"

"Do you feel like you need new talent, or can you deal with the misshapen lumps of clay you have now?"

He gave her the only explanation he could think of. "They're human beings."

He waited for his brain to supply him with further insight he could pass on to the listening audience, but none came. He shrugged with finality.

"Thanks for the time, Coach."

Francesca dropped the microphone and hit a series of buttons on the recorder. "Sorry if that was a little aggressive. I've found it best to keep the questions moving, before you realize what's going on."

Charlie nodded, defeated. "Interview by bulldozer – sure, no problem."

"You can dig it?" She shot him a rakish grin.

"Wow," he said, "I guess I'd laugh at that – I deserve it."

But Francesca had already turned her attention to a thorough scan of the locker room, a newsy predator in search of quality interview prey. He watched her, perhaps a second longer than he would have had she known he was watching her. She quickly homed in on the skipper, who was busy demonstrating a wide batting stance to Javier on the other side of the clubhouse. The large first baseman laughed at his manager but indulged him the lesson.

"I'm gonna go catch Whalen before he stuffs the towel under his office door," she said, already halfway to the other side of the room. Whalen spotted her approaching. His eyes widened at the sight of the recorder she was brandishing. Charlie watched him make a deft beeline for his office, only to find himself trapped within by the intrepid reporter, who followed him without an invite.

All of this was nearly amusing, all things considered, but the comedy was immediately sucked from the room, as he felt the vacuum of a familiar presence.

"Charles Michael-Margaret Conroy! You have some explaining to do."

Charlie closed his eyes for a moment, with a foolhardy wish that he could somehow vanish in a puff of smoke. He admitted to himself it would never happen and turned to face his outraged accuser.

"Mom, you made it!" he said, taking a stab at expressing relief in seeing Margaret briskly making her way across the room. He found it curious that she appeared to be clutching his blazer but brushed it aside as she neared. "Homeland Security let you go, right? You didn't escape?"

Margaret huffed as she neared him. "That ticket taker got exactly what was coming to him," she said with a dismissive wave of the hand. "It was worth every hour I spent in handcuffs. And yet I arrive to find this!?" She held out the blazer, giving it a shake, as though that explained anything. "You're in some deep water now, Jacques Cointreau."

"Mom, I think it's 'Cousteau'–"

"I don't care if it's 'Bongo A-Go-Go,' do not sass your mother."

Charlie assumed the garment rattling was being done for effect and chose to ignore it. "Listen, I'm really sorry we lost again, but it *is* going to take some time–"

Margaret's hand darted into the jacket. "I found *cigarettes* when I was going through your pockets."

The words didn't register with Charlie. "What?"

She withdrew her hand from the pocket and held up the crumpled soft pack of Whalen's confiscated cigarettes.

"Oh, Mom – those are just the Skipper's! I took those away from him earlier," he said, taking them and stuffing them into his shirt's front pocket. "And why were you going through my jacket?"

"I can't help it, I'm your mother – I get mad."

Charlie frowned. "You mean, you worry?"

She frowned back. "I said what I said. Now listen to me: I'm having the cab brought around to take us back to Herbert's place in ten minutes. Do not be late." She jabbed her index finger at him to drive the words home.

"Mom, please don't treat me like a child," he said, softly outraged that she thought of him as such a goof. "I'm a grown-up and I need you to take me seriously, okay?"

Margaret arched an eyebrow. "Oh, I see. You're a big boy now."

"Exactly. I'm a big boy now." He immediately felt like this could have been phrased better. "I'll meet you out front, okay? I just gotta get my bag out of my locker."

Margaret snorted in disgust and left the clubhouse without another word. Charlie was used to this behavior and didn't question it, but decided he was not looking forward to the evening ahead. As he slid his arms through the sleeves of his incriminating blazer, he eyed Francesca, who was now departing from Whalen's office. She was looking down at her recorder in one hand and typing notes into her phone with the thumb of the other. He made the tactical move of slowing his movements down to a pace more dramatic, in the hopes she would speak with him again.

No sooner had he formulated and begun executing his plan, then he looked up to see her watching him move in slow motion. His jacket hung awkwardly over his head as he worked it onto his body with a motion that could only be called graceless. She seemed curious.

"Oh, hey," he said, maintaining the casual tone of a man who was not oddly engaged with his clothing. "That was quick."

"Yeah, well, you know what a chatterbox Gray is," she said. "I'm happy if I can get a complete sentence out that doesn't feature him chewing his prime rib. He wants to see you, by the way. You've been summoned." She looked down to check the recorder display once more, allowing Charlie a window of opportunity to shrug the jacket fully onto his torso. "All part of the glamorous life of a radio nerd. How about you – long day?"

Charlie huffed a weary breath. "Long game."

"Hey, just hang in there," she said, offering him a playful sock on the arm. "It gets worse."

His face fell. "Really?"

"'Fraid so. It's the Coelacanth way." She watched, curious, as he dragged a hand down his face. "You need a drink? On me."

This took him off-guard. Despite his many years in the lowest league, it could be argued that Charlie's baseball-fumbling could be matched only by his eternal awkwardness around women. It wasn't as though these interactions never happened, but the opportunities were certainly rare. He decided to put his best cleat forward. *Women appreciate honesty,* he reminded himself. "I totally would, but... my mom's picking me up."

Francesca got to mid-smile before she finished reading his expression and realized he was quite serious. She froze her face where it was, awkwardly wedged between two feelings, and soldiered on. "You serious?"

"She's waiting out front," he nodded. "Gotta unpack and all that."

"Ah, right," she said. His eyes fell to the floor in self-disgust. He felt her watching him for a moment. Then she said, "Well, that's all right, we'll go tomorrow."

"Yeah?" He looked up at her, new hope in his eyes. "That's probably for the best – she'd be pretty mad if I ditched her."

"You mean worried?"

"I said what I said."

She laughed despite his morose tone. "Come on, guy! It's not like she can *ground* you, right?"

His eyes darted to the side and he coughed up an anxious chuckle. "Ha. Riiight..."

Francesca smiled and made for the clubhouse door. She paused, considering something, then turned back to him. "Not to be 'that' person, but the cigs set a pretty bad example for the kids, you know?"

She pointed at the pack of Whalen's cigarettes, peeking out of his breast pocket.

He looked down at them, mortified, and made a brief sputtering of excuses before looking up to find that she had already breezed through the exit.

CHARLIE ENTERED WHALEN'S office to find the old man seated, a napkin tucked into his shirt collar. On his desk sat the remains of his dinner, the rest of which appeared to be stuffed into the side of his mouth. Charlie had spent the better part of the day with the skipper, but he had yet to see him as satisfied or enthusiastic as he now appeared to be. The rhythm of his chewing did not slow as he watched the new bench coach slide into the room and close the door behind him.

"Hey, Skip – Francesca said you wanted to see me?"

"Hm? Oh yeah. She's tough, that one. I like her. Asks all the hard questions."

"You've got that right," Charlie said, flashing back to the ringer of inquiry she'd just put him through. "How do you deal with it all season?"

Whalen wiped his mustache with the bottom of his napkin and waved him off. "Ah, I just give her the ol' runaround. It's pretty standard issue. 'We should've scored more runs,' 'It's a long season,' 'They're still developing…' And you can deny any accountability by saying 'Sometimes you just have to tip your cap to the other team,' which shoves all responsibility onto them. *Or* you can offer my favorite: 'We need to play like a team and start winning again.' Totally on-message, but still pretty vague because there is no message."

Charlie nodded, considering this. "Kind of like saying, 'Tomorrow, we've just gotta come in here and put on our gloves and hats and play some baseball.'"

Whalen's eyes lit up. "Yeah, that's a good one – can I use that?"

"Listen, Skip, about tonight–"

"Ah-ah-ah, we don't talk about it," Whalen said, putting his hands up. "You just said it yourself – we've got games all summer. We'll try again tomorrow."

Charlie frowned. "Okay, sure – but don't you want to factor in tonight's numbers for the–"

Whalen gave him a look. "Charlie. Come on." He stared at his new coach for a moment before pushing his chair away from his desk with a groan. He stood, and Charlie was relieved to see the manager had his trousers on. "You want some numbers? 10-8-1956. Game 5 of the World Series."

Charlie's brain whirred as it associated the digits. "Don Larsen throws a perfect game against the Brooklyn Dodgers for the New York Yankees."

Whalen nodded his approval as he made his way around the desk. "Classic Brooklyn Dodgers, right? I once heard a story about that afternoon. It was the bottom of the 7th, the Bombers were up, and Mickey Mantle walks past the exit to the tunnel in the dugout, where Donny Larsen's ducked out for a quick smoke."

Whalen drew near, raising a finger to accent his storytelling. "Now, at that point in the game, everyone in the house knew what the deal was: 21 up, 21 down, two frames to go. And, this game being superstitious as it is, all the Yankees are doing their duty and ignoring the hell outta ol' Donny, acting like nothing's going on, but, you know, *not.*"

Charlie understood. "Of course not, it's a no-no."

Whalen nodded. "A *perfect* no-no! So, the Mick looks over and Larsen says to him, 'You think I'll make it?'"

Charlie waited a moment before his curiosity got the better of him. "What'd Mickey say?"

Whalen stopped in front of him, his voice lowering into something more dramatic. "Nothing. Not one word. He just walked away." The manager watched Charlie's face as this sank in. "Now, do you get where I'm going with this?"

Charlie nodded slowly as he replayed the scene in his mind one more time. This was certainly a test, and he wanted to impress his new skipper with his analytical acumen. After all, this was the man who would be shepherding Charlie's new career. "I *think* so..." he began, teasing a little drama of his own. "You're saying that, despite all of the probability projections and statistics, sometimes there's still a place for superstition and magical thinking. Even if its only effect on the game is how it impacts our collective mindset. Is that right, Skip?" Charlie was certain he'd nailed it.

"What?" Whalen frowned at him. "No – I'm saying he was *smoking*. Gimme these."

Whalen reached toward Charlie and pulled the confiscated cigarette pack from his front pocket. He tapped one out with a grin and lit it up as Charlie watched, helpless.

The manager gave him a good-natured slap on the arm, then brushed by him, followed by the gray billows of smoke. "See you tomorrow, kid."

IT HAD BEEN the briefest of rides down the street to the private pier where Herbert Tinley's East Coast domicile was moored. As the driver unloaded their suitcases, mother and son surveyed the legendary man-about-town's yacht. This was to be their new home for the time being, but Charlie found the idea difficult to accept.

The *HTIII* was the sort of ship that would have been rented for a music video shoot in the early-1980s. It shone through the dark of night with a gleaming white that was not unlike the marble that now covered Herbert's corpse. Never one to let fancy things be simply fancy, he had custom ordered it to be detailed in the deep amber color that only the fakest of gold could provide.

They made their way up the precarious, rope-lined gangplank and began soaking in the so-called 'vibe' of this physical manifestation of a rich man's excess. It was somehow more gauche than even they had expected.

Charlie could feel the slow roll of the tide beneath his feet. It was a sensation that required him to keep his legs perpetually locked, making the experience of merely existing in this place exhausting. Meanwhile, his mother crossed the length of what would be considered the living room without a worry of balance. Charlie wondered if the deep pile of the blindingly white carpet was chosen because it offered additional ankle support.

Stepping away from the stairs, he ducked through the doorway to follow her. The ceiling was low – not so low that he needed to hunch over, but low enough to where it was uncomfortable knowing there was little room for error when fully upright. What if he needed to jump more than three inches, what then?

He pushed the thought away, knowing he needed to concentrate on more pressing matters, a conversation that the appearance of this nautical absurdity had interrupted.

"Mom, I understand that cutbacks were needed, but you got rid of the entire staff."

Margaret rolled her eyes. "Oh, please – I would've sold the seats and made everyone stand if I thought it would cut down on the overhead."

"I thought Herbert got the city to pay for all the refurbs?"

"Of course he did," said Margaret. "They would've funded a flight to the moon if he'd told them it would revitalize the harbor district. But tax bonds don't pay the utilities on that obscene fishing pole they plugged in out there. As if losing was any more watchable when branded by HerbCo." She barked a laugh of contempt.

"But did you need to get rid of *everybody?*"

"Charlie, the people of Cape Haddock deserve to see their tax dollars hard at work," she said. "By which I mean, we need to literally keep the lights on so they can see the ballpark they paid for."

"Okay, this is a great point – *seeing* things," said Charlie, happy to be reminded of what he felt was an obvious flaw. "How is our team supposed to know where they're going without base coaches?"

"People who point for a living are a luxury this team can't afford," she said. "You'll just have to suggest your players pay attention to what's going on when they're out there. They should know which base to run to by now – they're *numbered,* for the love of Pete."

"But this can't be allowed, rules-wise—"

"Charlie, the rule book explicitly states: 'The team at bat shall station two base coaches on the field.' 'Shall,' not 'Will.'"

"It's a question of *verbiage?*" Leave it to his mother to find the grey area in a black-and-white issue.

"It's a question of how long our lawyer can keep the matter tied up in league meetings while we're busy *not* paying those salaries."

They stared at each other in silence for a moment while Charlie regrouped. True to form, she had an answer for everything. "You're pretty cutthroat, Mom, you know that?"

"Aw, welcome to the real world, my boy – nice of you to finally join us," she said, patting him on the cheek. "You can call me a pirate if you need to, but there isn't a team or a player out there who isn't looking for an edge. Corked bats, overwound baseballs, stolen signs, steroids, segregation, the reserve clause – it's *all* cutthroat. But no one cares about the ugliness if it brings in the gate and pads all the right bank accounts."

"You're so cynical," he said.

"I'm a *realist,*" she corrected. "And why shouldn't I be? Look at where airheaded fantasy gets you – a honeymoon suite booked on Aaron Spelling's wet dream."

She turned to open a door, revealing what was unmistakably the master bedroom. "Of course," she sighed.

Charlie joined her in the doorway and was immediately struck by the velvety ambience. "Oh god," he said, taking in the leopard-print fabric that lined the walls and part of the ceiling, where it was interrupted by a garish, circular mirror. Charlie looked at the bed, piled high with earth-toned pillows. "Is that what I think it is?"

Margaret shook her head. "Leave it to Herbert to have a waterbed on a goddamned yacht." She turned to him. "This can be *your* room. I'd wait a half-hour after eating before going to sleep if I were you." With that, she departed for the decks below.

CHAPTER 8
The Gilded Cage

A SMALL SCHOOL of Coelacanth players gathered around the netting of the batting cage, watching as Javier took his immaculate swings. Charlie was among them, clipboard in one hand, forehead in the other, massaging his temples. He watched the soaring arcs of the infamous Coronado hitting prowess and shook his head in wonder.

"'I swing the bat electric!'"

Turning at the sound of this bellowing proclamation, Charlie saw Whalen ambling toward him. The skipper grinned, slowing as he approached the cage. He took in Javier's elegant swing and nodded. "'...And if the bat does not do fully as much as the soul?'"

Holy hell, the old man's gone crackers, Charlie thought as he puzzled over this odd performance. "I'm sorry?"

Whalen ignored him. "'And if the bat were *not* the soul... what *is* the soul?'"

Charlie frowned, the words now somewhat familiar. "Who's that, Walt Whitman?"

"Nah," Whalen said kicking a clod of dirt from his spikes. "A Whitman's Sampler, more like."

"You learn that from Susan Sarandon?"

Whalen looked at him, puzzled. "Who?"

Charlie shook his head. "Sorry, never mind. I'm not feeling so hot today."

Whalen looked him over with the practiced eye of a man who had spent his life diagnosing twenty-somethings who were not taking care of themselves. "Did you and moms get a batch of bad clams last night?"

"No," said Charlie, trying not to linger on that thought. "I just don't have my sea legs yet. Turns out that sleeping on a boat doesn't really suit my, uh, constitution."

"Tummy trouble," Whalen nodded. "Gotcha. It is a *lot* of boat, I'll give you that."

"Have you ever been on that thing?"

"Only against my will," said the manager. "Herb's yacht parties always brought to mind the phrase 'ship of fools.'"

Charlie nodded. "And now I'm the cabin boy. Great."

As he squeezed the bridge of his nose, Javier knocked a pitch deep into the outfield. Charlie released his face and watched in amazement as the ball flew. One of the Coelacanths uttered a falling-bomb whistle as the ball clanged against the right field bleachers. The other players hooted and high-fived each other, as though they'd been responsible.

"Goddamn..." Charlie shook his head, watching as Javier grinned and said something in Spanish to his teammates.

"The legend in his youth," Whalen nodded. "Enjoy it while you can."

Charlie watched as the young man dug into the batter's box, scratching the toe of his cleat into the dirt like a bull about to charge. "You really think he's the Chosen One, huh?"

Whalen shrugged. "Well, the usual qualifiers apply, of course."

"Such as?"

Whalen gestured to the young man with the mighty swing. "The kid has his whole career ahead of him, right? But there are plenty of opportunities for him to screw it up. Plenty of temptations along the road he'll be traveling. *But,* if he ignores the demons and behaves himself, drives in runs, stays healthy... as long as he entertains the fans who'll pay to see him... then he'll be able to do what he's capable of doing."

The crack of Javier's bat drew their attention. They craned their necks to follow another perfectly placed double. Charlie had never seen such confidence in a minor leaguer. Javier held the bat as though he'd been born holding it. As though it was an extension of his body.

"That's... quite a swing."

"The echo has echoes." Whalen nodded. He watched the young giant rock the bat into two sharp practice cuts across the plate, then turned back to Charlie, a glint in his eye. "And the kid's only 20 years old. You remember that feeling, I'm sure. The beginning?"

Charlie nodded; he remembered it all too well. "I had my whole career ahead of me. I was going to be a player, you know?"

Whalen nodded. "Sure you were – I was too. All of these guys are." He gestured to the young men gathered around the cage. "Or *were,* anyway." Whalen paused, considering his team. "It's that feeling of the beginning that keeps you going. Through the bus rides, the rented rooms, season after season. That feeling that if you just keep going, just ride out the drills, the slumps, the blowout losses… your game will come together, and you'll get a call from the Big Club. It's just that simple in the beginning."

Charlie found the statement to echo feelings long passed. "Yeah. I remember."

"And the hard part's not even the end, but the middle," said Whalen. "You wake up one morning and realize that you're three seasons in and that call hasn't come, and your skill set has flatlined... and it occurs to you that your game might never come together the way you or the team want. And it becomes clear that, if you keep going, you are now thoroughly in the *middle* of your career. And that's a hell of a decision to face: end at the beginning, knowing deep down that the express train you want isn't gonna stop at your station... or choose the middle and shuttle back and forth on the local until you just can't take it anymore."

Charlie gave him a sad smile. "Not exactly *Field of Dreams,* is it?"

Whalen shrugged, turning back to the practice session. "Well, it's where *we* live anyway – grown men, enabling each other while wearing numbered pajama outfits." He paused, lost in a thought, before emerging and giving Charlie a backhanded slap on the arm. "But hey, we're the lucky ones, you and I."

"How's that?"

"Well, coaching is the magic loophole to prolonging the middle for *ages,* if you want. We actually live in the Middle Ages. Like Chaucer."

Charlie frowned. It was a truth he'd had a difficult time accepting; though he was now middle-aged, he felt as though he'd hardly lived at all. He shook the thought from his mind. It was still too overwhelming for him to process, so he turned back to his new mentor. "You made it up to the Big Club, didn't you?"

Whalen shrugged with a carelessness that suggested he had little to brag about. "Oh, sure – I yo-yoed back and forth for a few years. There were a couple of seasons where it felt like I was just getting paid to experience the joys of transportation."

The manager turned away from the plate action and leaned back against the metal frame of the cage. He crossed his arms and stared out at the bleachers, sinking into the past. "I'd get called up, give a guy a day off, warm guys up before the game. Get sent back down, get on the bus, ride all night, show up at my home park, only to get a note calling me up again..." Charlie waited, watching as Whalen's eyes quivered for a split-second. "Quite a life, that is." He returned to the present and turned back to his coach. "As you well know."

Charlie shook his head. "Can't say I ever got a note like that."

Javier lined another ball up the gap in right-center. Whalen spat, as though to punctuate the hit. "Yeah, well, it ain't always what it's cracked up to be, I can tell you. Never knowing where you stand, which league you're in, where your home is." He looked up and squinted into the sun. "It's better to have a team, you know? The team is everything. It's family." As if on cue, the players gathered around the batting cage hooted as Javier launched one into the center field seats. They exploded with cheers as the ball hit the deep bleachers with a *clang!*

"By the way, did you do your homework?" said Whalen, glancing behind them.

"My homework?"

"Just asking," Whalen said, throwing a thumb over his shoulder, "because it looks like your mom's here."

Charlie's stomach sank as his eyes darted past the skipper. True enough, Margaret had emerged from the dugout and was now stalking her way across the field, a clipboard tucked under her arm. She carried a hand-painted, cardboard baseball diamond, upon which were taped several baseball action figures of about four inches in height.

Whalen's bottom lip curled up over his mustache in curiosity. "...and she seems to be carrying a diorama?"

"Here," Margaret said as she reached them. She shoved the homemade baseball field into Charlie's hands. "You forgot this on one of the bulkheads this morning. What have I told you about leaving your toys lying around?"

Charlie could feel himself turn red as Whalen raised an eyebrow, the smallest hint of a smile peeking from beneath his whiskers.

"They're not toys, Mom, they're models – it's a *model,*" he said, cradling the tableau.

Margaret wasn't having any of it. "We got you the dolls from the toy aisle, Charlie – they're toys."

Whalen stared at the slapdash scene, fascinated. "Wow, are those Starting Lineup action figures?"

A line of flop sweat began to form on Charlie's forehead. "No! No, they're three-dimensional avatars. I was using them to visualize some potential strategies."

"You sure?" Whalen said, bending down to examine them more closely. "Look, you've got Lou Whitaker, Dan Quisenberry, Carney Lansford–"

"They're *not* toys, I was trying to plan ahead!"

"He says goodnight to them before going to bed," Margaret said to Whalen, shaking her head.

"Mom!" In a long career of embarrassing moments, this conversation was rapidly making its way up the list.

Whalen piled on with a chuckle as he tipped his cap to Margaret. "How are you, Maggie?"

Charlie shook his head. "*'Maggie?'*" he muttered to himself. It was completely foreign to him.

"Why, Gray Whalen – who let your corpse back in here?" Margaret gave him the once-over. "Escaped from the funeral home, have you?"

Whalen grunted another laugh. "Still alive, I'm afraid."

Margaret's lip curled as she homed in on his facial hair. "Sometimes I think those things on your face keep you that way, just so they can have something to walk them around."

Whalen grinned and smoothed his sideburns. "They do get more looks than the rest of me, I can't argue with that."

"Looks of *concern,* Gray – it's just people wondering which retirement home to call. How's Iris?"

"Well, you know, I'm out of the house for the next three months, so she's doing great."

"You know, I don't understand why she bothers with you," said Margaret.

Whalen nodded as though this was fair. "I know, Maggie, I know." He paused for a moment. "I was sorry to miss Herb's funeral. We had to get our asses handed to us in that spring training series with Alewife, you'll recall."

Margaret waved him off. "I can't say you missed much – the wake was as dead as the body. But, how is Charlie doing?"

Charlie was about to respond on his own behalf, but Whalen carried on. "Oh, he's seems all right. He just got here, so it's kind of hard to see where his baseball I.Q. will fit in."

Charlie couldn't believe it. "You guys know I'm standing right here, correct?"

Whalen continued, taunting Charlie with an amused smile. "Plus, he forgot his diorama, so..." He tilted his head, as though this was a sure sign of inevitable failure.

Margaret seemed to agree, her lip curling. "Ugh. He's a good boy, Whalen – he's just lost without a map when it comes to living his life."

"Mom, I can hear you."

Margaret continued, unphased. "I'm hoping him working with you might ground him a little bit, if that's even possible."

"Oh, don't you worry, Maggie," Whalen said, scratching his chin, "no one who's ever seen a Coelacanth game can say they haven't been slapped across the face by the cold hand of reality."

Charlie had had enough. "Hey! Listen to me: I exist, and I *will* be heard–"

"Uh-huh," said Whalen. "Listen, meet me over at the cage when you're done with your chores, yeah?" He turned back to Margaret. "Great to see you, Maggie. I look forward to you telling me how to do my job on a daily basis."

Margaret arched an eyebrow. "Do I tell you, or the muskrat under your nose?"

Whalen chuckled once more. "You're a class act, Maggie. Through and through."

Whalen departed, moseying his way back to the world of practice swings. Charlie watched him go, wishing he'd stay and further occupy his mother's attention. The thought had barely crossed his mind, when Margaret raised her clipboard. With the click of a pen, she surveyed the ballpark and began taking notes.

Charlie eyed her warily. Experience had taught him that her attentions rarely led to his own life becoming easier. "Um…w-what are you writing there, Mom?"

She neither broke from her writing, nor looked at him. "I'm putting together a handbook for the organization."

Yes, because that's what this fiasco needs, he thought. *Mom-rules.* "Like, an operator's manual?"

"Mmm," she said continuing to write. "I was thinking I could call it The Coelacanth Way, or some such nonsense. It's going to lay out how we'll be doing business around here. Provide some focus for the brand."

"*Is* there a Coelacanth brand?"

She sighed and stared into the distance. "I swear, if this was 75 years ago, I'd start by changing that goddamned name. No one can pronounce the thing, let alone spell it! Unfortunately, there's this 'legacy' the league is hell-bent on preserving. Not to mention the sunk cost in merchandise that nobody buys."

"Well, at least you've got Steve-O-Canth the Coelacanth to lean on, right? People seem to like a good mascot."

"Then they can stare at the ballcap logo and use their imaginations," she said, making a note on her clipboard.

"What does *that* mean?"

Margaret shrugged and continued writing. "I'm afraid the Steve-O-Canth has been given his swimming papers."

Charlie was aghast. He leaned toward her and whispered, "You *fired* the mascot?"

"Sorry, Charlie – extinction is quite a bitch." She turned to him suddenly. "Listen, I want you thinking of new t-shirt ideas we can use. Something ironic and ostentatious that the hipsters can adopt."

"Um, I'll try, I guess..." Charlie had no idea what she was talking about; far from hip, his most outrageous fashion choices typically came down to inadvertently pairing a black sock with a navy one. He followed as she began crossing the field, making further notes as she took in the park and its players. "So, I guess this means you'll be hanging around some days, huh?"

"Most days," she said. "It's time to bring order to chaos, Charlie." She turned and pointed the business end of her pen at him. "I sat by and watched Herbert auger this organization into the dirt because of his love affair with being a big shot while remaining wholly incompetent. I will *not* be left holding the plug to be pulled while there's still blood pumping through this thing."

Charlie considered this portrait of an oppressive past she was painting. "How much of that sitting by and watching was done at the spa, Mom?"

Margaret poked a menacing index finger into his sternum. "It was the desert, Charlie – you know I need to stay moist."

"Because you're my Mummy." Charlie grinned.

Margaret stared at him in disgust. After a moment in which Charlie began questioning his little joke, his mother reached out and slapped the diorama from his hands. It landed hard, eliciting a gasp of infield dirt, and lay there, thoroughly defeated. He looked down at it aghast, his hands still out before him, cradling nothing but the wind.

Margaret leaned close to him, her eyes steely. "That's for the pun. Now pick up your toys."

Accustomed to a lifetime of obedience, Charlie crouched on command, a sad man gathering plastic. He grimaced, dismayed to find Andre Dawson's face had been scratched to hell. *I am so sorry Andre,* he eulogized in his head, hoping his mother would not see him paying his respects. *You were always the most awesome.*

"Margaret!"

Charlie looked up to see Francesca and Dip across the field from them. Dip had his hand up as though hailing a cab back to the 1960s. "Excuse me, Margaret!"

Margaret clenched her jaw and turned to them. Dip and Francesca immediately began trying to outwalk each other to reach her.

"Oh, good lord," said Margaret. "I thought I felt my skin crawling..."

His mother had returned to her notations, ignoring the pair of broadcasters as they raced their way over to her with fire in their eyes.

FRANCESCA HAD SEEN Mrs. Tinley see them, just as she had seen her new boss immediately turn back to whatever she was writing. She also saw a player in his batting practice uniform, crouched beside her. Either he was tying his shoe, or Margaret Tinley was demanding complete supplication, as had always been rumored.

Beside her, Dip pushed his pace into another gear. She found herself wondering how someone so used to others doing everything for him could be so *spry* when needed. Tapping into some long-forgotten reserve of energy, he was fast-walking as though his career depended on it. Francesca hoped hers did not. She sped up, lengthening her stride, just to be sure.

Mrs. Tinley remained focused on her writing as they reached her, and as both Francesca and her co-worker wound up to voice their many complaints about one another, the owner held up a finger of silence. Dip stopped himself, mid-inhale, and began tapping his foot impatiently. The kneeling player stood up, and as Francesca glanced at him, she was surprised to find it was Charlie.

"Oh, hey!" she said, smiling at him. She looked down to find he was cradling the remains of a battered baseball playset. *This is interesting,* she thought. "Nice toys."

She watched as his face fell; apparently, she'd struck a nerve.

"They're avatars," he said. "And they're collectible."

"They're dollies," Mrs. Tinley said without looking up from her clipboard, "and I paid $3.99 for them in 1987."

Francesca frowned, her eyes darting between Charlie and Mrs. Tinley as the picture became clear. *It couldn't be...* "Wait, so... Margaret Tinley's your *mom?"*

Charlie sighed. "When she admits it."

Francesca laughed. "Well, that's pretty crazy. What, is your dad, like, the Mayor of Cape Haddock too?"

"My dad's dead," he said, staring down at his spikes.

"Ha! Good one." She liked the fact that he was good for jokes that didn't involve jockstraps.

He looked up at her, his expression pained. "No, seriously."

Her heart sank. "Oh god, really?" *Nice instincts, Madame Reporter,* she thought.

"It's true, dear," Mrs. Tinley chimed in, her tone disinterested, "they're both dead."

Francesca felt a plunging sensation in her gut as something clicked in her mind. "Wait, so that means your first dad was–"

"Jackie Conroy," said Charlie.

"Wow," she said, as the various threads came together. She was of course familiar with the Conroy-led playoff teams that had earned them the right to fly their sad outfield banners. Not to mention that Jackie Conroy had died in his prime under tragic circumstances. "He was like Cape Haddock royalty."

"Yeah," Charlie said, avoiding her gaze.

Beside them, the infamous widow made a final stab of punctuation, before finally looking up from her clipboard. At this point, Dip was nearly vibrating with frustration, his arms crossed.

Mrs. Tinley turned to the man who was apparently her son. "Charlie, would you please give us a moment?"

"Yeah," he said, futzing with a particularly unbalanced figure. "I'm gonna go find the Skipper before he yells at me too." He turned to Francesca. "See you later?"

She smiled at him, hoping it would help with what appeared to be a challenging day. "You bet."

As Charlie skulked off with his toys, Mrs. Tinley finally turned to address the broadcasters. She seemed to relish that Dip was close to exploding with frustration.

She turned to Francesca. "Now. What is this?"

"Well–" Francesca began, only to be immediately steamrolled.

Dip's voice rolled out of him in his default, bossy way. It was always a proclamation rather than a conversation. "Margaret, I–"

"I don't see our hands down each other's pants, Dip," Mrs. Tinley said, her tone bone-chilling. "What on Earth are you calling me?"

Francesca was astonished to see him wilt in the face of her interjection. "Oh. I, uh…" he sputtered, "uh… Mrs. Tinley?"

She nodded. "There it is."

"Mrs. Tinley," he continued, promptly rebounding into his vintage, voice-pushing form, "first allow me to offer you a warm Cape Haddock welcome home! It's been far too long since you've graced us with your menace." Francesca stifled a laugh as Mrs. Tinley's eyes bulged in disgust. Dip ignored this and leaned in conspiratorially. "You just let me know if you need anything while you're here, okay? When you're in Cape Haddock, you're in Lockerbie Country. These people would do anything for their Big Dipper!"

"Out with it, Dip," Mrs. Tinley said, checking the time on her phone. Francesca began to feel a certain kinship with this powerful woman who had taken a flyer on her talents.

Dip seemed less enthralled, his gregarious mood melting into one of outrage. "Well, whose idiotic idea was it to bring a-a-a-a-a *non-player* into the broadcast booth!?" he blurted, all radio-friendly pretense now gone.

Mrs. Tinley's eyes narrowed. "It was *my* idiotic idea. Why?"

Dip threw his hands up in surrender. "Whoa, there! Let's just calm it down with the aggressive rhetoric, Mrs. Tinley – nobody's calling anybody *idiotic...*"

"I'm getting bored, Dip," she sighed.

"W-w-well, darn it all, Mrs. Tinley! I have done Coelacanth broadcasts by myself for decades! And the folks at home, you just ask any of them–"

Mrs. Tinley glanced back at her clipboard. "Ten seconds."

Dip moved from pleading to full-on whining. "Well, why am I suddenly sharing the microphone with some... some..."

"Tread lightly," said Mrs. Tinley.

"...some *amateur?*" he concluded, inexplicably pronouncing the last word with a French accent. "Mrs. Tinley, there's just no need for it, that's all! There's *no* need and *no* room for it in the booth."

"No room," she echoed, unreadable.

"Exactly!" Dip smiled and clapped his hands together as though he'd just cracked his way into a bank vault. "There's no room for her *thoughts* and her *ideas* and her *opinions* and her *hair* and her *breasts* – I mean, how am I supposed to get a word in edgewise?"

"Mmm..." said Mrs. Tinley. She considered him as he gathered himself, having now vented his frustrations. To Francesca's surprise, Mrs. Tinley suddenly turned to her. "And you?"

"Me?" Francesca found herself wildly unprepared, now that she was being sighted by Margaret Tinley's laser focus. "Oh." She pondered this a moment. "Actually, I think he's said it all." *Take that, Lockerbie.*

"I see." Mrs. Tinley fell silent. After an agonizing moment, she turned to the old man. "Dip, allow me a moment to bring you down from the orbit of delusion you've launched yourself into." Dip's face collapsed, but she did not stop. "I've seen your numbers, and the truth of the matter is that when the radio dial lands on Coelacanth baseball, the drone of your nostalgic buffoonery immediately turns off *half* the listening audience."

"Hockey fans?" he blurted.

"No, you antique idiot – *women.*" She drew this last word out in a way Francesca found delightfully condescending. "The numbers don't lie, Dip. There's only so much market share, and if we're ignoring half the market, then that's *half* the market share not being shared. And, to be perfectly honest with you, I don't *care* if you like one another or not. If people had to like their co-workers, then *this* conversation..." She made a circular pointing motion at the three of them, "...would not be happening, the government would be more useless than it already is, and business across the globe would grind to a halt. So, my advice to you is to get over it."

Dip was flabbergasted. "But, Mrs. Tin–"

"Get. Over it."

Francesca felt a flush of embarrassment. Their conflict seemed petty now. Childish.

"You're both allegedly adults," Mrs. Tinley continued, "figure it out. And bring me numbers, I don't care how you do it. Sit back-to-back and watch the game through mirrors if you have to, but get it done and *be compelling.*"

"Now Mrs. Tinley, you play it straight with me," said Dip. Francesca could hear the strain in his voice from having to walk the fine line between addressing and demanding something. "We go back a long way, you and I."

Mrs. Tinley appeared unmoved. "I am, unfortunately, well aware of this."

Dip squinted behind the lenses of his glasses. "Does it help any?"

"It does not."

"Come on now, Herb was like a brother to me! I consider us family."

Francesca scoffed. "You didn't even recognize her son the other day."

"Now, we all know Herb didn't have any children," said Dip, shaking his head. "It's what makes his death even more heartbreaking. They broke the mold with that man."

"If by 'mold' you mean 'bathtub,' then yes, you're correct," said Mrs. Tinley. "He had a very difficult time finding objects that would support his weight."

"He's *Jackie Conroy's* son!" said Francesca, almost laughing out loud at her partner's complete refusal of reality. "How are you missing this?"

Dip flashed her his most condescending look yet. "I know, we *all* wish Jackie Conroy was our dad, but that doesn't make it true."

Mrs. Tinley's sigh announced the end of her patience with this conversation. "Dip, you may be the so-called 'voice' of this team, but that also means you're at least partially responsible for what the team is saying to its fans."

"I beg your pardon, *Mrs. Tinley,*" said Dip, his voice dripping with contempt, "I am *fully* responsible for what the team is saying to its fans."

"Interesting…" Mrs. Tinley tapped her pen on the edge of the clipboard. "If the dismal record and low gate receipts are any indication, then the team has been saying that they don't give a good goddamn about entertaining these people. I shall make a note that *you're* the one turning all of these Cape Haddockers off."

"Herb would've wanted me–"

"Herbert isn't *here* anymore." Francesca could see Mrs. Tinley's words hit Dip like a bucket of cold water. "Just as Herbert is no longer the big wheel in this organization. *I* am. And you can move with me or be rolled over but understand that the wheel is in motion."

The owner gave them each a final, pointed stare, then brushed past them. While Dip stood, frozen, wondering what had just happened, Francesca saw her window closing and reacted. "Um, Mrs. Tinley?" she called, rushing to catch up with her employer.

Mrs. Tinley didn't look at her, or break pace. "Please, call me Margaret."

Francesca was taken aback by the warmth of her tone. "Okay… Margaret. See, the thing is, the way you just described our, uh, current setup back there, it kind of feels like you've hired me as a token."

Margaret came to a halt as they approached the batting cage and turned to Francesca. "You can call it tokenism if you want to. But I choose to call it 'exploiting a deficiency in the marketplace.' And if I was you, I'd choose to call it an opportunity to transcend tokenism and achieve a different title."

"Which would be…?"

"A *pioneer,* dear." The owner's tone was gentle, but firm. "The funny thing about the way things are is that they're always one step away from being the way things *were.* And it's clear to me that the future of this place has been waiting far too long to become the now. Best be prepared if you would like to be a part of it. There's a reason you're here."

Now, it was Francesca's turn to be left frozen in the wake of this powerful woman. A woman who was now walking the few feet to where Charlie and Whalen were watching as Javier Coronado launched another shot to the opposite field.

"Is this him, Whalen? This is the lobster-boy?"

Francesca watched as Whalen leaned over to Charlie and mumbled, "Told you." The skipper then gave a sharp whistle toward the plate. "Hey, Javi!"

Whalen waved the colossus over to them as Margaret flipped to a page on her clipboard. She turned it to the manager, shoving it mere inches from his face.

"Seriously, Whalen? We have a tank of live lobsters in the budget?"

"Come on, Maggie," Whalen said, peering around the clipboard. "He's a growing boy! He gets hungry!"

"*Two* lobsters a day, Gray? Are we all under the impression that arthropods grow on trees?"

Whalen put his hands up, his tone measured. "Maggie, I'll tell you the same thing I told Herb: he's worth it. Trust me."

As he spoke, Javier arrived, looking somewhat confused by this meeting. Francesca had been around the team long enough to have noticed he did not do much beyond eat, work out, eat, play baseball, and eat. He was shy and uncomfortable with his English, despite speaking it fluently, and avoided most of her interview attempts. Which was a shame, since Francesca, like the rest of the organization and its major league affiliate, could see his greatness from a mile away. His story was her white whale. It was the one tale that *needed* telling on this team. And it was all bottled up and stored on a shelf by a soft-spoken apothecary keeper whose only joy seemed to come at mealtimes and from sending baseballs to the moon.

Margaret stepped closer to Javier. She stared up at him as though examining a monolith. Her eyes narrowed. "Is it true, Javier? Are you worth it?"

Javier stared back at her, his face neutral. He shrugged. "I give everything."

"Well," Whalen said with a nod. "There you have it, then." He turned and gave his slugger a pat on the arm. "Javi, m'boy, let's get you ten more swings, huh?"

Whalen tipped his cap to Margaret and walked Javier back to the plate.

Francesca watched with interest as Charlie turned to his mother, his posture slumping. She still could not believe this passive man and this no-nonsense woman were related.

"You let that big kid off pretty easily, Mom," Charlie said. "Remember when you wouldn't let me have a hot dog between innings on the old team?"

"Please," Margaret said, shaking her head, "it's hardly the same thing. He's the one the Majors actually want, and they have to go through *us* to get him." She swept the end of her pen over the entire spectrum of ballplayers spread across the field. "He's the gravy train all of us ride, Charlie. He's a *winner*. And I've certainly seen enough losers to know the difference."

She gave him a pointed look then walked away, making further notes on her clipboard.

"I love you too, Mom," Charlie said, under his breath. He turned to Francesca with a sad smile, and she felt for him.

"You still good for drinks tonight?" she said.

His mood seemed to lighten. "Oh yeah! You thinking milkshakes or something?"

She laughed. "I was thinking more along the lines of bourbon."

"Oh, great," he said, "I love wine."

"Uh, I don't think..." She gave him a look, uncertain if he was joking or not. "Well, whatever – I'll see you across the street, okay? Latimer's Seafood."

He beamed. "Yeah, see you there."

Behind them, Javier swung again, lining the ball perfectly up the middle, bisecting the diamond. Whalen nodded his approval, and Francesca swore she could hear him muttering a line.

"'The universe is a procession with measured and perfect motion...'"

CHAPTER 9
Nectar Of The Odds

THERE WERE ONLY a few non-diner restaurants open in Cape Haddock, but the hip, warehouse-chic sign and brickwork of Latimer's Seafood were making a case for it being the most sophisticated in town. The menu posted beside the meticulously varnished and repurposed antique door was brief and featured dishes Charlie was largely unfamiliar with. He entered, relieved to have noted something called a 'beef tartare patty,' which he hoped was a burger.

The interior of Latimer's was dimly lit and working a calculated industrial maritime aesthetic of raw wood flooring and roughhewn tables supported by factory steel. The nautical maps hanging from the walls may have been vintage, but they had also been displayed within heavy frames that Charlie suspected were worth hundreds of dollars. He briefly wondered if he would be able to cover the check he was walking into – his per diem allowance was decent, but not exactly ideal for a grown man who was now, quite possibly, on a date.

He steeled himself, drawing a deep breath as he was led to a table in the corner, where sat Francesca, engrossed by the menu, and flanked by an open bottle of red wine and two glasses. This was somewhat intimidating – as a drinker, he was very much a lightweight. *Don't mess this up, Conroy,* he said to himself, as had so many managers and coaches before him.

"Ahoy there," he said as he seated himself, immediately messing things up. *Nice one, Ahab,* he groaned inwardly. "Thanks for inviting me to the, uh... the cannery?"

Francesca smiled and nodded. "Yeah, this town pushes the sea angle pretty hard – they've kind of hitched their dinghy to it."

Charlie nodded and surveyed the antique buoys hanging from the open rafters, and bare Edison bulbs emitting their coppery light over the swank bar nearby. "I grew up in Arizona, so replace the fishing gear with chaps and branding irons, and it's probably the same kind of thing."

Francesca raised an eyebrow and sipped her wine. With a mischievous grin, she set the glass down and drawled, "I have two guns – one for each of you."

Charlie felt like this might be a reference to something but was unsure of what. He faked a knowing laugh, poorly, then changed the subject. "Listen, help me out here: do we know *why* they went with the coelacanth? As far as I can tell, it is unpronounceable and repulsive to look at."

Francesca laughed and leaned in, eager to spin a yarn. "Well, unfortunately, the team's branding instinct has always been about as strong as their baseball talent. They used to be called the Cape Haddock Pocket Squares."

"How sporty."

"Right? These people couldn't *buy* a good idea. So, as the story goes, the Cape Haddock baseball teams have always been unpopular – like, historically unpopular. So bad that they spent over 50 years trying to rename the team."

"Really?" Charlie felt a ray of hope at this news.

Francesca nodded. "So, in the mid-1800s, for whatever reason, it was very fashionable to just name yourself after fashion: the Red Sox, the White Sox–"

"The Red Stockings, the Red Caps–" said Charlie.

"The Brown Stockings, the *Green* Stockings – exactly," she said, seemingly pleased he could play along. "So, initially they were the Cape Haddock Top Hats, but obviously that's not where headgear went in baseball. Then they cycled through the Cape Haddock Cummerbunds, the Cape Haddock Epaulets, and the Cape Haddock Tricorners – all of which either fell out of fashion or were never *in* fashion for baseball uniforms. They go with the Pocket Squares for a while, but then the front pockets on the uniforms die off – you see what I mean?"

"I see that this team might have been better off as a Halloween store?" Charlie took the second glass and drank deeply. The wine hit his tongue with a rich bitterness he had not anticipated – he'd always assumed it to taste like fancy grape juice. *This might have gone off,* he thought. *Be strong,* he cautioned himself. *Maybe it's supposed to taste like this.*

Meanwhile, Francesca ramped up her story. "Ah, but it's not just fashion for names anymore, but characters and objects too – the Pirates, the Stogies–"

"The Brewers, the Crackers – sure."

"So, apparently they decided to open their eyes and look at the biggest object of them all: the ocean. And they decide 'Hey, this dump's by the seaside, let's go full-nautical.'"

Charlie nodded, now feeling a warm sensation creeping its way across his skin. He eyed the wine glass as thought it was a feral cat.

"So," Francesca continued, "they reboot in quick succession as the Cape Haddock Tars, the Cape Haddock 'Paulins, the Cape Haddock *Tar*paulins, and briefly the Cape Haddock Tar-*gills,* before seizing the moment and switching to the Cape Haddock Chum during the Atlantic coast shark attacks of 1916. *However,* in a stroke of incredible fish-related luck, the coelacanth pops up after having screwed off from the fossil record for about 80 million years. It was just this hideous creature nobody thought was still around but got everybody all hot and bothered for a couple weeks in 1938."

"It was a pretty big deal around here, huh?"

Francesca shrugged and took another sip. "Apparently it didn't take much to rename – that was a headline for one day. The thing was caught off the coast of South Africa!"

Charlie nodded – this was odd.

"But the owners ran with it, figuring they could cash in on the popularity. You know how that worked out. Team got passed around for ages, wound up in your stepdad's pocket, and that was it. The Dead Fish have lived ever since."

"He liked the fishing tie-in," Charlie nodded. He was impressed; she was an encyclopedia with an incredible voice, while he was...

what exactly was he? "I guess I am yet another classic entry in the team's history." He sighed, his head drooping slightly.

"Hey, cheer up," she said, her voice playful. "Just because you lost doesn't make you an actual loser- well, I guess it kind of does, doesn't it? But it doesn't mean you're a *complete* loser. It's just Coelacanth baseball."

"Lucky you, forced to watch it every day. You like what you do?"

She pondered this a moment. "It is… challenging. I mean, I love the work. I love radio, it's exciting to be a part of. And I love the game, so it's even better that I get to tell the story of the plays to people who can't see it."

"But?"

"But... imagine having a conversation where you're interrupted every two seconds…"

"Okay…"

"…the interruptions are framed in the third-person…"

"Okay…"

"…and the other person isn't listening to *anything* you say."

Charlie frowned. *"Is* that technically a conversation?"

Francesca offered a sad smile. "Unfortunately, it's my career. My partner – that guy, Dip – he's on the mute button like it's his wife and it's 40 years ago." She sighed, her gaze losing focus. "Once he gets going, it's just a tsunami of words hitting you. There's no room to say anything, you just get swept aside by this wall of talking."

"That sounds nightmarish."

"Eh," she shrugged. "Nobody alienates like the patriarchy, right?"

Charlie's mind flashed to Herbert. "So, how did you end up here?"

She ran the tip of her index finger along the base of her wine glass. "You know, sometimes, when Dip is neck-deep in one of his longer monologues, I ask myself that." She paused, her eyes falling to the glass. "And then I ask myself to repeat what I just asked so I can hear my own thoughts and desires over his droning."

"And then what happens?"

"Usually we cut to break."

"Ah," he nodded. "A dream come true, huh?"

"I used to call D-1 field hockey tourneys and softball – you know, the lady-shit that's just as competitive as guy-shit but without the same shine. Anyway, I did that for about seven years, had my demo tracks out there, and got a call from the office of the infamous Margaret Tinley."

"Bone-chilling, I'm sure."

"Oh, *absolutely,*" she said, grinning. "But she hired me sight-unseen, and here I am." She gestured to their surroundings, "In a fancy cannery. Not bad for a retired softballer from the Midwest"

"Did you really?"

"Oh yeah – eye black, coordinated cheering, streamers in my hair – I loved it. But this Lockerbie guy..." She shook her head at the very notion of her partner. "It's like it's physically impossible for him to take me seriously as a broadcaster."

"He refuses to acknowledge your baseball I.Q.?"

"He refuses to acknowledge I'm a woman!" She laughed at the absurdity. "I mean, I expected to hear it from the trolls in the audience, but not my broadcast partner, you know? This business is all about teams, right?"

"Wait, so you get it from the fans too?"

"Oh, you should see these guys on my Blither feed, they *love* tearing me down. It's mostly comments about my looks, which... you know, I'm on the radio." She shook her head at the idea.

Charlie had long ago accepted his own role as a target for hecklers. He wasn't necessarily comfortable with it, but he'd grown accustomed to it. This, though, was unexpected. "Who would spend their time commenting on this?

She laughed and shook her head. "Oh, are you sure you want to get into this?"

Reaching for her phone, she pulled up her Blither feed with a few taps and handed it to him. His eyes went wide as he scrolled through the comments.

It was a hideous display of humanity; for every complimentary message of support for Francesca or the Coelacanths, came nine more that raged against any number of seemingly inconsequential things related to either. Most of them seemed to be of a particularly incongruous strain of commentary regarding Francesca's womanhood being affiliated with a team they disliked.

"Um," he began unsure of how to respond, "are you sure this isn't a police blotter? It's just death and rape threats."

To his surprise, she laughed. "Yep! All day, every day."

"Over sports."

She pointed at the phone. "These guys take it all very seriously. And they liked the fact that for *years,* no stupid lady could get 'girl' all over their games. Sports were supposed to be where 'men do men-things, and you'll never understand, *rrrahr!*'"

"Huh." Charlie was stunned. "Sounds like a garage full of assholes to me."

"My guess is you're not far off," she said, nodding. "The saddest part being that there is nothing new about any of this. I was at home one night, like, a month ago, and I was watching this episode of *Murder, She Wrote*–"

Charlie nodded. "Mom loved that show."

Francesca shrugged. "Of course. And this is the exciting life I'm building for myself in Cape Haddock, you see."

"Hey, Jessica Fletcher always came out on top in the end."

"She's a role model, no doubt," Francesca said, beaming across the table at him. "Anyway, it's a minor league baseball episode; Fletcher shows up, somebody's murdered – you know the drill." Charlie nodded. "But, wouldn't you know it, the victim is this marginalized lady sportscaster who gets all caught up in a web of team manipulations and harassment. And this was made over *thirty years ago!* It was like I was watching my life with an Angela Lansbury cameo thrown in."

"Whoa, that sounds like a dream come true… *and* one of the worst things ever? Is that even possible?"

"Turned out that Paul Sorvino killed her on accident, so it's all very disappointing," she said, shaking her head.

Charlie tried to process this, put himself in her shoes. He found it difficult. "So, do you report this stuff? I'd be afraid to even show up if I was getting this all the time."

Francesca shrugged as he gingerly handed the toxic delivery device back to her. "Nah, they're relentless, so why bother? If I actually paid attention to them and didn't show up, that's just giving them what they want.

"And seriously–" here, to Charlie's surprise, she reached across the table and seized his forearm, staring deeply into his eyes, "dudes of America: it's just me, talking on the radio. I'm not slashing your tires or stealing your credit card, so chill out, you know?" Charlie nodded. "*Also,*" she added, "maybe there are fans out there who actually want to hear what I have to say. So, whatever." He felt a twinge of sadness as she released his arm and began swirling her remaining cabernet around the bottom of her glass. "Dip doesn't even let me say anything aside from play-by-play, which I guess explains missives like..." She put the glass and down and picked up the phone, scrolling anew. "'*...I hate the way you call strikes with your bitch mouth.*' My bitch mouth!"

She laughed and shook her fist like a grandfather whose lawn had just been parked on. "'Ooh, those darn girls!' They can't even come up with creative insults, these guys." She chucked the phone back onto the table in disgust. "And mind you, this is all happening in a world where *Dip Lockerbie* is taken seriously."

Charlie rubbed his temples as he acclimated to all of this. His head was now decidedly fuzzy. "But... why? It has literally no impact on the game."

She nodded. "Mmm, but Charlie, I will never *really* know what it's like to put on a uniform and run out there, onto the field. And it wasn't *done* like this back in 19-blah-blah-blah... to which I say: yeah, I get it. I will *never* know that feeling. *However,* I'm also seated right next to you, looking down on the game from a box in the sky, *and* I know the rules!

"As if Dip could run onto the field and snag some grounders without dragging an oxygen tank behind him – come on!" She threw her hands up in mock despair. "I'm a human being! I have eyes and critical thinking – why shouldn't I describe what's going on with the baseball game? It couldn't be any worse than Dip repeating the one line on the back of his baseball card over and over and over again."

Charlie nodded. "Yeah, is he *always* like that? What is going on there?"

"Oh, he played for the Coelacanths back in the 60s, and spent two games with the Big Club when their shortstop had polio." She rolled her eyes at the notion.

Charlie frowned. "Two games – that's a pretty quick turnaround time for polio."

"Apparently his fielding was considered to be more of an epidemic. But he's been sailing that two-game boat ever since."

Charlie rolled this over in his mind as Francesca topped off both of their glasses with the remainder of the bottle. Her situation seemed untenable. "So... what're you gonna do?"

"I don't know," she shrugged. "I mean, I kind of figured it'd be a little like this, since female sportscasters get a world of shit across the country. There's a ceiling for women in this business, you know," she said, pointing a finger at him with the hand that raised the glass. "Doesn't matter which field you're broadcasting from, it's a grass ceiling." She took a drink, then smacked her lips as though this dismissed the entire situation. "Whatever. Dip can talk over me all he wants, it won't stop me from trying."

Charlie could not help but admire her resilience in the face of such an imbalance. He shook his head in disbelief. "You're totally a boss," he said, awestruck.

She grinned and tilted her head to the side. "I am totally a boss."

"I mean, don't say that around my mom – I don't even think my dad would've disputed that *she's* the boss."

Francesca took a drink and shook her head. "I'm sorry, I'm still very fuzzy on the details of what happened to him – Jackie, I mean. Whenever people talk about it here, it's always clouded up with the tragedy aspect. I'm sorry, I don't mean to make you relive this trauma over drinks–"

"Honestly, it's okay," he said, fully believing her curiosity to be genuine rather than muckraking. "The whole situation was too weird for it to be as traumatic as it could have been."

Charlie's head fell as he summoned the remaining details of that strange week, thirty-odd years ago. The memories he maintained were now mixed with the anecdotal details he'd learned from others over the ensuing years, those who'd been adult, active participants in one of the more bizarre chapters of Coelacanth history.

But what he could identify as his own experiences were small fragments of feeling represented by flashes of sights maybe seen and probably exaggerated in their vibrancy when recalled for examination through the lens of time. His mother crying in their little apartment. The crowds of grown-ups who filled the space with their consolations. The confusion of something so every day and familiar suddenly coming to an end with seemingly no reason. The void that existed in his father's place ever after, now so much more familiar than the man who once occupied it.

Finally, he clawed his way back into the moment at hand. "He had a boat," said Charlie. He paused as he realized this phrase was the very simple, silly heart of the matter. "It's funny, because I don't even think we had a proper car that worked all the time."

"But you had a boat?" said Francesca.

Charlie nodded, understanding this must be a confusing statement. "Yeah, it was a gift. Herbert gave it to him after one of the playoff runs. Like, as a thank you, or something. It wasn't even really much of a boat – just a three-person thing with a little trolling motor, you know?"

"Not exactly a Corvette," she said, nodding in understanding.

"Right, probably more trouble than it was worth to insure or take care of, but, you know… something tangible that said 'Good job' from the boss." Charlie's mind flashed to the grotesque pleasure barge he and Margaret were now occupying. "Anyway, I guess he liked to go out after day games, before the sun set. He'd take me and my mom out sometimes, but mostly he'd just go tooling for a bit, enjoy the boat by himself. And he went out one night, buzzed out into the ocean… and never came back."

Francesca's face fell in a shock of sympathy. "Oh god. Did they ever find… um–"

"No," he said, giving her a sad smile. "They didn't find him, they didn't find the little boat… they didn't even find any clues as to what happened. He was just out there one night and then he was gone. They put his cause of death down as 'Lost at sea.' Which I guess is a rare sub-category of 'Death by misadventure.'"

"Holy shit," she said. "That's so… archaic."

"I know – Poseidon's revenge, right?" he said, shaking his head in disbelief. "Not even a body left to stick in the ground and throw a headstone over."

"Charlie, I am so sorry."

"It's okay," he shrugged. "Like I said, it's so weird, it's not as bad as you'd think. I didn't have to watch him wither away through illness or see him go through some violent thing. There was no corpse that needed comprehending… Cemeteries are pretty depressing anyway. I kind of feel like Dad's better than that, you know? The ocean's so scary in how big it is and how it doesn't seem to care what we think at all, but at least it's nice to look at."

"Don't you find it odd that there's no sign of your dad in the park? No tributes or anything?"

Francesca had a point. He'd never really considered it before, but there was something off about this. Baseball had always struck him as being more in love with its own legacy than any other sport. It was constantly holding the present up for comparison with the past. Why would Cape Haddock's team not do the same with one of its most beloved players?

"Herbert was always kind of weird about it. I get the feeling there was a resentment there. Like, Herbert didn't like the fact that Dad was the one people loved, when it was his team."

"His team to buy, his name on the stadium, his fishing pole in the outfield–"

"Exactly. He was desperate for people to take him seriously, but I guess it doesn't work that way." Charlie considered this a moment while Francesca examined him across the table. "That said, I guess it's better to be remember by the fans. That's like a living tribute to him."

Her eyes narrowed as she considered him, and he now felt incredibly *seen.* It was almost uncomfortable, this dissection. Almost.

She began swirling her drink again, the rhythm of the motion hypnotic. "You know, I looked you up online."

"Oh, really?" he said, now even further on edge. There were so many embarrassing things he'd been affiliated with (some would argue, directly responsible for) that he'd lost count.

"Turns out I do remember hearing about you before."

Sadly, this could have been for many reasons. He decided to go with something random, hoping she might not remember what she'd heard. "Something about that triple-play I was a part of in '07?"

She shook her head and his heart sank. "No, it was about some record."

"Oh. That." His eyes fell to the table. *Of course, she would pick that one,* he rued.

"Yeah," she continued, "it was kind of a big deal, right?"

He shrugged. "Well, it's not really anything to brag about."

She leaned toward him, smiling. "The minor league player hit by the most pitches? That's huge!"

"Is it?" he asked, daring to look up at her.

"How many was it again?"

"Come on..." he said, his tone weary as he straightened in his seat.

"You come on!" She was not the least bit deterred by his reluctance. "Please? How many?"

He sighed and looked away again. Finally, it came. "87."

Francesca choked back laughter. "Oh my god. *87?"*

"Yeah..." his head fell again as he became lost in an unfortunate reverie of tower buzzings.

"87 hit-by-pitches... in one season! Charlie, that's, that's... that's amazing."

"It's not exactly a skill-based thing, is it."

"You had to pick yourself up and walk to first. That's pretty tough."

He looked up in disbelief. "Yeah? You think so?"

"Definitely," she said with a nod. "You're like a boxer. A boxer who can't punch back."

"So... a punching bag."

She laughed. "Hey, punching bags *never* get to first."

He nodded, mulling this over. "You know, my on-base percentage was never higher than that season..."

"Hey, .207 is nothing to sneeze at – the numbers totally prove that you got on base."

".207? Really?" He was shocked – surely, she couldn't have that taking up space in her brain? "Wait," he said, looking at her sideways, "so, are you a statistics person?"

She scoffed and leaned across the table again. "I *love* statistics."

Charlie leaned in as well, suddenly excited. "That's amazing! Sometimes it's hard to find baseball people around here who care about any of those numbers. It feels like you're dragging them to the odds, kicking and screaming, you know?"

"Whalen, huh?" She gave a wine-soaked wave, dismissing the problem on Charlie's behalf. "He's just old school, you know? Did he tell you about the Brain Test?"

"Yeah, I heard that one."

"He does okay by it. I understand not wanting to bring math into it. Now, the new guys should know better, but some of them wouldn't know an Ultimate Zone Rating from their elbows."

"Whoa," he said, raising an eyebrow. "Nice UZR reference. That was spicy."

"Please," she said, "that was nothing." Her devilish grin challenged him.

He thought a moment. "Okay then, how about... BABIP."

She started answering before he'd even finished, trampling him with glorious accuracy. "Batting Average on Balls In Play."

"Touché." He was wildly impressed. "RF/9?"

"Range Factor per 9 Innings."

"What's the formula on that?"

She didn't hesitate. "Putouts, plus assists, times nine, divided by innings played. Your turn – WHIP."

He was not as quick but rebounded neatly. "Walks and Hits per Innings Pitched – don't you hold back now." *This woman is incredible.*

Her head dipped slightly, and she stared up at him with a professorial gaze. "Formerly known as...?"

"Uh, Innings Pitched Ratio?"

"OPS–"

Charlie gave her a look. "Come on now."

"Wait, let me finish!" she said, her tone delightfully bossy. "OPS...*plus.*"

He nodded. "On Base Percentage, plus Slugging, adjusted for player's ballpark. VORP?"

"Value Over Replacement Player."

"Define 'replacement player.'"

She waved him off. "Psh – get real."

He leaned closer. "Okay, Hot Wheels: Bob Gibson's ERA in 1968."

"1.12."

"Joe DiMaggio's hit streak?"

"56 games."

"Ted Williams' lifetime on-base percentage?"

".482."

"All-time home run leader?"

"Hank Aaron."

He tilted his head. "What about Barry?"

"Come on," she said. "No one takes Barry seriously."

Charlie grinned and leaned back. It was quite possibly the single greatest interaction he'd ever had with… well, *anyone*.

The two considered one another for a moment, electricity dancing between them in the silence. Finally, she straightened and cleared her throat. "So, I guess I'll be seeing you in a couple days, huh?" she said.

"What do you mean?" he said. "You're not going to Alewife with us?"

"Not since the cutbacks, no," she shrugged. "Dip and I have been staying back here to call the road games."

"How could that ever make sense?" he said, shaking his head. "How?"

She sighed, the very idea of the new setup clearly exhausting her. "We listen to the streaming version of the game off the local broadcast's website, and Dip tries to rephrase everything the home announcers are describing. It's quite a scene."

"Really? Huh." He pondered this. "So, what kind of broadcast delay are you getting when you do it like that?"

"You'd be better off having me mail you the score."

"Ah."

Francesca paused and stared down at the tabletop as though weighing something in her mind. "Dip keeps calling me 'Frank,'" she said, looking up at him.

"Seriously?" He could not believe how sincerely bizarre this man was.

"I wish I was joking."

"Damn." Charlie thought for a moment. *Are we at this point now?* He decided to take a cue from her and be bold. "If it makes you feel any better, everyone back in the day always called me 'Connie.'"

She laughed. "Your nickname was 'Connie?'"

"Yep" he nodded, feeling okay about letting that particular cat out of the bag. "Just like my mother's hairdresser."

"But you go by 'Charlie,' right? You never said 'Hey, guys, I'm Charlie – just call me Charlie?'"

He shrugged. "My skipper told me that you don't get to choose your nickname."

"And they chose 'Connie.'"

"Yep."

"Well, hey – Connie Mack, right? Winningest manager of all time? That's something."

"Yeah…" Charlie sighed. "Turns out he's not as popular these days as Connie Chung. I got that one a lot."

Francesca snorted, covering her mouth as though to catch it before it escaped. "I'm sorry – believe me, I'm laughing with you."

He grinned. The wine was making all of this a very smooth experience. "Oh, is that what this is?"

"She's a very influential woman!" she laughed.

Charlie nodded, pleased that she was somehow still seated across from him. "And Connie Francis – boy, she's a talent, huh?"

Her mouth open in faux outrage. "Hey, I *like* 'Where the Boys Are!'"

He smiled at her. "Oh, Frank. You are one adorable guy."

CHAPTER 10
Snooze Lagoon's

"ANOTHER ROUGH ONE today, huh?"

Charlie was comforted by the sound of Francesca's voice coming through his headphones. It was rich and warm, a three-dimensional tool of expression that flowed effortlessly from her. The headphones enhanced the closeness of her mouth to his ears, and it was obvious to him that she, unlike himself, had chosen a profession in which her natural talents could be maximized.

And she was correct in her assessment of the day's bludgeoning by the Alewife Amberjacks: it *had* been a rough one. After pouring himself into his bunk on the rolling yacht the night before, he'd managed approximately three hours of blackout sleep and had barely been able to dress himself for the day's travel. His head felt as though nine marching bands had taken up residency behind his eyes. A five-hour bus ride up the coast had begun before the sun rose, replete with the sounds of cantankerous early-morning bitching from the players and Windy's phone blooping as he uploaded useless post after useless post onto Blither. It was also accompanied by great plumes of cigarette smoke from Whalen, though the rest of the team seemed to accept this as part of the job. All of it had distracted Charlie from the data deep-dive he'd been planning, to see if there were any unexplored angles to work that could help break the skid.

He'd foregone his dramatic stack of papers, now accepting that even physical evidence would not be swaying the skipper from his usual routine of throw-'em-out-there-and-see-what-happens. Yet, the hangover, combined with the reading of his tablet, combined with the rattling of the 1980s-vintage bus and Whalen's stale nicotine fog had troubled his stomach, and he'd spent much of the last few hours on the sticky floor with his head in a bag.

"I've had better days," he finally said into the phone. He was now pacing the walkway outside his room at the Zero Motel. It was a humid night and his blazer was both absorbing the heavy atmosphere and locking in his body heat.

"I'm just glad you made it up that gangplank," Francesca said, implying that she had walked him home. "It looked touch and go for a minute, but you really held onto those ropes."

"Oh, yeah…" he said, trying to pull this memory up with little luck. He decided to pivot. "How was the broadcast?"

"Totally tragic. I would say a solid third of it was just Dip contradicting the Alewife broadcasters. Who, of course, our listeners weren't hearing."

"How do you contradict something you're not even looking at?"

"He does it to me every day," she said.

"Fair point."

"So, what're you doing tonight?"

"I've been looking for Whalen, but he's not in his room." Charlie had done enough low league traveling to know he should tread lightly when knocking on teammates' doors. He, of course, had always traveled with Margaret, who had consistently made a point of booking the room next to his. He supposed he should have been flattered that she would be so concerned with what he was doing, but it had always limited his exposure to the vices his fellow players sometimes found on the road. "I guess he's pretty old, so maybe he's asleep already."

"Did you try Snooze Lagoon's?"

"Maybe?" he said, perplexed by this arrangement of words. "Is that a, uh, website or something?"

She laughed and he could not help but smile. "It's a restaurant – right down the street from the motel. There's no way you can miss it."

Charlie crossed the motel parking lot, realizing he *had* missed it while being carsick into a crumpled pharmacy bag. He stared down the road that lead into Alewife, another small seaside community that was barely distinguishable from Cape Haddock. It seemed an average, poorly lit outskirt street. "I am not seeing it…" Turning to face the other direction, all became clear. "Oh."

A few hundred yards away, crouched the silhouette of a low building with a dramatically peaked roof. A sign of buzzing neon bent into the shape of a tribal mask sat perched upon two crossed oars. Beneath this was a series of martini-shaped lights that lit up, one after the other, offering the illusion of tipsy movement.

"I'm going to guess the portal to 1962 is the place I'm looking for?"

"Yeah, they don't give him a hard time about smoking outside, so he's there a lot," said Francesca.

"Right," he said. "Well, I should go."

"Sure," she said. "Let's get together when you're back, okay?"

Charlie felt lightheaded and nodded before realizing she could not hear this over the phone. "Yes, we should definitely do that."

"Maybe we'll do a white wine next time though, eh?"

"Probably a good idea."

"Oh, wait…" The sound of rustling followed by a digital beep could be heard on her end. "Another tough loss tonight, Coach." Her voice was now in full broadcaster-mode. "What kind of adjustments would you like to see the team make?"

"Oh, uh… Well, when it comes down to it, we really just need to string some hits together and, uh… you know. Try to score some more runs." He frowned at his own boilerplate – was this really all people wanted to hear? "All good?"

"Yeah. Nicely phrased dodge there, you're really getting the hang of this."

They said goodnight and Charlie proceeded down the road to the relic that was Snooze Lagoon's Tiki Bar. Pushing through the dark-stained door, he found it was a museum piece from a bygone era, dimly lit by pools of colored light. The aesthetic was chintzy South Pacific, all palm fronds, demon masks, and island bamboo.

Whalen sat at the bar in rumpled tweeds, the restaurant's only patron. A massive cocktail was planted in front of him, and he appeared to be lost in thought, his foot tapping along to the faint sound of a Hammond B-3 organ oozing from speakers hidden overhead. Charlie leaned on the counter next to him with a sigh.

"My sentiments exactly," said the manager, running a hand over his mustache. "Hence the drink."

Charlie tugged anxiously at the sleeves of his blazer – he'd never had to dress up in Single-A, and it felt strange to be wearing such an 'adult' uniform. "Always nice to take in the local flavor after a road game, huh?" he said, glancing around the vacant lounge.

"Exactly," Whalen chuckled. "And what are you doing this fine evening, young Conroy? Blow through the dirty movie menu at the motel already?"

"Actually, I, uh..." He paused to double-check the bar was empty and lowered his voice. "I was just talking to Francesca."

Whalen's eyebrow arced upward. "From the radio? Radio-Francesca?"

"Yeah. We went out last night."

"Oh, this makes sense," the manager nodded. "I thought you looked a little rough this morning while you were tripping up the bus stairs and passing out on my shoulder and leaving for the bathroom every four batters–"

"Yeah, I remember the day, Skip, thanks," said Charlie, motioning for him to keep his voice down. "And dinner last night was great, but…but, I don't know if I'm, like, *allowed,* you know?"

Whalen looked at him like he was an idiot. "No."

"We work at the same place, my mom's the boss – it might look bad."

Whalen waved him off. "I wouldn't worry too much about it, Charlie. She's a sharp woman, that Francesca. I don't think she'd do anything to get either of you into trouble." Whalen looked back to his drink, then tilted his head toward his bench coach. "How, uh... how'd it go?"

Charlie shrugged, the hazy memory of the night's conclusion coming back to him in fits and starts. "I got dizzy and she dropped me off at the boat."

Whalen nodded knowingly. "Ah. Yep, she is definitely one sharp woman. So, you're already at the check-in-with-me-on-the-road stage?"

"She wanted to do a phoner for the post-game."

"Ah. And what a game it was, eh?"

"Well, we only lost by single digits this time, so that's progress, right?"

The skipper snorted and took a drink. "Okay..."

"But, hey, are you going to get kicked out of *every* game? It almost feels like you're doing it on purpose." Whalen had put on a tremendous show in the top of the seventh.

"Well, Charlie, I *was* screaming in a grown man's face about how I hoped he'd die because of his lousy strike zone, so... yeah. Kind of on purpose." He smiled at the memory.

"And this is you maintaining good relations with the umpires, huh?"

"Ah, they expect it from me," he said, waving Charlie off. "It's almost a part of the job description. And better they run *me* than one of the players, right? We don't exactly have many to spare."

Charlie sighed and rubbed his temples, knowing this was all too true. Reg Pretzel had thrown a sterling five innings of seven-run ball that day, leaving Manny Hulacox to mop up the rest. This meant that Hayden would be pitching the crucial Fourth of July tilt on less than three days' rest. It was wildly irresponsible, and they would be lucky if his arm didn't fall off in the process. Charlie had a sneaking suspicion that J.J. would probably have a good laugh if it did.

He took in the antiquated surroundings while Whalen took another drink. "What is this place?"

"Eh," Whalen said with a shrug. "Just the watering hole I hide away in whenever we're in Alewife. Nice place to get away from the team for a minute. Pull up a chair, these are actual Witco barstools, you know!"

Charlie didn't know what that meant, but gamely tilted the stool back to examine the grimacing tiki idol face carved into the side. He set it back down and gingerly sat himself atop it. It felt like any other stool.

"Kinda like you're hiding in the early-'60s, huh, Skip?"

Whalen's eyes went wide at the suggestion. "Good lord, if only. I mean, sure, you had the racism, the B.O., and the Bay of Pigs, but whoo-boy, I'll tell you what..." he looked over at Charlie, his expression alive in a way the younger man had rarely seen. "Back then you could knock out a doubleheader, slide right into a turtleneck and blazer, while running on nothing but greenies and Brylcreem fumes. Then you'd find a place like this to stretch out the five bucks in your pocket, just knowing you were gonna have a hell of a night. In Toledo, no less!" He shook his head at the thought.

"That sounds incredible."

Whalen nodded. "Indeed, it was."

"So... what happened?"

"Mostly the '70s."

"Ah."

Whalen raised a hand and flagged down the bartender. "Hey, Tommy, get my friend here a, uh..." Whalen glanced at a yellowed, laminated menu on the bar. "...an 'Arthur Lime-Man,' huh?" He turned to Charlie. "You like limes?"

"You mean, do I enjoy eating raw limes?"

"What?" Whalen scowled. "No, you stupid son of a – uh, son of my boss."

Charlie nodded to Whalen's highball glass, filled with a tropical-colored liquid of unknown origins. "Whatcha got there?"

Whalen removed the drink's cherry-and-pineapple garnished cocktail sword and spun it between his fingertips. "That's an 'Easter Island Iced Tea.'"

"Ouch."

Whalen nodded and studied the fruit-spear. "Yeah, the puns are awful, but it kinda comes with the territory. The kitsch factor, you know?"

Charlie looked around the bar and frowned. "This place has a kitchen?"

Whalen plunked the decorative garnish back in his drink. "Now, what's going on – you were looking for me?"

"Huh? Oh! Yeah, I wanted to show you something." Charlie held up the smallish newspaper clutched in his hand.

Whalen eyed the paper, his expression dubious. "The hell is that?"

"It's the Alewife Annual. They have a rack of them in the lobby."

Charlie handed the paper to Whalen, who surveyed the cover with tepid interest. "Published bi-weekly, by the way, not annually, but whatever. Page 13."

Whalen shook the paper open and began perusing. "Mmm... Oh, I see. You're looking into this guy who wants to trade a set of snow tires?"

"Huh?"

Whalen nodded, deep in thought. "Well, it says they're barely used, but you're definitely gonna want to check the tread–"

"No, Skip, down at the bottom." It was like herding an enormous cat.

"Oh, right..." Whalen's eyes moseyed south. "Hey, look at that! We made the free paper that people use to line their birdcages. Top of the world, huh?"

"Just read it. That part there," Charlie said, pointing to a lower-third article, and wondering why the bristly manager had to constantly bust his chops. He was only trying to save their jobs.

Whalen gave him a look, but turned back to the blurb without further comment, and began reading aloud:

" 'Be sure to take the kids to Amberjack Field this weekend, as the "floundering" Cape Haddock Coelacanths stumble into town, playing a brand of baseball so lousy that the Coelacanth faithful have taken to social media, calling for Manager Grey Whalen to be fired, among other punishments unsuitable for publishing in a family bi-weekly circular...' "

Charlie shook his head in disgust, fully prepared to enable Whalen's inevitable outrage. "Can you believe that? I mean, what's this guy's problem?"

Whalen nodded, skimming the paper further. "Yeah, that's a run-on sentence. You'd think with two weeks between printings, they'd have somebody copyedit the thing."

Charlie gave him a look. "No, Skip, you're missing the point – the fans are turning on us. On *you!*" Where was the outrage? Could Whalen not see that he was being tried in the press without even being asked to defend himself?

Whalen looked at Charlie as though he'd just offered to paint the skipper's name on the moon. "Oh, for fuck's sake, Charlie, you can't take this stuff personally. You've gotta toughen up a bit!"

Charlie's face fell. "This doesn't bother you at all."

Whalen sighed and began refolding the paper. "Listen to me: every year – *every goddamned year* – you're gonna have to endure this shit if you want to manage a ballclub. They come with the job, articles like this." He held the paper up, then handed it back to his coach. "In fact, this sounds word-for-word like the same article that circulated *last* year. And the year before that, and on and on and on."

Charlie couldn't wrap his head around the idea. There was an inherent unfairness to being judged by people who were only partially informed, at best. "But… how do you *deal* with it?"

Whalen shrugged. "How did *you* deal with two decades spent looking up at the Mendoza Line in low-A Ball?"

This was a cheap shot, but Charlie couldn't deny the wily manager was right. How *had* he dealt with it? "Well… no one cared how any of us were doing," he said, thinking back on those days, not far behind him. "And I suspect my mother hid the paper from me every morning."

Whalen frowned. "So, she went over to your place and stole your newspaper every morning?"

"Oh, no, no – she'd just throw it out before I came downstairs."

Whalen stared at him for a long moment. His face was blank, but Charlie could almost see the gears in his head grinding. "Because… you were living at home."

Charlie nodded. "Well, yeah. I mean, between college courses and the Tumbleweed season, it's not like I was exactly raking it in anywhere, you know?"

Whalen didn't move. "Huh."

"You sound… surprised?"

"Huh."

Charlie looked at him sideways. "...And maybe somewhat embarrassed for me?"

Whalen squinted at him. "And this was the whole time you were playing?"

Why is he so fixated on this? "Well... well, yeah. I guess so."

"What about the internet?"

Charlie was briefly impressed that Whalen even knew what the internet was, let alone that it had news on it. "She had a filter on it."

"Of course she did." Whalen nodded as the bartender placed a hurricane glass of pale, green liquid that was, in fact, garnished with raw limes in front of Charlie.

Charlie stared at the citrus monstrosity in shock and offered one last line in his defense. "You know, it's very common for millennials to live at home." He tried to color this statement with as much conviction as his pride would allow.

Whalen looked unconvinced. *"Are* you a millennial?"

"I'm close." Charlie tugged at the collar of his shirt, the bar suddenly feeling extra warm.

"Well, anyway," the manager continued, "I've had more than my share of bad press over the years, and I'm sure you will too when it's your turn in the hot seat. The point is, you walk it off, like a fastball to the ribs."

"It seems like an issue with maybe more nuance than a sports analogy can cover?" said Charlie.

The skipper turned back to his coach. "Listen, no one likes having their every decision questioned and dismantled, but that's kind of the job."

Charlie shook his head and turned back to the paper. "They just get so *mean."* It was a feeling he was not unfamiliar with, but having it published was a real slap in the face. He could only imagine what had been published about him during his playing days.

Whalen nodded. "Sure, the fans get frustrated when you can't win games. Or if their favorite player isn't doing the thing they're so good at doing, or whatever goddamned thing it is." He pointed at Charlie. "You've gotta remember that these fans are paying their hard-earned money to escape reality and have an experience that they can get lost in. *With* their team. They want to be lost in the beauty of the thing that is this game. And when you fail to deliver a quality effort on the field, they get pissed off. But they're pissed off because they care so much. Because they're invested in the team and want us to do well." He turned back to his drink. "So, from that angle, you can take it as a compliment."

Charlie nodded and chewed this over. He fiddled with the slice of lime dangling from the salted rim of his drink. "So, what happens if you can never live up to the greatness they think you're capable of?"

Whalen snorted into his drink and set it down, barking a mighty laugh.

Charlie frowned. *Oh god, is he drunk?* "What's so funny?"

Whalen wiped his mouth with a cocktail napkin and shook his head. *"You,* kid. You're a real stitch, you know that?" Charlie had been called many things in his life, but this was not one of them. "The joke is that you'll *never* live up to the greatness they expect of you. From Little League in grade school, to that busher league you were playing in, out in the atomic testing grounds, and all the way up to the Big Club, there has never been a team that has lived up to the expectations of the people. Ever."

Charlie considered this. "But somebody's gotta win, right?"

"Yeah, but that's the thing though! The people want to see you win *every* game. All of 'em. Especially the ones they've paid to come see. But the reality is, no team wins all the games in this sport – not even close. Any team's bound to lose *a lot* of games over the course of a 162-game season. It's just gonna happen."

Charlie nodded, the picture becoming clear. "And when your best hitters only hit the ball three out of ten times, these things can add up."

"Shoot, if a guy in our league's hitting .300, the Big Club swoops in to collect, and we're back at square one."

"And I thought you weren't a numbers guy, Skip."

Whalen tilted his head. "Even *I* respect batting .300."

Behind them came the jingle of the doorbell. Both men turned to see J.J. Pike enter the bar. He looked oddly adult in his street clothes. Charlie felt like he could just as easily be mistaken for a realtor as a baseballer.

Whalen hailed him with a wave. "J.J.! Hey, take a seat."

J.J. joined the party, nodding to each of them. 'Hey, Skip, hey Tommy, hey... whatever your name is."

Charlie's face fell, but Whalen chuckled as he moved over one stool, allowing the backstop to sit between them. "Ah, he's just screwing with you, Charlie."

J.J. gave Charlie an examining stare and slowly shook his head. Charlie's eyes went wide.

Whalen turned to the grim catcher. "What're the fellas up to?"

"Ah, they went into town to pick up girls."

Charlie shook his head. "Those poor girls."

"Ha!" J.J. blurted. "You got that one right, Chester. Fucking idiots..." J.J. flagged down the bartender. "Tommy, can I get this 'Mai Tai To Shine?' Thanks buddy."

Whalen ran a hand down his mustache, grinning. "Now, J.J., as I recall, *you* had your share of dangerous liaisons back in the day."

J.J. waved him off. "You make it sounds so exotic. And it definitely was *not.*"

"Any port in a storm, huh?" Charlie said, always curious as to what that type of life was like. His mom had never let him have sleepovers.

J.J. shrugged. "You can put into as many ports as you want, but that won't stop it from raining. That said, you could've tracked my movements up and down the Eastern Seaboard over a season and come back with a goddamned nautical map."

"Would've made my life easier," said Whalen. "I was the one who had to chase you down when you broke curfew." He leaned over the bar to see Charlie. "J.J. helped me learn every trailer park and budget apartment complex in New England. I spent *hours* trying to dig him up."

"You were like a shitty Sherlock Holmes, chasing down what's-his-face..." said J.J.

"The Professor?" Charlie offered.

The catcher nodded. "Yep, that's the one – Professor What's-His-Face..."

"Moriarty?" Whalen tried.

J.J. snapped his fingers. "That's the one! I was like a very horny Moriarty."

"You were a Horniarty," said Charlie.

"I was," J.J. nodded. "And I made the old man chase me everywhere."

Charlie found it curious that these adventures were spoken of in the past tense. "But now you're having drinks with us at Snooze Lagoon's?"

J.J. didn't respond for a moment. He stared down at the drink that Tommy the barkeep had slid across to him, balancing the tip of his index finger on the end of a pineapple spear. "I'm 34, I'm in decline in every way. Physically, professionally, socially, mentally... I just want some quiet at this point. I wanna not hear about what a shitty husband I'm being from my wife, or what a shitty part-time boyfriend I'm being to my shitty part-time girlfriends, or about how their seats are too sunny, or how they're not sunny enough… all while trying to keep the wife on the third base side and the girlfriend on the first base side, or vice versa...

"And then listen to my pitchers harp on about snap throws and shaking my signs off like the fucking spoiled idiots they are. Like I haven't been rotting in this circuit for the past 10 years, watching these kids swing through outside-inside-top shelf sequences over and over and over again." He shook his head. "Fucking kids, man. And if it's not any of *that,* it's my *other* wife calling, berating me for being a lousy father–"

"Wait," said Charlie. "I'm sorry – you have two wives?"

"Well, *ex*-wife, I should say," said J.J.

"Mmm..." Whalen nodded too, as though this fact was inevitable.

"Actually," said J.J., "they're both ex-wives at this point."

Charlie nodded. "And how many kids do you have?"

"I am 99% sure that I have somewhere in the neighborhood of three to four kids. Tops."

"Oh, wow," said Charlie. "So, you're kind of a monster, huh?"

"Oh, yeah, I'm a pretty awful human being. Definitely not a role model, that's for sure." J.J. paused, his eyes darting upward as he made a further mental tally. "Maybe five kids? Eh, it could be five."

Whalen gestured to the drinks sitting before them. All were now melting their spectrum of tropical colors into a shade of reality-tinged puce. "You'll notice he still spends half his time on the road, doing exactly what we're doing right now"

"Hiding from reality beneath your drink's umbrella, huh?" said Charlie.

J.J. scoffed. "Do you see the fucking bamboo and wood paneling in this heap? Yeah, this is a reality-free zone if ever I've seen one, and cheers to that." He raised his glass, the motion as sarcastic as the man making it.

"Cheers," Whalen said, doing the same.

"Cheers," said Charlie. They drank. It was the most camaraderie Charlie could remember feeling in his many years of baseball.

Whalen drained the last of his cocktail. "What's your take on the kid, Pikey?" he said, flagging the bartender for another.

"Chandler? Oh, he's a real piece of garbage, Gray."

Charlie found the assessment to be brutal. "Whoa."

J.J. shrugged. "I mean, it's not his fault he's kind of a shithead – you can blame his parents for that."

Charlie could not believe what he was hearing. In theory, the lower leagues were supposed to be where talent was nurtured and allowed room to grow and develop. Where your failures would only make you stronger as you found the strength to push through them until success was finally earned. The minors were supposed to be a place here wisdom was passed down from generation to generation, like skilled craftspeople did in days of yore. There was something timeless about this methodology, a thread of continuity that could be followed all the way back to mammoth hunts on the glacial plains. And here was one such elder, easily dismissing a rookie who knew no better and was lost in the woods. Helpless. Waiting for guidance. *Their* guidance.

"You don't think that appraisal's a little harsh? I mean, these are just kids." He thought back to his own disappointing years of aimless swings and misses. Kurf Plunkett. The errors and strikeouts. "I thought we were supposed to be offering them some kind of encouragement at this phase in their careers–"

Whalen sighed and looked away as though his bench coach had just built a log cabin on some train tracks. "Oh, Charlie..."

J.J. put his drink down with enough force to make Charlie start. "Fuck. No."

Whalen shook his head. "Here we go."

The catcher stared at Charlie, his gaze allowing no room for nonsense. It bored into Charlie like an oil rig. "Listen. That dirty diaper of a human being might only be nineteen years old but make no mistake about what he is and where he comes from. This kid's been treated like he's 'special' since the day he could even *look* at a baseball, let alone throw one.

"His parents own a string of car dealerships that hold the Mid-Atlantic in a used car headlock. Second generation lot owners at that, so even his parents didn't have to earn anything. So, they buy their way into the travel leagues and they have him conditioning with ex-major leaguers by the time he's in middle school. They have him breaking down his windup at some slow-mo, biomech lab when he's

16, and by 18 he's nine months into his rehab for Tommy John surgery. After that, it's winters in SoCal so he can play with a team year-round, just like he'd done the previous six years.

"He's had *every* advantage there is to have, from raw talent, to being a rich, white dude, surrounded by enablers and sycophants. And all these people around him thought it was perfectly okay to sacrifice his humanity with this non-stop pampering, in order for him to become one of the greats. I mean, everybody works hard to get here – there's nobody this close to the Big Club who hasn't given their blood, sweat and tears to be here, but man..." J.J. finally broke his gaze and shook his head in disgust. "When everyone's already treating you like you've already done something, but you haven't done shit... When your life's a blank check while the rest of these guys go back to the lumberyard, or whichever farm they were pulled from, well... fuck that guy."

The trio sat in silence for a moment, processing this take. Finally, Whalen said, "His stuff is electric though, you gotta admit."

Charlie nodded. "Yeah, it is..."

"It *is!*" said J.J. "Dammit, that's the worst part of all this – his stuff is really fucking electric! It's only a matter of time before he gets the call-up, that son of a bitch."

"But he's so wild," said Charlie.

"Mmm – but *effectively* wild," J.J., nodded. "Sometimes!"

"Which is enough," said Whalen, turning to his coach. "Charlie, I know you're kinda new to his level of play, but you've got to understand two things about the Big Club: If you can hit, they'll find a spot for you to play, and if you've got the velos to throw 100 miles per hour in the general vicinity of the batter's box, they'll make room for you."

"You think so?" said Charlie. "Last time, he threw eight pitches that gophered all the way to the backstop."

J.J. barked a laugh. "Yeah he did. Honestly, I just stopped trying to catch 'em after a while." Whalen chuckled while Charlie looked at J.J. in disbelief. "What?" said the catcher. "C'mon, lighten up, it's all I can do to keep him in line. Kids need boundaries – it's good for him!"

"Builds character," said Whalen, draining his second drink.

Charlie gave him a quizzical look. "I *think* it might be building a damaged psychological profile."

"Oh, you're one to talk, Mr. Bean Ball," said J.J. "Guys were throwing at you just because they hated your face. What's it say about the self-esteem of a guy who keeps letting them do it?"

"Score a run for J.J." Whalen said, nodding. "The point is, if the kid can hang in there through all this shit down here, he'll be fine up there. Eventually." The trio stared at their glasses until Whalen cleared his throat. "I mean, if he misses the strike zone and hits some poor bastard in the head, it's gonna be like the Zapruder film all over again, but barring that... he's gonna be all right, that kid."

As though he'd been conjured, Hayden burst through the door. "Skipper!" They turned to find the young pitcher wide-eyed with panic. "We've got a huge fucking problem."

CHAPTER 11
Zero Motel

CHARLIE, WHALEN, J.J., and Hayden crossed the motel lawn and adjoining parking lot at a brisk clip, soon arriving outside of room 27. The lights were on, but the curtains were drawn.

"I heard noises," Hayden was saying, relaying his story with the earnestness of a campfire tale. "There was shouting, and something that sounded like a water buffalo crashing through a lamp store."

J.J. and Whalen exchanged a knowing look. "Javi," they said as one.

"Who's he rooming with?" said Charlie.

"Windy," J.J. said, shaking his head as though this was the stupidest thing he could conceive of.

Charlie knocked on the door as Whalen ate pieces of fruit off the toothpick from his drink. "Javi? Windy? You guys all right in there?"

From behind the door, the sound of a table collapsing was heard, followed by a moan. Charlie and Whalen exchanged another look, then began pounding on the door.

"Windy, it's your Skipper!" Whalen's tone was stern. "Open this door or I'm... grounding you and taking away your phone privileges!"

Charlie gave him a look and received a shrug in response. Finally, the door opened a crack, revealing the panicked face of Windy Turner staring out at them.

Charlie was alarmed by the sight of the second baseman's nervous eyes, but quickly regained his composure. "Hey! What is going on in there?"

Windy's hand shook as he raised it in a warning gesture. "Coach… Skipper... don't be mad, okay? I'm only one man."

He pulled the door open wider, revealing Javier sprawled over one of the beds, clutching his stomach. He was wailing in agony, surrounded by fast food trash and broken motel furniture.

Charlie and Whalen must have looked completely dumbstruck, for Windy quickly held up his phone to get a picture of their expressions. The digital click snapped them out of their stupor, and they rushed to the aid of their first baseman.

The rooms at the Zero Motel were as classy as the name suggested; shag carpet and wooden paneling ruled the decor, while the twin beds wore blankets featuring enthusiastic, tropical patterns.

Charlie was aghast at the sight of Javier's massive, ill form. "Oh god, what happened!?"

J.J. turned to Windy and shook his head, tsking in mock disappointment. "What did you do?"

Whalen crouched next to his fallen player and began lightly slapping him across the face. "Javier? Javi? Wake up, buddy – speak to me!"

Javier moaned in response but didn't open his eyes. With a guttural moan, he somehow flung his gargantuan body to the side and rolled into a facedown position.

Whalen watched in horror. "Oh, goddammit, he's on his stomach – Javi, no! Sit up for me, big guy!" He grabbed Javier by the shoulders and pulled at his torso. The bulk refused to yield to his efforts.

Windy sidled up to Charlie, who was observing all of this from within a state of deep shock. "Coach, you've gotta believe me, there was nothing I could do!"

Charlie turned to him, desperate for answers. "But how did he *get* like this?"

"Are you kidding?" Windy shouted over Javier's groans. "He went 4 for 4 today! Javi does a lot of running like that and he gets *extra* hungry!"

Whalen checked Javier's pulse against his watch and turned to Windy. "Did you let him order for himself?"

Windy's face fell, disgraced. "Skip, you see how much bigger he is than me, right? He's like the size of three Windy Turners!"

Whalen shook his head, disgusted. "Dammit, Windy, you know he can't order for himself – it's too much! It's always too much!"

"I know, Skip, but he likes it! I can't take away a man's joy like that."

Charlie patted Windy on the shoulder. "I know, buddy, I know..." He looked around the room, hoping for an easy distraction from the panic. "Why don't you get me some water. Hayden, get me some towels from the bathroom, okay?"

Whalen looked up at him as the two players scurried to the bathroom. "You planning on doing surgery, Doctor?"

"What? No, it's just in case he's thirsty or gets sick all over the place."

"No, no, no," Whalen said, shaking his head. "Out of the question. We don't travel with that kind of insurance – we get sick in the toilet like the rest of America. J.J., get his feet, we've gotta move him."

J.J., who, until this point, had been leaning against the dresser, observing the unfolding chaos with his arms crossed, reluctantly joined the fray. He grabbed Javier's legs and tucked them under his arms, awaiting Whalen's signal. Windy and Hayden emerged from the bathroom, supplies in tow.

Windy held out an ice bucket filled with tap water to Charlie. "You want me to boil it, Coach?"

Charlie gave him a look. "Put it in a cup so he can drink it – what are you thinking?"

"Oh." Windy considered this. "Well, can I splash him with it? See if it wakes him up at all?"

Now it was Charlie's turn to think it over. After a moment, he shrugged and nodded. "Yeah, I suppose you can try that."

Whalen straightened at this. "I really wouldn't–"

He was interrupted by a cascading splash as Windy emptied the bucket at Javier's face. It slapped the fallen giant's skin, soaking him. The big man gasped and sat up at the waist like a vampire, then just as quickly collapsed back onto the now-dampened bed.

Whalen's eyes went wide as the attempt resolved itself into failure without further incident. "Jesus, you fellas are a real Mayo Clinic over here."

J.J. sighed, shifting the weight of Javier's lower half. "Gray, his legs are like pylons – what are we doing here?"

Sensing a moment of crisis, Charlie leaned toward Whalen, his voice low. "Skip, I hate to be redundant, but what *are* we doing? Can't we just leave him to, like, sleep it off?"

Whalen raised an eyebrow at him. "Can you really conceive of a universe in which your mother pays for a complete scrubdown of this motel room?"

Charlie frowned and thought for a moment. "I can't imagine that's in the budget–"

"It's *not* in the budget, okay?" The skipper's tone left no room to argue. "And I don't want to hear about it, which I *will*, if this goes down – or comes up – the way I think it's going to, you read me?"

Charlie paused for a second to consider this. "Let's get him into the bathroom."

Whalen slapped him reassuringly on the shoulder. He turned back to the ground zero of his team's hell and leaned into Javier's sweaty face. "Javi, can you hear me? Moan once if you can hear me, kiddo." Javier moaned, the noise weak, tenuous. Whalen nodded as if he understood completely. "Listen, buddy, we gotta get you into the bathroom so you can puke up your regrets, all right?"

Javier moaned again, shaking his head violently.

Windy looked up at his manager, eyes wide. "How much time we got, Skip?"

Whalen grimaced and bent over, placing his ear against Javier's stomach. After a moment, a menacing rumble came from the bloated abdomen. It was the growl of a territorial predator, challenging all who dared intrude.

Whalen straightened and began loosening his tie. "We've got about three minutes before he blows. Maybe two."

J.J. peered at Javier's face, appalled. "Oh man, is he drooling?"

Charlie snapped his fingers without peeling his eyes from his fallen soldier. "Windy – towel."

Windy grabbed a towel from the stack held by Hayden and started dabbing at Charlie's forehead.

Charlie recoiled. "Will you *stop* that, please? I'm not doing surgery!"

Whalen pointed at his first baseman's face. "Wipe Javi's mouth, he's got some, uh... spit-up burbling."

J.J. looked down at the pile of man before him, lolling on the comforter like a helpless baby. "We're not going to have to, like, *change* him or anything, are we?"

Whalen stepped back and raised his arms for their attention. "Okay fellas, here's the situation: we've got to move him into the bathroom and we've gotta do it quickly. But not so quickly that we jostle him and set off, uh..." he waved his hands in the direction of Javier's ample midsection, "you know, something we'd rather not deal with."

Whalen turned and paused in his instructions upon finding Windy recording video of him with his phone. He leaned close to the young man, his voice low. "Windy, I love you kid, but so help me god, if that phone doesn't disappear for the next 30 minutes, I will personally throw it into the goddamned ocean."

Windy's face fell, apparently wounded by his skipper's lack of interest in historic preservation. "It's just for posterity, Skip–"

"The ocean, Windy – I'm not even kidding."

"Gotcha, Skipper." Windy sheepishly tucked the device into his back pocket as Whalen continued.

"Now, remember back in spring training when we spent an afternoon doing lift and carry drills? You want to lift with your legs and keep the weight close to your center of gravity. Now, we're gonna do a combination carry, got it? We're gonna blanket-pull him on to someone's back, and then logroll him into a stretcher lift."

Charlie was surprised to see the Coelacanths nod their heads, as though these terms made all the sense in the world. "Whoa, whoa, whoa – we're going to put him on someone's back?" He looked to the others for shared disbelief but found none. "He's 275, Skip," he added, as though this might inspire a re-evaluation.

Whalen was unphased. "Actually, it's closer to three bills. But it's only for a couple seconds, so why don't you get down there and, uh... gird yourself. Windy, J.J. – grab that blanket." He nodded to the tropical comforter.

Charlie gasped at being suddenly thrown into the middle of the maneuver Whalen had planned. "Me? But... but... I'm the bench coach."

Whalen sighed. "So you keep saying."

"Shouldn't we, you know..." Charlie leaned close to Whalen again, voice lowered, "get the rookie to do it?" He nodded in Hayden's direction. The young hurler's jaw dropped.

Whalen looked at him in complete disbelief. "Oh, I'm sorry, you're right – what was I thinking? Yeah, let's put the million-dollar arm down there and drop a metric ton of Venezuelan on him, huh?" He pointed a stern index finger at Charlie. "You're the bench coach – *be a bench!*"

Charlie rolled his eyes and tossed his blazer across the back of a nearby desk chair. He got on his hands and knees as Windy and J.J. each took a corner of the comforter, and Whalen and Hayden took the other. Javier moaned.

Whalen spoke over the prolonged grunt. "You just hang in there, Javier, okay? Sí?"

Javier waved him away, the motion weak, his eyes closed.

Whalen huffed and addressed his cohorts. "All right boys, time is of the essence here. Let's do this before there's some other essence happening, all right? One... two... *three!*"

The quartet of movers groaned in unison as they dragged the blanket, along with Javier, off the foot of the bed and onto Charlie's back.

The weight was crushing. It was as if a semi-trailer had jackknifed itself across his spine. "Oh, you've got to be kidding me," he groaned.

Whalen bent down to meet his coach's eye-level. "Charlie, I get that this is less than ideal, but give me two shakes of a lamb's tail to get him wrapped up for the stretcher lift, and–" He was cut off as Charlie's phone rang from inside his jacket pocket. The muted, digitized melody of Ozzy Osbourne's "Mama, I'm Coming Home" leaked into the room, a harbinger of beeping doom. "Charlie, your jacket's ringing," said the bemused manager.

Charlie's head emerged from beneath the comforter. "Outstanding," he said, his tone stressed. "Say, could you do me a solid and *answer it,* please? It's my mom."

Whalen shot him a wicked grin and gestured to the bulk of his first baseman. "Charlie, I'm kind of in the middle of something, if you wouldn't mind waiting–"

"Skipper, please!"

"Okay, okay..." Whalen chuckled at his bench coach's anxiety and turned to his players. "Start wrapping, boys – shawarma-style."

As the players began carrying out his orders, Whalen plucked the phone from Charlie's blazer, and answered. "You've got Charlie's phone – go."

Margaret's voice came blaring over the speaker, impatient to find an audience. "Hello? Charlie? Who is this? I don't *do* ransoms."

"Ah, Maggie!" Whalen said, trying to sell a scene of upbeat normalcy through his voice. "It's Whalen."

"Whalen?" Charlie could sense her frustration at having to speak to another person. "Oh. I'm using your office, by the way – it's disgusting."

"Uh-huh," Whalen nodded, as though this was to be expected, "I could see that being the case."

"Where's Charlie – did he get lost in the grocery store again?"

Whalen gave Charlie a skeptical look. "'Again?'" he mouthed off-phone, before turning back to the conversation in-hand. "No, he's fine, Maggie, he's just doing some team building exercises."

"Don't you bullshit a bullshitter, Whalen – I know very well what happens on the road. Do you have everything under control there?"

In the background, Javier moaned. Every person in the pathetic motel room froze. Their eyes darted from one to another, before resting on the phone in Whalen's hand.

The old man reacted quickly, defaulting to a leadership tactic he'd honed over several years in minor league management. He cupped his hand over the microphone-end of the phone and drew it near his face, mimicking a series of static bursts. "Uh, what's that, Maggie, you're breaking up, *skkrrrrk* – gotta go, here's Charlie."

Whalen held the phone out to Charlie with a shrug. Charlie glared at his superior, who was clearly standing further away than he could reach. "Thanks. Would you mind?" He nodded his head to the side, grimacing as the movement and the weight of a full Coronado crossed paths. Whalen dutifully maneuvered his way around the players and held the phone up to Charlie's ear.

Charlie's head dropped for a moment as he gathered himself. "Hey, Mom–"

"Charlie, what the hell is going on over there?"

Charlie sighed. It was in situations like this, when her domineering side would require nothing short of all the answers, that he was sometimes forced to lie to her. It was the only defense he had against hearing about everything, all day. "Nothing, Mom. Just teambuilding, like the skipper said."

"Good lord, you are the worst liars," she said.

Meanwhile, Hayden, J.J. and Windy lined up alongside Javier. Whalen, still holding the phone, made motions with his free hand, guiding the big man onto his side and into the arms of his teammates.

Hayden immediately dropped the head-end onto the matted carpet, where it landed with a *thud.* Javier's moaning was replaced by the pitcher screaming through a clenched jaw.

Charlie's head snapped to the sound, where he saw his star player half-grounded, and possibly concussed. "Oh shit."

"What was *that?*" His mother was relentless. Charlie knew he needed to provide answers as quickly as possible before he was rightfully accused of lying again.

"Uh... what was what, Mom?"

"That thump – it sounded like someone dropped a bag of concrete from a helicopter!"

"No, no," Charlie said, struggling to keep his voice airy and casual. "Just a, uh – a trust fall. All part of the bonding."

Meanwhile, Whalen and the others proceeded to scold Hayden in raspy whispers.

"What are you doing, dipshit?" J.J. asked his batterymate.

Hayden clutched his hand to his chest, his face a mask of pain. "He *bit* me!"

Windy nodded knowingly. "Javi gets hungry. Even when he's not."

"Yeah – betcha that million-dollar arm tastes delicious," J.J. said, glaring at Hayden. "Even if it can't hit the fucking strike zone to save its life."

Windy cracked up at this, his laugh a wheeze that threatened to loosen his grip on his passed-out teammate.

Hayden turned on both, his hands clenched into fists. "Hey, fuck you guys."

"J.J., Hayden, take it easy," Whalen said, scowling at the pair.

Charlie waved his arms as he boosted himself to his feet again, imploring them to keep it down. He took the phone back from Whalen and straightened with a wince. His back cracked audibly. *That can't be good.*

His mother was still demanding attention. "Charlie? Charlie!"

"Yeah, Mom, I'm here," he said, rolling his eyes and stepping away from the blanket-wrapping fracas.

"What is going on there? Who is biting who? Why is *biting* happening at all!?"

Charlie felt fortunate his mother was leaving none of these questions room enough to be answered – it allowed him to gather his thoughts to create the most effective white lie. "No, Mom, we're all good. Nobody's biting anyone."

Four feet away, Whalen leaned over and into Javier's sweaty face. "Javi? No biting, comprendes?" Javier mumbled something incoherent in any language. Whalen nodded, as though this was the response he was looking for.

"There! *Right there,* with the biting!" said Margaret.

"No, he said '*no* biting,' Mom."

"Charlie, I will not have the brand of this team debased any further with local headlines talking about our hooker-biting scandal! It's bad for business and it's *weird.*"

Charlie briefly registered the oddness of discussing prostitutes with his mom, then promptly brushed it aside. "Will you relax please? I swear to you, this is a perfectly normal night."

As he spoke, he turned to find Whalen and the others attempting different handles on Javier's bundled form.

"Okay, he's already on the ground so the stretcher-lift is out," Whalen said, orchestrating everyone with waves of his hand. "We're gonna pivot into a shoulder-pull, two a side."

"What is that old goat talking about?" said Margaret. "I'm switching to video." Charlie's stomach dropped – she was not playing games.

"Mom, do *not* switch to video!"

But it was too late; her voice now came over distant, and it was clear she was looking at the phone display. "Where is the goddamned– oh, here it is. I'm pushing the button!"

"Mom, no! Do not push that button!"

"There!" she said with triumphant finality. "I've pushed it! It's pushed."

"Goddammit..." Charlie couldn't believe her persistence.

"Accept it!" Margaret shouted as the beeping vibes theme of her video request joined in the sonic melee. "Accept my video feed!"

"I will *not* accept it, I have everything perfectly under control," he said. "I am 39 years old, and I don't need my mother to feed me!"

Charlie's words registered with him immediately, and he turned to find the faces of his players staring at him in disgust. He waved them off and returned to his pacing. He was fuming by now – fuming about how Margaret constantly belittled him, constantly kept him in her pocket and treated him like a duckling who could neither fly nor swim. Sure, they were dealing with a minor health issue on their roster – this was normal baseball business. Why would she not trust him to get the job done?

"Oh, you'd better have things under control, Mr. Big Boy," she said. "Because according to the conference call I just had with our major league overlords – a call where they *did* accept my video feed, I might add – there's a hurricane of shit coming your way."

Charlie did not like the sharpness of her tone. "Wait, what? What are you talking about, Mom? We don't have room for more shit – we have a *surplus* of shit!" He needed her to grasp the dire straits in which their team was currently ensnared. "And you've got to understand that I think everything around this team is probably a chaotic situation. It could take *years* to rebuild."

"You have one day," said Margaret.

Charlie could only assume she was joking. "I'm sorry?"

"They're sending their moneymaker to us. The one everyone talks about."

Charlie couldn't tell where she was going with this. "Their moneymaker? What, like, a new kind of bratwurst, or–"

"The *player,* you goof. The famous one. Does charity work, dates all the actresses – the only one anyone gives a hoot about?"

"The *Franchise?*" Charlie could not believe the words he was hearing. Why would this ever be the case, the most famous of all the Big Club's players, playing for him? Madness. "Are you serious? Mom, you can't be serious."

"Does this seem like one of my jokes?"

"Well, I guess it's not particularly scathing or hurtful–"

"Exactly."

"I'm sorry, *why* is he coming down here?"

"Oh, he's pulled his Achilles' hamstring, or some such nonsense," she replied, as though this was as simple as cracking a knuckle. "They want him to get playing time with us during the All-Star break."

The entire situation was stunning. "So, wait," he began, clutching his forehead with his free hand, "the Franchise is coming to play with the Coelacanths, instead of the Major League All-Star Game? Mom, you didn't 'arrange' for him to get hurt or anything, did you?"

"No, for the love of god," she shouted. "He's a national heirloom! What kind of gangster do you take me for?"

"The kind of gangster who raised me to believe all my hopes and dreams would come true as long as I subscribed to your ambiguous moral code, that's who!" Charlie marveled at how quickly these phone discussions seemed to spiral out of control.

"Well, it certainly kept *you* quiet for 39 years, didn't it?"

Charlie shook his head. "Yeah, I'll send you a bouquet on Gangster's Day, Mom."

"By the way," she said, her voice pivoting back into the realm of professional, "is it raining there?"

"What?" *This is new,* he mused. *Maternal weather prognostication.* "No, why?"

The words had hardly escaped his lips, when the sound of thunder was heard rumbling in the distance, pushing its way through the Zero Motel's paper-thin walls. Everyone in the room froze, listening as the subsonics came and went.

"Whoa," said Charlie, turning back to his call. "Did *you* do that?"

"I'll never tell," said Margaret. "I just spoke with NOAA."

"'Noah?' Who's Noah? You're not already dating again, are you?"

His mother's sigh was deafening. "Sometimes it's *insane* to think I gave birth to you. NOAA. The National Oceanographic Atmospheric Administration."

"Oh, of course." *I have no idea what she's talking about.*

"They're tracking a hurricane that's bearing down on the east coast as we speak, and it's due to make landfall sometime during the game. Happy Fourth of July."

"Wait, I'm sorry – there's a hurricane coming and we're playing baseball in it?" It was a proposition only his mother would endorse. "Jesus, Mom, you're really upping the stakes here."

"'Hurricane Hannah' it's called – and no, I didn't have a hurricane whipped up just to keep things interesting for you."

Meanwhile, Javier had finally been successfully dragged into the bathroom. His teammates emerged from the nightmare of coral and turquoise tiles, breathing heavily from their labors. Windy clutched the bathroom door jamb for support.

Charlie could hear Margaret's frenetic typing on a keyboard. "This Hannah storm is a real troublemaker," she said, apparently lost in a cloud of weather reports. "Which I can respect." And then she was back, in full, threatening voice. "But if The Franchise comes up here from the city and gets dicked around by *your* awful team and the Big Club hears about it, this whole thing collapses like it was built by the Soviets, do you understand me? Now go to bed!"

She hung up, leaving him in the middle of a divey motel room, thoroughly shocked. Whalen emerged from the bathroom, wiping his hands on a towel. "What's wrong now, Charlie? You grounded?"

Charlie turned to him and glanced at his fellow Coelacanths. He felt like he'd just seen the ghost of his career's future, lingering in the doorway of his mind. It was chilling.

"The Franchise. The Franchise is coming here."

Thunder and lightning rattled the outside world, swallowing the reverberation of Charlie's words as they hit the pavement of reality. From the bathroom came the sound of his star first baseman, heaving vomit while his teammates stood in the doorway, observant and helpless. Just like the national audience that would soon be tuning in to watch all of them go about the underwhelming business of playing Coelacanth baseball.

CHAPTER 12
Designated For Assignment

ONE OF THE greater follies to be born out of the boondoggle of the HerbCo Field stadium rehab was known as the Courtyard of Champions. The red brick atrium found just beyond the turnstiles was ostensibly built as a place for Cape Haddock fans to be welcomed to their day at the ballpark with a splash of legacy. At least, that was how it was described when presented to the local government, accompanied by some terribly romantic watercolors of the soon-to-be-bustling stadium district.

The future painted was one of Coelacanth banners hanging from every wall and lamppost, well-manicured foliage strategically placed to break up the monotony of parking lots, and smiling, diverse crowds of people meandering the streets, visiting charming shops and bistros that were promised but never followed up on. It had been an irresistible pitch, and the town had swung big to make it happen.

Of course, the real reason for the courtyard's construction was to build out a corner of the park to support a larger HerbCo sign that would be angled out so its neon glow would be seen from multiple directions. Herbert Tinley had been *very* into neon. The sign had lived up to the hype and could easily be seen from the moon, a glorious example of taxpayer-funded corporate advertising. It appeared that the pros had outweighed any objections; Herbert had gotten his name on a thing and the fans got a bit of open-air class added to their ballpark. The only things missing were the champions, of which there were none.

As Charlie and Whalen slid through the service gates at the end of the turnstile row, Charlie could not help but feel that the empty atrium was serving more as a reminder of their lack of quality history, then a celebration. The Coelacanths did have past players who'd accumulated respectable numbers, but they were mostly from over a century ago, when the players were rough men, somehow considered too volatile for either professional fishing or working on the docks. Sure, a high batting average was worth noting, but it was inevitability balanced into oblivion when weighed against an inordinate number of stabbings. If anything, the highlight of this space was the masonry itself; no one could deny that the brickwork had been executed in fine fashion. *It's really more of a Courtyard of Bricks,* thought Charlie as they crossed the space to a utility door.

The low rumble of the team bus could be heard passing as it rounded the block behind them. It had been Whalen's idea to make a low-key entrance upon returning to Cape Haddock. He had achieved a point of stress that required a lit cigarette remain ever-present in his mouth like a scuba mask underwater. Their sleepless night added to the delirium, and Charlie had to take a moment to establish the reality of the pointed throat-clearing that came from the shadows of the nearby concourse.

Charlie and Whalen turned from the half-open door to find Margaret emerging from the darkness, her expression as grim as the low cloud cover overhead.

"I can't imagine you two are avoiding me…"

Charlie's palms began to sweat. "Hey, Mom, we were just going to look for you in the, uh…" he gestured to the door behind them, "…in the stairwell."

"Smooth," said Whalen. "Good to see you, Maggie. How's life on the Love Boat?"

"Please, don't remind me. I'm seven seconds from scuttling the damned thing," said Margaret. "Meanwhile, I can't help but notice that the entirety of our offense is not in the ballpark today."

"Your eagle eyes have not failed you, Maggie," said Whalen. "I just sent Javi home to digest."

"I can't let either of you out of my sight for a minute, can I," said Margaret. "Do I even want to know?"

Charlie grimaced. "Not really, Mom. It's kind of gross."

"I was married to Herbert Tinley for over two decades," said Margaret, tilting her head. "Try me."

Whalen exhaled a plume of smoke with a grin. "You see, when the diaphragm is unable to quell a geyser of stomach acid–"

"That's enough." Margaret held up a hand.

"But you didn't let me get to the part about the esophageal sphincter–"

"Enough. What is the bottom line?"

Charlie could sense they had worn her patience down to its last micron. "We propped up the head of his bed with a stack of phone books, like the internet said to, and stuffed him full of antacid tablets the rest of the night."

"Ah yes, the sage Dr. Internet," said Margaret. "Will he be ready to play tomorrow?"

"Once he's had some time to, uh, *process* a bit, he'll be right as rain," said Whalen.

"Fine. He's just about the only thing lending us any credibility at this point, I can't have him super-sized into extinction before The Franchise shows up."

"Not to worry, Maggie, it'll take more than a bag of sliders to bring that guy down. He's tough," said Whalen turning back to the door. Their escape was so close, and yet, so far.

"Oh, and one more thing, Gray," Margaret said, her eyes scanning her ever-present clipboard anew.

"At your service, madam," he said, offering a taste of careless sarcasm Charlie had never seen used with his mother without blood being shed.

"With the recent staffing shortages, it has become imperative that our remaining employees take a little more responsibility onto their plates."

"Ah, of course," said Whalen, grinning. "The old downsizing two-step. I don't suppose they'll be making any more money?"

"You watch your mouth, Gray Whalen, or I'll have you retired and back with Iris so fast you won't know which yard to mow."

"Whoa," Whalen raised his hands in surrender. "Let's not get crazy here, Maggie – and I'm not saying that to be condescending–"

Margaret scoffed. "I'm saying it because you and I both know I'm not ready for that to happen yet. Not until my youngest is out of the house. I mean, she's 27, it has to happen at some point, right?"

"I'm sure I have no idea," said Margaret, tossing a withering look at her son. "Needless to say, life flounders on and we're left to do the best we can with what's available. Which does bring me back to the matter at hand." She held up the clipboard, revealing a short list of names Charlie did not recognize. "I need to delegate some of the outstanding tasks to what's left of our staff. Now, who is Arnold Hot Dog and where can I find him?"

Whalen peered at the list. Finally, he nodded. "Ah, you mean old Terry Arnold. The hot dog guy," he added, seeing that more clarity might be needed.

"Fine," Margaret said, rolling her eyes. She pulled a manila envelope from her clipboard and handed it to him.

Whalen accepted it but was clearly puzzled. "And this is…?"

"The thing you're delivering to Arnold Hot Dog."

"I see," he said, nodding. "Because we all need a little more on our plates."

"Precisely," she said. "That is cash for the purchase of Fourth of July decorations and one unit of firework. The television people will be here, and they'll want to see something patriotic and colorful that is not a goddamned light-up fishing pole, so we'll give them just that. And Mr. Hot Dog is now also in charge of Stadium Operations Coordination."

"That's kind of a leap from handing out food, isn't it, Mom?" said Charlie.

"He can thank me later, when he's able to put that title on his sausage resume," she replied.

"Is that not a key position to be cut from the payroll, Maggie?" asked Whalen. "Ops is kind of a big–"

"He was making almost as much as you were, Gray, he had to go," she said, stabbing the air with her pen. "Besides, this joint is as good as brand new with the refurb. It practically runs itself."

Behind her, Windy walked at a leisurely pace while holding out his phone and recording a Blither video of himself. In a smooth motion, she turned, yanked the phone from his hand and held it up over her head.

"There, see? Just look at that beautiful WiFi signal. It's as good as plugging your phone directly into a wall – who needs coordination?"

She brought the phone down and quickly posted the interrupted video to Windy's timeline, provoking a tinny goat bleat from the app. She tossed it back to the nonplussed second baseman. Windy shrugged and kept walking.

"Can't say I noticed the WiFi," said Whalen. "You know I–"

"You don't '*do*' email," said Margaret. "Oh, I got your snail-mail letter about that, Gray. That was very clever of you, wasn't it?" Whalen grinned. "Thank you for reminding me of the analog pleasure found in crumpling up handwritten nonsense and throwing it into an actual garbage can."

Whalen's laugh echoed across the field. "You're a real pistol, Maggie."

"I also gave you something to do," she said, unamused. "You run along now, Gray. We need to at least give the *impression* of festive things happening on this so-called festive day."

"Of course, Your Majesty, we'll go right now." Whalen beckoned Charlie to follow him across the courtyard to the concourse.

From behind them boomed the final command: "And don't think I don't know *exactly* how much money is in there, you two – I want receipts!"

"IT'S $60," SAID Terry Arnold, holding out the contents of the envelope to Charlie and Whalen. "What the hell is she expecting I get for $60 that's gonna do this whole park?"

Whalen shrugged. "Dunno, Terrence. Swing by the party store, I guess. And there's a guy by the pier who's selling those supernova cakes, you could check that out."

"Uh-huh." Terry seemed less than impressed with the entire situation. He stood behind his food prep station with a white apron and a frown pulling at his weathered face.

"Hey, I'm just the messenger," said Whalen.

"And, apparently, I'm the Ops Coordinator?" Terry said, staring blankly at the letter that had been folded around the bills. He looked up at Charlie. "Is your ma serious about this?"

"'Fraid so," he said, feeling for him. Terry Arnold was old – as old as, if not older than Whalen. He was probably close to calling it a part-time career, and now he was being tasked with this mammoth undertaking. To be completed with the help of three twenty-dollar bills. "Listen, she usually does a mid-week spa day, so if you can catch her in the twenty minutes right after *that,* you might be able to pry another sawbuck out of her."

"Yeah, I'm gonna pass on that," said Terry, turning back to Whalen. "You want the usual?"

"Yeah. And one for the new meat here," he said, gesturing to Charlie.

"You know your dad was one helluva a guy," said Terry. He began preparing four hot dogs, piling ample amounts of condiments on each. "He used to send the bat boy up for a dog during every fourth inning. Always had me and the kid split the change and keep it."

"Well," Whalen said, eyeing the chopped onions that were spilling over the buns, "a hot dog and the signs too, Terrence."

Terry laughed. "Yeah, that's true, he did do that, didn't he?"

"The signs?" said Charlie.

"Ol' Terry has a gift for cracking the other team's pitch signs," said Whalen, accepting two monstrous hot dogs from the vendor. "He's like a hot dog savant, ain't that right?"

"Well, having a stand with low traffic and a good sightline doesn't hurt."

Whalen and Terry chuckled while Charlie nodded. "This is nice, I'm glad to hear that cheating was fully institutionalized and that my father was a baseball criminal."

"Oh hell, he wasn't cheating," said Whalen. Chopped onions went flying as he waved him off. "That was gamesmanship! Yet one more quirk of the system that can't be tallied on your spreadsheets, I might add."

"You *are* making a case for an honesty index, you know," said Charlie, wondering if such a thing could be put together. The very notion was thrilling to him.

"You take it from me, young man, your dad didn't need those signs. He was the hardest working ballplayer I ever saw come through here. First one on the field for warmups and B.P. every day. Ain't that right, Gray?"

"Damned right," said the skipper, his mouth now full.

"But everybody knows you've gotta find an edge in this game," said Terry. "Especially on *this* team."

"Again," said Whalen, swallowing, "he is correct."

"But that business is all between the lines," Terry said, handing Charlie two hot dogs with the works. "Outside the game, Jackie was a champion good guy. Always treated people with respect – even the lowly hot dog man."

"Hear, hear," said Whalen, finishing his second.

Charlie was overcome, both by this spontaneous tribute to a man he could barely remember, and by the food in his hands. "Here," he said, passing a dog off to Whalen. "It's good to know that about him. That he was a decent human."

"Well, and look at you," said Terry, pointing at him with one plastic-gloved hand. "You were just a booger-faced, quiet kid when your dad was playing. And now here you are, a full-grown man who knows how to blow his nose!"

It was somehow odd to be acknowledged as an adult after so many years of playing a game for a living, but Charlie was again moved. He felt a peculiar sensation. Something unfamiliar. Was it… *pride?* He was, for the most part, an adult. And one with a job in which the booing was not for him directly.

"You're right," he said, taking a bite of his remaining sausage. "I can blow my own nose."

"There you go, young man," said Terry, grinning. "What's your ma got you doing aside from picking up after this slob?" He pointed to Whalen.

"I do the SABRmetrics and try to identify our undervalued resources."

"Is that right?" Terry gave a good performance of finding this interesting.

"Calculator ball," said Whalen, digging into his third serving. "He's our new edge."

Terry roared with laughter. *"He's* the edge?"

Charlie did not feel like this reaction was taking him seriously as an adult. "What's so funny?"

"Nothing, kid – if your ma says you're the edge, then you're the edge. I don't mess with that lady," Terry said, wiping a tear from his eye.

"Speaking of," said Whalen, indicating a watch he was not wearing, "we should mosey. You know she's timing us. Later, Terrence."

They walked and Charlie watched as Whalen chewed with a look of contentment he'd never seen before. "He seems like a good guy to know."

"I've worked very hard over the years to stay in Terry's good graces and maintain a steady stream of black market hot dogs. They're one of the few things in our world that *hasn't* changed," he said, taking another bite. "Hell, sometimes I hardly recognize this game anymore, with all of your pitch counts and shift malarky... How long before *these* are phased out, I wonder?" He held up the last bite of sausage and bun and considered it for a moment before finishing it off.

"You know, Skip, I'm kind of surprised we haven't run into each other before now," said Charlie.

"Oh?"

"The Coelacanths were always Herbert's favorite team. But I don't remember seeing you at the holiday parties."

"Yeah, well, I haven't really been one for parties the past 30 years. It comes with the territory when you're becoming an old crank."

"You weren't as old as Herbert."

"Aw, you flatter me, madam!" Whalen said. "I guess some of us know how to act our age." As soon as he'd spoken the words, Whalen frowned and shook his head. "Ah shit. I'm sorry kid."

Charlie was taken off-guard. "What for?"

"I run my mouth sometimes – it's kind of what I do, you know? I didn't mean to talk bad about him in front of you like that. The old man's not even cold yet."

Charlie was touched that the skipper would bother to consider this. "Honestly, I didn't really notice it."

The manager absentmindedly scratched a sideburn. "Listen, Herb and me..." He stared into the distance as though memories were hanging there for his evaluation. "Well, before I say anything, let me ask you: How did *you* see Herb? Or, what do you call him anyway? Is he, like, your dad, your stepdad? Creepy uncle?"

Charlie pondered this a moment. How *had* he seen Herbert? "My dad's my dad. Jackie, I mean." Whalen gave a nod. "Herbert was more of a distant grandpa, I guess? Maybe not so much a grandpa as he was your grandpa's neighbor, if that makes sense?"

"Not yet but go on."

"It always felt like your grandparents lived in the same neighborhood, the same house forever. I mean, you're just a kid when you know your grandparents, so a year feels like ten." Whalen grunted as though this read true. "But, they're in the same place they've been for 30, 40… 50 years. And everyone around them is in the same boat, so they're always around at parties and barbeques and all that. So, you know them, and they're familiar fixtures, like neighbors on a sitcom. But they're not family."

"You wouldn't hang around the hospital to hear how the surgery went–"

"You'd wait for the phone call. Yeah. That was Herbert."

"Did you hang around the hospital?" Whalen asked.

Charlie tilted his head as he searched for the details of that day. "We had a day game – spring training reps in Groom Lake. I went 1 for 4 and it was one of the best games I had this year."

They reached the edge of the concourse and leaned on the railing that separated the walkway from the seats. Charlie followed Whalen's gaze out to center field where the four playoff flags rippled in a lazy breeze beneath the massive HerbCo fishing rod.

"Memories?" he asked the skipper. Charlie had done the math and knew Whalen had been on the roster for at least some of those postseason teams.

Whalen grunted, his gaze fixed on the flags. "They should take those down."

"Seriously?" Charlie couldn't believe what he was hearing. "You're kidding me."

"Uh-uh," said Whalen, shaking his head. "They're pathetic. Never won a series, rarely won a game… They're just reminders of how we've never done anything worth a damn." He turned to Charlie. "And that's not a knock on your dad, either – he did everything he could to get us there, and we never sealed the deal for him. He deserved better. Better than us. And you should know that."

Charlie looked to the sky where a seagull was hanging in the air, held in place by a steady headwind above the light towers. "It feels like everyone has all these memories of him except for me."

Whalen nodded and ran a hand over his mustache. "Yeah, I'm sure you've been hearing it since you've been back. People really loved him around these parts."

"Sometimes I worry that if I can't help us get turned around, maybe they'll stop loving him."

"Listen to me, Charlie," said the manager, his tone as serious as Charlie had ever heard. "If anyone has a chance of turning this thing around, it's you, because you care the most. And you've got to trust that people will see that."

"You think so?"

"They saw it with your dad, even though he never won them a series. Just like they started to see the opposite with Herb when the community didn't come back after they funded the refurb and that goddamned fishing pole. And no offense to your house, but a yacht the size of Rhode Island stands out in a place where folks are having trouble keeping the lights on."

"I thought people loved Herbert here," said Charlie. "He was always such a man-about-town and all that."

Whalen rolled his eyes and stared out at the HerbCo advertisement. "You take it from a guy who knew *both* of your dads pretty well; Herbert was the kind of guy who liked to surround himself with guys like him. Other Herbs – lesser Herbs, if you will. Lockerbie's one of 'em – loved going on that big boat and pretending to be a big wheel. Don't ever tell him anything about anything, by the way – he's not to be trusted."

"Yeah, I had a feeling."

"Anyway, Herb liked to throw a party, right? But nobody who's invited to the party wants to upset the party. Which is why your mom inherited nothing but this… *shell* that is not looked on too favorably by the town these days. He was a taker, you see? But Jackie was a giver. He left it all out on the field and everyone saw him do it. That's why they love him." Whalen turned back to him, and to Charlie's great surprise, put a hand on his shoulder. The manager looked him in the eye, his gaze carrying the weight of hard-earned wisdom. "Don't be a Herb, son."

CHAPTER 13
The Franchise

PREPARATIONS FOR THE Franchise's arrival reached their apex on the morning of July fourth. A harbor bell clanged good morning as Charlie made his way down the gangplank of the *HTIII*. He noted the extra stars and stripes flying from the poles and masts of the nearby pleasure cruisers and could not help feeling a dash of national pride on his country's birthday. This stirring of patriotic fervor was promptly quashed by the wall of storm clouds that had bloomed frighteningly close to shore from the distant horizon.

He shivered as a hard gale of Atlantic wind rattled his bones through the yellow of his rain slicker. He'd dug the jacket out from one of the yacht's storage compartments, and while it looked like a prop that belonged on a box of fish sticks, he hoped it would serve him well in the forthcoming squall.

Minutes later, he was crossing the stadium's parking lot to the staff entrance, where he noted his mother, who had left for the ballpark before dawn. She was now fussing over a group of headphone-clad people who were diligently unpacking a semi-trailer filled with cables, hard-shell road cases, more cables, tripods, and still other cables. The Network had arrived.

So, they did *show up,* he thought as he slipped through the door and made his way to the clubhouse. The arrival of cable television's most successful sports-themed channel now began injecting a bit more tension into his body. He'd not let himself believe they'd actually journey to little Cape Haddock, and now that they had, the tentacles of pressure to not act a fool before a national audience were attaching themselves onto his chest.

The next three hours were spent trying to ignore this lump of anxiety by tidying the locker room. His mother had made it clear several times over the previous 36 hours that things had to be *perfect* for The Franchise's arrival. The notion of an all-time great hopping onto their roster was rather exciting. Charlie had played with a handful of guys who had managed to climb all the way up the ladder to the Big Club, but this was not the same as walking in with so much history already made.

Aside from the initial conversation laying out the rehabilitation visit, there had been almost no further information from their major league affiliate. The first baseman's schedule was always busy, so there would be no locked-in schedule, no way to know when he would be arriving, or how. These unknowns were also loaded with nervousness, and Charlie made the best of it by making sure The Franchise's uniform was neatly displayed in his guest locker. He straightened chairs and benches, and vacuumed the carpets with an obsessive level of detail.

These tasks completed, he then headed out to sweep the loading dock, just in case The Franchise decided to use it for making a low-key entrance. He wondered what that would entail. Was he a limousine guy? Town car? *Helicopter?* As he paused mid-sweep to eye the loading area and make mental measurements of the dimensions to determine whether or not it would be able to support the footprint of a chopper, he realized it was time to get out of his own head and return to the duties of coaching a sub-par baseball team.

He re-entered the clubhouse to find that most of the players had arrived. Taking the temperature of their muttered greetings, he was puzzled by the decided lack of enthusiasm for such an auspicious day. He glanced over to Windy and J.J. as he unsnapped his slicker and caught the odd feeling of a conversation interrupted. "What're you guys up to?"

"You're looking at it, Coach," said Windy, gesturing to them sitting around in their underpants and high socks. "Let me ask you this: How many people you think are in The Franchise's entourage?"

"I like that you're just assuming an entourage."

Windy shook his head. "Come on now, this dude is going to the *Hall of Fame.* He's making $25 million a year and has a penthouse in the city overlooking the park. The *park,* Coach! Trees in the city!"

"Sure," Charlie said. This logic was indeed unimpeachable. "But he's still just a guy, right?"

The pity telegraphed by Windy's slow headshake was palpable. "A 'guy' with an ex-girlfriend roster featuring some of the finest women this planet has ever seen. Models, gymnasts, actresses–"

"Friends of those actresses," J.J. threw in.

"Heads of state–"

"I feel like you might be exaggerating a bit," Charlie said, though, admittedly he'd never considered the notion. Was an aptitude for knocking down hot grounders a road to diplomatic immunity?

"You keep telling yourself whatever you need to sleep at night, Coach," said Windy. "Just don't be surprised when he shows up with lawyers and sponsors and starts big-stuffing it in the clubhouse. We've seen guys do that before."

"Don't listen to him, Starch Man," J.J. said, shooting him a malicious grin and pushing Windy's shoulder from behind. "He's just burnt because of the Alewife Roadhouse incident last year."

Windy turned and pushed the bigger man back. "Shut up, J.J. – you don't know me!"

J.J. chuckled and threw his arm around Windy's neck, headlocking him into submission. "Actually, after seeing the shit you put on Blither, I feel like I know too much." Windy slapped at him, but quickly gave up with an awkward shrug. J.J. released him and turned to Charlie. "We had a guy come down from the Big Club last year, and he took us out to the Roadhouse for steaks. Mind you, he never once told us he was picking up the bill, but genius here orders one of everything on the menu."

"He was very unclear about his intentions, Coach," said Windy.

J.J. turned to him, exasperated. "He was a utility guy playing nine outs worth of backup positional play every two weeks! Phil the Peanut Guy makes more than that dude!" Windy shrugged again as J.J. continued. "Anyway, this doofus wraps up his meal two hours later, only to find that the backup to the backup in left field has cabbed it back to the motel without footing the outstanding sampler tab."

"It was disrespect, Coach, nothing but! He knew I wasn't gonna eat steak fries *and* waffle fries – read between the fries, man! I'm *still* paying that meal down."

"Okay, so lesson learned: don't order double-digit entrees when Number 9 gets here, right?" said Charlie.

"I'm only a sucker so many times, Coach. Couldn't live with myself any other way." Windy held up his phone. "Unless my Blither followers think I should."

"Well, that's... great to hear," Charlie said, slapping him on the back before crossing to the other side of the locker room. He'd been finding the young second baseman's energy to be promising, but also exhausting.

As he surveyed his players going through the motions of pre-game preparation, he noticed Hayden, sitting, removed from everyone else. This in itself was not unusual, in that he seemed to stew on days he was expected to pitch, but also on days he was not, implying a shallow spectrum of emotional variance. However, the cloud that seemed to hang over him today appeared to be raining more anxiety than normal. Charlie eyed the hurler's restless leg as it bounced a cleat against the clubhouse floor in a relentless *clack-clack-clack-clack-clack.* He saw the thousand-yard gaze boring through the cinderblocks, focused on some distant, but fresh hell in the offing. Charlie found it torturous to observe and guessed the firsthand experience must be far worse.

"Hayden, you seem... well, more alienated than usual, if that's possible?"

Hayden's head snapped up in response, but he did not make eye-contact. "I'm fine."

"Yeah?" The pitcher's tone implied anything but. His hands worried a clear, plastic sleeve holding a baseball card. Charlie thought he recognized a Topps border from several years prior but couldn't make out the player. "Whatcha got there?"

Hayden froze, as though caught beneath an overpass with a can of spray paint. "This, uh... it's my favorite baseball card."

Charlie leaned down and craned his neck to get a better look. In an instant, the reason for his player's nerves became clear. "The Franchise?"

Staring down at the card, entranced, Hayden nodded. "Yeah. It's his rookie card. When I was 10, he was signing stuff at the mall by where I grew up. He was my favorite player."

The confession was a glimpse of raw humanity that Charlie had never seen from Hayden. He was typically such a cauldron of rage, it seemed impossible for something as vulnerable as hero worship to survive amidst the flames.

"Did you meet him?"

Hayden nodded. "Yeah, he said I should keep practicing and I could be like him one day." He stopped, considering his next words carefully. "At the time, I wasn't having any fun playing, so really... I probably wouldn't be here if it wasn't for that."

Charlie suddenly felt as though a new dimension had been slotted into place with this young, spoiled, talented man. Even the young and talented had their share of angst. And who was he, a former player who was neither young nor talented, to judge the relativity of it compared to people with real problems to worry about?

"Well," said Charlie, as if this was a complete, meaningful sentence. He quickly aspired to dig deeper. "And, uh, look at you now, right? You're gonna be his teammate. That's... that's pretty amazing."

"It makes me anxious."

Charlie could hardly contain his excitement over getting a response that did not include the words 'Fuck off.' It was probably as close as he was going to get to an invitation to bestow some quality advice. "Nerves, huh? I guess that would be tough, having to play with your personal hero watching your every move while you're busy trying to not... well, to not screw it all up..."

Hayden went pale as Charlie questioned whether he had nailed this impromptu counseling session. It had started strong, and then spiraled beyond his control.

"I'm getting dizzy," Hayden said, bending over. His elbows propped up his torso on his knees as his breathing became ragged.

Noticing the other clubhouse eyes darting their way, Charlie grabbed the back of Hayden's jersey and hoisted him onto his feet. He grabbed the pitcher's glove and hat, and stuffed them into Hayden's arms before ushering him toward the clubhouse door.

"Why don't you, uh, go warm up in the 'pen, huh? Atta boy." The last thing the team needed was to see the man who would be leading them into battle having a nervous breakdown.

Hayden stumbled out to the tunnel, nearly colliding with the jamb as he left. Whalen stepped out of his office and watched as his pitcher exited into the dimly lit hallway. He looked to Charlie. "Pre-game yips?"

"He's kind of freaking out about the whole Franchise-thing. He's a fan."

Whalen nodded and scratched a sideburn. "Sure, that'll happen. I broke out in hives when I got to play against Yastrzemski one weekend."

Charlie examined the skipper's face. He looked distracted. Ragged. "What were you doing in there? You look terrible."

Whalen shrugged with the carelessness of a man who was used to being pulled beyond the borders of his comfort zone. "Eh, I was just on a call with your Ma and the Big Club." Charlie nodded – this would explain the raggedness. "You know, she says we're 'sharing' the office, but she painted it and moved all my stuff into boxes while we were gone, so I guess I should take a hint, right?"

"What'd they say about the weather?"

The old man shrugged. "Apparently the league says the game goes on tonight short of the Titanic landing on the mound. The Network being here and all." He surveyed his players. "What's up with these goofballs?"

Charlie scanned the room; their players were strewn about the benches, some muttering to each other. Several others were completely absorbed in their phones, presumably taking in the stir of reporting that had hit the internet since word of The Franchise's imminent arrival had emerged. "They think The Franchise is gonna do a big-stuff routine when he gets here."

"That right?" Whalen looked at the clubhouse denizens in disgust and raised his voice. "All right, you guys, phones away or they're not gonna be here when you get back. You know I'm sick enough to let that happen, so shut it down." The Coelacanths grumbled various curses, but the sound of plastic cases clicking onto wooden shelves signaled their begrudging attention. Whalen nodded and began roaming the floor. "Let's just get this out of the way right now: This guy everyone is talking about… Number 9… The Franchise… is human."

The muttering began anew. Charlie could hear Windy's voice carry over the din: "He's got a fireman's pole in his apartment, Skip!"

Whalen scowled at him. "Of course he does – hell, wouldn't you? But yes, it's true. He's a guy, just like you're guys, and he's been down here before, just like you're all down here now." This easily forgotten shard of common sense seemed to calm the players. Whalen's gaze traveled from face to face. "So, when he does show up, I'm trusting you guys – begging, actually – to *just… act…*"

As the words dragged themselves out from beneath Whalen's trademark mustache with staccato precision, one of the most famous faces in the history of the game popped through the clubhouse doorway. The Franchise was a handsome man of middle age, dressed in a swank suit and flashing a blinding smile familiar to baseball fans the world over.

"Hey, is this where the baseball is?"

The tone of the room changed immediately. The players leaped from their seats and moved toward him with a cheer. Charlie watched as they were compelled to him; The Franchise was a baseball sun, and his gravity sucked all lesser masses into his orbit. They swarmed him, leaving Charlie and Whalen to stand by, flabbergasted.

"…normal," Whalen finished, throwing his arms up in surrender.

The Franchise emerged from the ecstatic scrum, laughing. He threw his hands up in surrender as the players pressed up against him with a relentless assault of back-patting.

"Whoa, whoa, whoa – easy, guys, I'm still technically in rehab!"

Whalen pushed through the throng like a nicotine-stained icebreaker prow, shooing the other players away. "Spread out, you sorry pack of hyenas! You're embarrassments to what is already an embarrassing uniform."

The Franchise squinted at the skipper in disbelief. "Coach Whalen? Man, I would've sworn you were dead!" He laughed and threw his arms around Whalen, drawing him in for a bear hug.

Whalen was caught off guard by the gesture and grinned. "Yeah, I get that a lot."

The Franchise appraised him as though the manager had just returned home from an arctic expedition. "And we're still doing the moustache, huh?"

"Yeah, yeah..."

Charlie stepped forward, his hand extended. "Good to see you, Number 9," he said, attempting to add some of Whalen's world-weary grizzle to the statement. "Charlie Conroy, bench coach."

The Franchise's eyes went wide as he shook Charlie's hand. "Wait a minute – *the* Charlie Conroy?"

Whalen arched an eyebrow. "You know Charlie?"

"Hell yeah, I do! I mean, I know about your dad too, obviously – that guy was supposed to be amazing. But the King of the Twin Killings – how could I forget? You're the only man in organized baseball to have grounded into a double play twice in every game of a season, right?"

The entire clubhouse collapsed into laughter. Charlie sighed as the body of another of his unfortunate records was unearthed for the world to see.

The Franchise was undeterred. He beamed at Charlie and slapped a hand on his shoulder. "Man, you're kind of a legend."

Charlie was completely taken aback by this news. "I am?"

The Franchise laughed as though this response was a joke. "Yeah! When I was in Double-A – right before I played for you, Skipper – me and the boys followed you for the whole back-half of that season. And you did it!"

Charlie nodded slowly, his tone morose. "I did."

"Anyway, it's an honor to meet you, Coach." The Franchise slapped him on the shoulder and flashed his million-watt smile before turning to the rest of the team. "It's great to meet all you guys! And listen, I know this is a huge distraction from your season, but I'll play as hard as I can for you, okay?"

Windy swaggered forth from the crowd of cheering players and threw his arm around The Franchise. "Well, Mr. Number 9, we *are* a finely-tuned machine. But in your case, I think we can make an exception."

Windy drew The Franchise's attention away, pointing to the left with one hand while raising his phone with the other. The selfie was taken in a motion so effortless that Charlie wished the second baseman could use those wits for fielding grounders. The Franchise turned to him, baffled, as Windy slunk his way back into the crowd.

"Yeah, he doesn't speak for us," said Charlie, shaking his head.

The Franchise shrugged, seemingly amused by the invasion. "It's okay. I've gotten used to it."

The din surrounding the famous arrival was pierced by a familiar voice echoing from the tunnel on the other side of the clubhouse door.

"Whalen? Hey, Whalen!"

Everyone fell silent. They were birds making no noise as an unappealing predator fumbled his way through the tall grasses of the ballpark and into their comfort zone.

"Ah, hell..." Whalen muttered.

Charlie turned to him with a whisper. "Lockerbie?"

The manager nodded. The Franchise turned to the skipper, alarmed.

"Wait – *Dip* Lockerbie? *He's* still here?"

Charlie watched as Whalen surveyed the clubhouse. Homing in on an apparent solution, the skipper beckoned for The Franchise to follow him over to Javier, who loomed quietly in the corner. Whalen grabbed The Franchise by his shoulders and moved him behind the first baseman, vanishing him behind the big man's bulk. Whalen patted Javier on the chest. "Don't move."

The words were barely out of his mouth when Dip burst through the door. "Whalen!"

The manager closed his eyes, gathering himself. Running a hand over his mustache, he turned to the broadcaster.

"Dip, what can I do you for, huh? I'm trying to get these guys ready–"

Dip was having none of it and walked briskly over to him. "Gray, I've received information recently that says The Franchise was spotted walking down the tunnel toward the Coelacanth clubhouse, not five minutes ago! I have heavily-embedded contacts who vouch for this, so no two-stepping, okay?"

"You mean Nancy, over at the snow cone stand?"

Dip scoffed at him. "You know I can't reveal my sources."

"Ah," Whalen nodded, "Phil, the peanut guy."

"God*dammit!*" Dip shook his fist like a foiled supervillain.

Charlie glanced at the clubhouse clock. "Dip, don't you have a pre-show to get ready for? I feel like you're supposed to be on the air pretty soon–"

Dip waved him off without bothering to look at him. "Ah, whatsherface does all that, and then I come in and do it the *right* way. Besides, I need to get *the scoop."* He leaned toward Whalen, his voice lowered into something conspiratorial. "The Network is here, you know." He nodded at the impassive skipper as though the subtext of this statement was being transmitted loud and clear.

"I did hear that," said Whalen.

"Then you know it's only a matter of time before our paths cross. You don't come all the way up to Cape Haddock and *not* seek out Mr. Coelacanth for the straight dope and all my timeless anecdotes."

"Uh-huh," said Whalen.

Seeing he was not receiving the desired amount of awe from Whalen, Dip turned to Charlie. "Now, according to Gladys in accounting, they're here because of that hotshot, Number 9. But between you, me, and the jockstraps, I think they were coming down here anyway, *if* you know what I mean."

"I never know what you mean," said Charlie.

Dip gave him an amused look. "Come on..." He presented himself, leaning back with his arms out and chin pointed skyward. Charlie and Whalen stared at him as he held this pose, waiting to be acknowledged for... something.

Charlie finally cracked. "Again, Dip, I don't know what you mean."

Dip tsked at the coach's apparent lack of vision. "Come on, kid – surely even *you* can see the opportunity they're missing by not having me lend my seasoned insight to their game analyses?"

"Okay, we're done here," said Charlie, walking away from him.

Undeterred, Dip turned back to Whalen. "But I have to get ahold of ol' Number 9 to kind of sweeten the pot a little. You know how television is – they have sound *and* picture. Radio can't compete with that!"

Whalen leaned up against the lockers, his arms crossed in casual defiance. "Now, Dip, I thought you were all about painting pictures with words and whatnot."

"Ah, horseshit, Whalen!" Dip waved the skipper off as though he'd asked the broadcaster for a hot air balloon ride. "Nothing beats a 'sclusie with a guy headed to Cooperstown on his first ballot! Besides, the kid loves me!"

Charlie allowed his eyes to flick over to the motionless superstar crouching behind Javier. The Franchise's eyes went wide. The rest of the players shifted uncomfortably, and Dip seemed to notice. Somehow, the last sliver of journalistic instinct that was left within his narcissist shell seemed to compel him to slowly walk in Javier's direction. Javier adjusted his position in front of The Franchise accordingly.

"Hey there, big fella!" Dip stared up at the massive first baseman, his expression one of deep pondering. He turned to Whalen, who was now warily making his way over. Charlie wondered if he was sizing the reporter up for tackling if need be, but Dip seemed to sense no such threat. "See, Gray, *this* is what I'm talking about! I would love to get the two of 'em together, you know? 'The old guard meets the new!' or some garbage like that. Whaddya say, Javi? You game for being a part of the biggest sports story of the season?"

Javier stared at him, impassive. Dip's round face, partially deflated with age, peered up at him with a nagging persistence, until the answer finally came: "No English."

Dip was dumbfounded. His jaw fell slack in a way that made Charlie feel as though his good ol' boy networking advances were rarely, if ever, rebuffed. Javier continued to stare at the broadcaster, his expression as cryptic as that of an Easter Island statue.

Whalen took the stunned Lockerbie by the arm and began leading him to the clubhouse door. "Okay, Dip, these guys need to get ready to rumble here..."

As they reached the door, Francesca entered, notebook in hand. The Coelacanth players covered themselves at the sight of her, uttering emphatic exclamations of protest.

Francesca rolled her eyes but raised the notebook to block her view.

She frowned at Dip. "And where are *you* going? We've got a production meeting with Margaret."

Whalen abruptly turned himself and Dip around, his tone cloaked in a perfectly executed false politeness that Charlie guessed must have served him well when Herbert was alive. "Well, Dip, we can't have you missing your big meeting, huh?"

"Wait, what–"

Whalen smoothly ushered him back across the clubhouse. With the gentlest of shoves, he cast the broadcaster through the frosted glass door of his now-shared office. Francesca followed his trajectory, stifling a laugh and waving to Charlie before closing the door behind her.

The locker room held its collective breath, half-expecting Dip to emerge from the office for more space invasion. Finally, The Franchise stepped from behind Javier.

"Thanks guys. I could never stand him back in the day. He was always trying to give me pointers that were...clearly not pointers."

"Not a problem, Number 9," said Whalen, slapping him on the back, "we can't stand him either." He turned to the rest of the team. "All right, you dingbats, let's get this pain parade on the road, huh? Number 9, you're playing first and batting third. Javi, you're the DH and I'm sliding you down to clean-up, okay? You all ready to do this silly thing? Then let's move it out!"

Whalen clapped his hands together and made for the door. He was stopped by the sound of Charlie clearing his throat.

"Actually, uh, Skip..."

Whalen's head sagged and he turned to his coach. "All right, Charlie, whatcha got?"

"Look, Skip, it's, uh... well, since you're moving some spots around, I figured–"

"Coach, remember we're literally fighting the elements out there."

"Javi should bat second."

The players looked at one another as this sank in. Charlie could hear the gears grinding beneath their ballcaps and knew he had to sell this while he had them hooked.

"I mean, not just today," he continued, "though he totally should. But it should be every day. He's always in the three-spot, right?"

"Sí," said Javier with a terse nod of approval. "I'm always third."

"Well, instead of sliding him down to four, just... why not bump him *up* to two? The numbers say he should be batting second." Charlie raised his hands in feigned innocence.

Whalen seemed to despair. "Charlie, not today, huh? There are people actually *here* today!" He gestured to the stands outside, which were indeed being filled with season-record numbers. "So, let's just flash freeze this idea for now, and you can have the rest of the season to putter around with your calculator-baseball."

There was a part of Charlie that understood exactly where the manager was coming from. Tickets were being torn, broadcasts were being broadcast on a national level, featuring a national sports hero – why mess with the formula today, of all days?

And yet...

"Skip, just answer me this–" He pressed through the mustache-filtered sigh uttered by the manager. *"Why* does Javi always bat third?"

"He's the best hitter. The best hitter bats third."

"Okay, wait," Charlie said, excited that Whalen had fallen into his carefully laid logic trap. "Let's go back; who bats first?"

J.J. nodded. "I know this one — it's 'Who's *on* first.'"

Charlie turned to Windy. "What's he talking about?"

"He's at second..." said J.J.

Windy shrugged at Charlie. "I don't know."

"...and he's at third," J.J. concluded. "Classic bit."

Charlie threw his hands up. "Okay, let's just get a grip here." He was losing the room. "So, the game starts, inning one, pitch one, and we bat..."

Whalen allowed him to trail off to a point where the ensuing silence had properly shamed him, then replied, "Windy."

Charlie nodded. "Because?"

"Because, I bring the flavor," said Windy. He waved his phone. *"And* I have the most Blither followers. I'm an icon."

Whalen grabbed the phone from his hands. "Technically, *I* now have the most Blither followers." He turned to Charlie. "It's because he's fast. When his face isn't buried in this thing."

"And because he gets on base, right?" said The Franchise. "He works the pitch count?"

Whalen chuckled and leaned toward the superstar. "There isn't really much of a strike zone, you see." He lowered his voice, "He's diminutive."

"Ah," said The Franchise, nodding.

Whalen shrugged. "He's wee."

Windy sputtered with outrage. "Come on, Skipper, I'm five-eight!"

"Yes, you're a real Paul Bunyan," said Whalen. "Mythological, even."

"In theory," Charlie said, doing his best to maintain the team's focus, "if he gets on base, he can run. If he can run, he can steal or make it from first to third on a whole lot of nothing. *Or,* he can just stay put, leaving the threat in the back of the pitcher's mind. Now, who bats second?"

"J.J. McNihilist," Whalen said, humoring him.

"Why is he second?"

"It's a great question," J.J. said to Whalen. "I'm not even that into it."

Whalen didn't flinch. "He's a hitter. He might get on base a fair amount, but it's really the fact that he's gonna move the leadoff man into scoring position."

"And the same with the three-spot, right?"

"Well, yeah, more or less."

"The point is, if three-spot's on base, he's hopefully knocking guys in, and he's out there to get cleaned up by Number four, who swings big and does big damage on-contact. Baseball 101." Whalen groaned at this, but Charlie persisted. "Now, let's say we're facing a pitcher who's just slicing through us like wheat, and we're going down one-two-three, one-two-three, one-two-three, and it's a perfect game. Now, in the perfect game scenario, everyone gets to bat three times. Three times up, three times down, three outs per inning, nine innings, 27 outs."

"Well shoot, Charlie – I think you might actually know the rules to this game." Whalen grabbed Charlie's hand and began shaking it. The team chuckled.

"However," Charlie continued, extricating his hand from the skipper's grip, "this almost never happens. As soon as someone gets on base, the cycle of the lineup is altered."

"But I'm still number one, right?" Windy asked. This seemed to be the most crucial part of Charlie's explanation for him.

"You *are–"*

"Then that's all that matters," Windy said, shrugging. "Flavor-1, you are cleared for takeoff."

"…and you aren't," Charlie finished.

"Wait, what?"

"As soon as anyone gets on base and assuming we can stay the hell out of a double play, you get bumped from that leadoff spot. So, while you're still 'number one,' that doesn't guarantee you'll always bat first in a frame. Which means that all this planning around the power spots of the three and four hitters is only good for the first inning."

Windy raised a hand. "Coach, I'm gonna have to take umbrage with that last statement; no matter what the numbers say, we are definitely out there, trying to play baseball for eight innings. Sometimes nine."

"I still get to hit, right, Coach?" asked Javier.

"Yeah, yeah, Javi, of course – that's the whole point!" Charlie moved over to a whiteboard that typically sat either unused or as a canvas for obscene doodles. He uncapped a dry erase marker and began writing stats. "Now, in the old days, you'd be batting clean-up, since you have the most power, as seen here with your slugging percentage, or how many bases you earn per hit, per at-bat. Batters one through three get on base and you knock 'em in, right?"

Javier nodded. "Sí."

"However," Charlie continued, his marker a blur of mathematics, "you're also our most *frequent* hitter, as indicated here with your batting average, which is easily a hundred points higher than anyone else on the team at any given moment."

The Franchise stepped forward, examining the numbers Charlie was furiously scribbling. He emitted a long whistle. "Oh, shit – these are your numbers?"

Javier shrugged.

"Javi's a bad, bad man," Windy said. His teammates nodded their respect and agreement.

Charlie turned back to the giant first baseman. "Now, with your batting average supplementing your superior on-base percentage – seen *here* – along with your power's ability to push runners across the plate, we'd normally have you in the three-spot to ensure you'll bat in the first inning. We do this, rather than watching the side go down like Sonny Corleone at the toll booths, and having you be leadoff the next inning with no opportunities for runs batted in." Charlie turned to Whalen for guidance, his energy high from the surplus of impassioned stat-chat. "I think I'm correct in saying that, right Skip?"

Whalen held his hands up as if to calm his protégé. "Charlie, I don't remember the *exact* equations I used to make that decision, but yes. I'd say that's pretty close as to why Javi's batting third."

Javier nodded. "I'm number three."

"Ah-*HA!*" said Charlie, raising his marker anew. "Now, at the risk of being *too* interesting, let's talk seasonal statistical totals..."

CHAPTER 14
Human Interest

FOR WHAT FELT like the millionth time that year, Francesca found herself seated next to a fidgety, scowling Dip Lockerbie. She loathed being made to spend time with him outside of a broadcast situation and would normally do anything to avoid this occurrence.

Back in May, she'd found herself not only accepting jury duty, but secretly hoping that the forensic evidence would drag the light-burglary case out for months. Discovering this urge living inside of her had been challenging (was it possible that she was actually a monster?) as was the wrestling with her conscience she'd engaged in when it was revealed that the defendant had left all sorts of fingerprints and DNA evidence at the scene of the crime. It had been with some reluctance that she'd cast her vote for guilty, all the while wondering why criminals no longer seemed to take pride in their work. She'd even lingered for an extra day in the gallery of the next trial, before finally admitting to herself that she needed to be back in the booth for pre-show preparation and interviews.

However, the circumstances of this current proximity to her archnemesis were different this time. Margaret had awoken her from a deep sleep with a text message, calling for this meeting. Why the text was sent at 2:00 a.m., Francesca did not know, and why the meeting time had been set, only to be blown past by at least ten minutes, was equally mysterious. At this point, the gathering was little other than a live demonstration of Margaret bashing out email correspondence. If Francesca had learned anything the past week, it was that Margaret Tinley was a shrewd player of people. And it made her apprehensive. *Which is exactly what she wants,* Francesca considered, taking a note.

Dip wasn't helping anything by bouncing his leg like a thumping rabbit. He had, of course, refused to acknowledge Francesca beyond the faintest passing of eye-contact as they'd taken their seats, and it had made for an increasingly awkward waiting period. But where Francesca was tense over the meeting to come, Dip seemed downright annoyed to be there at all. He made no attempt at disguising the checking of his watch, which he'd been doing on a minute-by-minute basis.

This was distracting, but not as much as the office walls, which had been stripped of Whalen's bleary decor and painted an intense shade of lilac. Francesca marveled at the difference the color made; the space seemed larger, less cluttered with framed 8x10s of Billy Martin and the like, and almost blinding in whichever frequency of light it lived within. Was it possible to paint a room ultraviolet?

Dip sighed in cartoonish fashion, but Margaret was unmoved from her work. Francesca imagined that if they'd had a healthy, semi-cordial working relationship, she and Dip might have taken this opportunity to exchange a glance of commiseration. As it was, both broadcasters knew enough to not call the team owner's ways into question, lest they find themselves on the wrong end of a now-infamous Margaret Tinley downsizing. Francesca shifted slightly in her chair, the paint fumes inciting a dull throb in her temples. Considering the cartons of cigarettes Whalen had downed in this space over the years, the room must surely have had *some* kind of ventilation, though it was not evident.

Meanwhile, Margaret typed furiously on her laptop, her attention focused on the wording of a presumably furious missive. Finally, her keystrokes slowed, becoming more staccato as she added the final flourishes to her work.

"And *that,*" she said, hammering home a final key, "is how you write an effective email." Her eyes flashed with unbridled glee as she moved the mouse a half-inch and clicked 'send.' "Eat my words, you bastard," she muttered, continuing to stare at the screen.

Francesca cleared her throat. "You wanted to see us? Or... anything?" She gestured to the room's new, garish layer. "This is quite a choice that's been made, this color."

Margaret grunted. "Whalen almost retired when he saw it, but this organization wouldn't know style if it pushed us into a swimming pool."

Dip cleared his throat. The resulting sound of viscosity was enhanced by the natural reverb generated by the bare, lilac walls. Margaret turned to him, her expression registering nothing but disgust, and for a moment, Francesca thought Dip might protest this assault on his organization's aesthetics.

"I hate to interrupt the gabfest, but I have a show to do, so can we…" he said, making a circular, wrap-it-up motion with his hand, "you know…"

Margaret's look of repulsion was quickly replaced by one that was having none of whatever this was. "This will take as long as it takes, Lockerbie. Or so help me, I'll call Mildred and have her come put you out to pasture for keeps."

Francesca was taken off guard by this; having almost no rapport with one another, she'd not been aware that Dip had a partner. Somehow, someone had not only agreed to *marry* Dip Lockerbie, but *remain* married to Dip Lockerbie? Francesca turned to him, curious to see how he would react. For a moment, he did nothing, his hand frozen in mid-circle. Margaret stared at him, her eyes locked into unblinking laser-mode. After a moment of epic length and a mutual loathing so thick, one could have spooned it onto a plate, Dip finally broke. He sat back in his chair, apparently resigned to listening to what the woman who endorsed his paychecks had to say.

Margaret continued, "The reason I called you in here is because you're streaming."

Dip bolted upright in his chair, his face now a mask of outrage. "Mildred *told* you that? For your information, the medication works just fine, and–"

"I *meant,*" Margaret said, holding up a hand, "you're streaming on the internet. I just got word from the IT team."

Francesca was again puzzled. "We have an IT team?"

"Technically, they're the groundskeepers," Margaret shrugged. "But yes, they're now doing IT as well. *After* the turf has been mown, of course."

Now it was Dip's turn to hold his hands up in protest. "I'm sorry, ladies, but I'm having a hard time seeing what in tarnation *any* of this means to the Big Dipper!"

Francesca almost felt sorry for him. She had never seen him use a computer, let alone the internet. He avoided this new, suspect technology that had now been around for 20 to 30 years, as though ignoring it might result in it being wished into the cornfield of obsolescence. It was all too much for him, yet this was most likely for the best regarding the online community. "It means we're going to be online," Francesca said, her tone neutral. "In the computer."

Dip refused to look at her, instead choosing to focus his outrage at Margaret. "Excuse me, but do I look like I spent 40 years talking into a microphone ad nauseum, just to be put through the floppy-optic googlebits of one of those... *doohickies?"*

"Dip, are you aware of another Pearl Harbor on the horizon?" said Margaret. "Because otherwise, nobody gives a goddamn about the radio."

He huffed in disbelief. "So, it's just radio everywhere then, is it? Plug into a melon and 'stream' all over the radio broadcast, is that what we're selling? What next – radio *on my phone?"* He mimed talking into a rotary handset. "'Ring-ring! Who is it? Oh, the radio? Sure, put him through!' It's absurd." He sat back, now oozing the smugness of a man who felt he'd thoroughly made his point.

Margaret tilted her head. "It will double your audience."

Dip's eyes lit up as he considered this for a half-second. "Okay then, streaming it is. Heck, I think I'm streaming right now!" He nodded and made to leave his chair. "I should go gather some news worth reporting on this 'stream.' You can point me at the computer I'm supposed to talk into later."

"Also," said Margaret, freezing him once more, "since The Network is here, I would ask that you *please* be respectful to them should you meet. As a professional courtesy."

For the first time all day, Dip turned to Francesca. "Probably best if you stay out of their way, Frank," he said. "They like their talent to be seasoned. Unflappable. What time do they arrive, Mar– uh, Mrs. Tinley?"

"They've been here all morning."

Dip straightened again. "Are you serious? Did they ask about me?"

It was now Margaret's turn to be surprised. "They absolutely did not."

"Seriously?" He shot her a rakish look. "I mean..." He pointed to his face.

Margaret waited, confounded. Francesca watched as he then tilted his chin a half-inch toward the fluorescents overhead. She watched as his eyes slid down to take in their response and smiled as though what he was projecting was the most obvious thing in the world.

Finally, Margaret broke the silence with a roll of her eyes. "Dip, they didn't ask about you!" His face fell like a building imploding as she continued. "Apparently, they're here because of the famous one, and how he's coming down to the minors before he goes to the Hall of Fame or something like that." Francesca laughed inwardly at this blasé attitude toward one of the game's all-time greats. Margaret flipped her hand, as though discarding the entire notion as the most useless of garbage. "It's all supposed to be terrifically 'meta' and they just can't resist."

"Really?" This take was new to Francesca. "Does 'meta' actually sell?"

"How should I know?" Margaret shrugged. "Ask the audience."

Dip cleared his throat again. Francesca noted that he now looked wildly distracted, his gaze distant, unfocused. "Ah, Mrs. Tinley, let me assure you that I have been combing the ballpark for the big scoop all day."

And by 'combing' you mean 'napping under the console,' Francesca thought.

"Obviously," said Margaret. "You've been scooping so hard that you must have missed the 23-man television crew setting up cameras all over the place."

In Francesca's brief experience, Dip and hard weather never seemed to mix well. Or at all. He may not have been addressing his broadcast partner directly, but he always made sure the room at-large was aware of his joint issues when the rain fell. Or even threatened to fall.

Now, he leaned toward the owner, his face a poorly constructed mask of seriousness. "Mrs. Tinley, don't you worry your withered little head about it. I, Dip Lockerbie, swear to you, I will land the big fish for some serious one-on-one time. We are going to keep AM 1371 on the map as the truest home for Cape Haddock Coelacanth baseball, and that's a threat you can believe in!"

"Does this mean you're leaving now?" she said.

Dip leapt from his chair, straightening his jacket and tie. "I've got a story to track down!"

Francesca bit the side of her mouth to keep from laughing.

Margaret gave him an equally dramatic wave of the hand, practically sweeping him from the room. "Then I love this plan. Goodbye."

His eyes bounced between the two women for a moment, as though suspicious he was missing something. After a moment's pause, he charged out the door and through the clubhouse. Francesca could see the players, currently huddled around the little-used whiteboard, pause as he rushed past them and into the tunnel. He did not give them, or the very man he was now looking for, a second look. As the office door swung closed, she caught a glimpse of The Franchise's astounded expression.

The frosted glass door creaked shut, leaving the two women to enjoy a brief silence.

Despite Margaret looking like a woman who was now considering the most cost-effective way to murder someone on her staff, Francesca risked addressing her as a human, rather than a boss. "Don't you ever feel bad about talking to him like that?"

Margaret looked at her and snorted. "Oh, please. He might be a doddering idiot now, but 40 years ago he was a skirt-chasing pervert like any other man."

"Ew, are you serious?" It seemed Francesca would be learning multitudes about her co-host today. "I can't picture him trying to pick up women with that hat on."

"Believe me, we all thought the hat was stupid in the '70s too." Margaret shook her head at the memory.

An unfortunate thought occurred to Francesca. "Did he ever... you know, try to put the moves on you?"

Despite being beyond the purview of a boss/employee relationship, Francesca was surprised when Margaret laughed. "Moretti, are you kidding me? *Of course* he did. I was the hottest thing any of those bozos had ever seen. And in those days for a young Dip Lockerbie, 'yes' meant yes, and 'no' meant 'Whoa, Dip.'" She spat his name with contempt.

Francesca laughed, delighted to find that someone shared her workplace angst. "Did you ever tell his wife what a scumbag he is?"

"Oh, god no," said Margaret. "In those days, who would've believed me? Who'd believe me now? Besides, Jackie would've murdered him." She chuckled wickedly at the idea. "All part of a life spent following a man who split his heart between me and this stupid, stupid game."

Surprised to find that they were now both laughing, Francesca took a bold leap.

"Margaret, may I ask you something?"

The owner wiped a tear away as her laughter died down. "Of course, dear."

"Okay. And this is officially off the record, mind you, but... how can you spend your entire life around baseball if you hate it so much?"

Margaret examined Francesca. After a moment, she said, "The first thing you need to understand is that I know what people think about me. The league, the other owners, my own players. I'm the axman, correct? The heartless black widow?"

Francesca had to admit to herself that this was the reputation she was familiar with but thought it best to assume the question was rhetorical. Fortunately, Margaret continued.

"Oh yes, I know all about the scuttlebutt. I'm a ruthless cost-cutter, intent on gutting an old, if not proud, franchise, all while profits for most teams have never been higher, and the fans have never had more money or leisure time to spend. I'm a cold-blooded, corporate murderer of the American pastime." Again, this lined up with everything Francesca had heard these past months. She found Margaret observing her closely and tried to remain neutral. "I know you know, Moretti. Everyone knows. And the scandalous truth is that

I *don't* hate it. I don't hate it any more than I love it. The game is purely incidental."

"I don't understand," said Francesca.

"I wonder how all of those clever fellows who know better than me would feel if they knew that their beloved Coelacanths were not only hemorrhaging the money we do have, but also the money we don't? Or what they would say when they found out that their Papa Bear, Herbert Tinley, fishing tycoon of the Northeast, had zero business sense for fishing supplies too? And how many of these brilliant baseball minds would be able to piece together the concept of emptying one pocket to fill another?"

These were the rumors Francesca had been hearing. *"Is* the entire family business bankrupt?"

Margaret offered a twitch of a smile – a sad one, but it was there. "Everyone in the front offices of the league loved Herbert, even if he didn't have a drop of common sense. He certainly didn't have two nickels to rub together."

"So..." Something troubled Francesca about this, but she could not place what it was. "Why do you bother at all? If there's no money in the thing, why not sell it for what you can and wash your hands of the whole enterprise?"

"Oh, you *are* a reporter, aren't you?" Margaret's eyes flashed in approval. "It's true, there's no common-sense reason I should remain entangled in the whole messy business. Nobody likes me, and I can't say I'm fond of any of them. But if I sell, there's a very good chance that whoever buys will eventually ditch the loser squad. And I can't allow that."

"Because of Herbert?"

"I knew what the financial situation was before I married Herbert."

"So, you..." Francesca squinted as the tumblers of the story fell into place. "You married Mr. Tinley *because* of the financial situation?" The words felt right as she spoke them, but she still could not comprehend why this would be the answer.

Margaret shifted behind the desk, leaning toward her young broadcaster. "As I said, the game itself is incidental. But, despite all common sense, the memories aren't. Think of the way people speak of this silliness, these grown men and women chasing after balls and following rules somebody made up, as though they might end up in prison if they didn't. There's the spirit of friendly competition, teamwork, fair play – all that garbage. None of it mirrors what real life is like. What real *people* are like. But what is real, is the power of memory that looms over it. The people and places shared in a particular space and time, where, *incidentally,* a game of baseball is happening."

The face of Francesca's father flashed before her eyes, and she felt a pull to her own set of baseball memories they had shared. It was vivid – a spectrum of sights, sounds, and smells that could only be found at a ballpark. Its power over her sense memory was undeniable.

"For me," Margaret continued, "baseball is the flyover state you move to after you marry the boy you met in college. You wouldn't normally do so, but if that's where his life is, you try to make the best of it. Of course, sometimes you end up with baseball *and* a flyover state..."

This felt like a rare personal tell from her boss, and Francesca decided to press. "So, your husband – well, Charlie's dad, I mean… he played most of his career up here, right?"

"Mmm," Margaret nodded, leaning back in her chair. "For ages."

"And you just stuck with him?"

The owner offered a small shrug. "Jackie was my best friend. I loved that man. And he loved me, and he loved Charlie. And he loved baseball." Her gaze grew distant as she grasped for memories of a distant time. "He talked about it constantly. When Charlie was a boy, we'd sit in the stands and watch his father play, and we'd try to piece together what was happening on the field. I had no idea what it was all about when we got together. It all seemed like tennis for idiots to me. But we'd watch the plays and try to figure out the rules and reasons for why things would happen, and then figure out what it all meant at the end. Just so we'd have some idea of what Jackie was talking about afterward. It was an easy way for us to be close to him."

There was an unexpected softness in the visual of Margaret and her boy sitting together, trying to connect with this man. "That's really sweet," Francesca said.

"It was *something,* anyway. It was something for a time when we had nothing. Or nearly nothing. We had each other, and, because of Jackie, we had baseball. And the numbers on that scoreboard helped us to understand. And believe me, just because nobody asked, that doesn't mean that I didn't see the inefficiencies on the field."

"Oh, I believe you." If anyone would be able to eagle eye an inefficiency, it would be Margaret Tinley. "But if you and Charlie were so into the numbers, how, um... how do you explain Charlie's playing career?"

She knew this could be an easily misinterpreted question, but Margaret did not flinch. "What do *you* think it is that defines the value of a person's life?"

The question came from left field, catching Francesca off-guard. She had no response. Margaret carried on. "It's a ruthless talent that succeeds in this game, you know. There has to be a fire within you to do whatever it takes to win."

"And you don't see that in him?" It was a needless question in that Charlie had never 'won' anything, but this conversation seemed to be about something greater.

Margaret waved her off. "Charlie was never going to be that person. And he knew it too. He's not stupid. Simple – *easy,* if you will – yes. But not stupid. He figured out he was rotten at the game. And he's far too trusting and kind to ever be ruthless."

While this admission of the obvious was refreshing, it didn't explain why Charlie had gone on, year after year, scraping by in the desert for no one. "So... Why did he keep playing?"

"Charlie felt like he was protecting me by playing," said Margaret. "It was him offering me some kind of security, if you will. And why shouldn't I let him think that? It was a noble effort, even if it was a wasted one. It was what his father would have wanted him to do."

"Charlie really loved his dad, huh?"

"There was a lot to love with that man. Good things and bad."

"How do you mean?" This was the first time Francesca had heard the owner speak so openly about her first husband.

"As a professional baseball-talker, I'm sure you're aware of the 4-A model player?"

Francesca was. "Too good for the smalls, not good enough for the bigs."

"A cigar for the lady," said Margaret, waving an index finger across the desk.

"And that was Jackie," said Francesca. "4-A."

"He was a goddamned unicorn," Margaret replied, looking away. She spat the words out like the husks of seeds. "Always hit .300, usually over .320 – *.340* in *this* barn. But never felt comfortable on Broadway, under the spotlight. And he could never understand why. It drove him mad, of course. The one thing about the game he could not wrap his head around."

"But *you* knew."

"My husband had *miles* of talent–"

"But he wasn't ruthless."

Margaret pointed approvingly at her again. "Of course, all of this worked out swimmingly for Herbert. He got himself a local star who could put asses in seats and would never be called up for too long. And Jackie occasionally managed to drag the Coelacanths across the finish line and into the playoffs."

"Bonus gate," Francesca said, nodding.

"Ugh," said Margaret, rolling her eyes, "Herbert *loved* that extra gate, let me tell you. Not that they ever got out of the first round."

"But people still love Jackie around here."

Margaret scoffed and leaned back in Whalen's creaky chair. "For all the good that ever did him, the beautiful bastard." She leaned forward, her tone suddenly serious. "Love gets you a beer at Latimer's, but it doesn't pay the rent, Moretti. Never forget that. Jackie made Herbert a small fortune and we never saw a dime of it."

Francesca was stunned. There were few names that managed to dry in the pavement of the minor leagues. Most fans simply didn't have the bandwidth to commit the scrappers to memory. That Jackie Conroy was appreciated by the few people left from his day said something about the man's character as well as his play. "Surely, there must have been a bonus–"

"League minimum," said Margaret. "From day one to year twelve. Herbert had little mind for business, but enough to know he should hold onto as much of the black as he could. And who would complain? Most of his players were just happy to have jerseys and short pants to wear, a place to play their game." Francesca knew this to be the sad truth. Margaret leaned back again. "Meanwhile, we lived in poverty. Needed for the team – the business – but with no leverage to move any place other than where we were. But... Jackie was happy, so I was happy. As was Herbert. He got everything he wanted from my husband. Squeezed every last drop of blood from that stone with one hand while patting him on the back with the other. And then, one day, Neptune decided to have his say in the matter, leaving Charlie and me with nothing."

And here was the knot of the story that Francesca had yet to untangle – the great mystery of Margaret Tinley.

"And you fell in love with Herbert?" she said.

"Ahh..." Margaret said, offering her a sly smile. Francesca swallowed; she should have known Margaret would spot such bait. The owner rocked her chair in a slow, shallow motion and stared into the distance. Finally, "Herbert was a charismatic man, there's no doubt. He'd never have been allowed by the league to run his teams otherwise."

Francesca instinctively knew this was not enough. Margaret Tinley was no cocktail hour bimbo. "But..." she prompted.

Margaret nodded. *"But...* there is more than one way to call in a debt. Some just happen to be more unsavory than others. That doesn't mean they're any less effective."

Francesca frowned at this cryptic assessment and Margaret took notice.

"I saw an opportunity. He was 62 when we married. I thought he was three years from retirement and five from the grave. Shame on me for learning too late that the decadent ones always have a buffer of cash to protect them from time's sharper edges. But Charlie was 16 and wanted to be like his dad. He wanted to be a baseballer. And as odd as it seems now, all these years later, I did feel something for Herbert."

"Vengeance?"

"Of course. But also, something more. Not romance exactly, but... gratitude. Herbert gave me a job when Jackie died. No pension, mind you, and I was only his secretary, but this was as generous as I'd ever seen the man, or would ever see him. And when you're at the bottom, love and gratitude can be easily confused. The drowning woman does not question who is at the other end of the rope that's been cast out to save her."

"I don't think many people would do any different," said Francesca.

Margaret shook her head. "But most people are incapable of understanding the cost of such an act. It's not the decisions made that will deter a person, but the time that passes *in between* deciding and reaching one's goal. The playing out of the thread to its end. But I was patient. For 22 seasons of rotten, desert Single-A, I waited. And now..."

She gestured at the space around them and all was clear. Francesca beheld the owner, now seated in the throne of whatever power a small-market minor league team could afford, with new eyes. The woman who had been left with nothing, now had everything. It was a fabulous con – the longest Francesca had ever heard of, but there could be no arguing the results.

"Why, Margaret..." she said, shooting an awestruck smile at this shrewd woman, "you are *ruthless.*"

Margaret smiled across the desk. "Someone in this family had to be."

THE COELACANTH PLAYERS were clustered around the whiteboard as Charlie finished writing down a lineup with projected yearly at-bat totals.

"And so, we can see, with each descending position in the batting order, each player gets 15 to 20 *fewer* at-bats per year than the player in front of him. As such, the optimal placement for the best hitter to score the most runs and have the most runs batted in is..." The marker squeaked as he underlined Javier's name. "...batting second." Charlie turned to the team. "You get it?"

Each Coelacanth – from J.J. Pike, to Malcolm Watts, to Turp Salazar, to The Franchise himself – gave the board a final, prolonged examination. Their eyes traced over the hastily scrawled mathematical schematic until, finally – barely... it clicked.

"Ohhhhh..." came the response.

The Franchise patted Charlie on the back. "You know, I've had that explained to me a dozen different ways, and I've never understood it before now. Nice job, Coach."

Windy turned to Whalen, who was stroking his mustache. "Skip, we gotta bat Javi second. It just makes sense, right?"

They turned as Margaret came through the office door and crossed the clubhouse, Francesca following close behind. "Excuse me, Bert Convy," Margaret said to Charlie. "I hate to interrupt this round of *Win, Lose, or Lose Harder,* but don't you have a baseball game to be punishing yourselves with?"

"Mom, I'm kind of in the middle of something here."

Margaret eyed the whiteboard. "The old 'Best Hitter Bats Second' routine?" she scoffed. "I've been pushing that bit since the '80s."

Whalen clapped his hands together. "Well, Maggie, any last words of encouragement for the fellas before they take the field? It's your team."

Margaret was taken aback. She surveyed the faces of her players before clearing her throat.

"Oh. Well, I suppose." She began to slowly meander through the clubhouse as she voiced her thesis. "You know, I've been sitting around this game, spectating like some kind of disinterested sports pervert for 45 years. And while I may know what everything happening on the field *means,* that doesn't mean I particularly care about any of it. If anything, I find it an amusing little world that's been created for you here. In essence, you put on an outfit and run around while the rest of us powder your bottoms and tell you you're special."

Charlie watched as the players eyed one another and looked to Whalen for help. The skipper shrugged.

She ignored this and continued her meanderings. "This is a game of hang-ups, you understand. You're all hung up on one thing or another – yourself in relation to the past, or what your legacy will be like in the future. But none of it is an actual *'problem.'* Chasing the numbers of dead people to please your daddies isn't splitting the atom, you see. I never even knew my father, let alone 'had a catch' with him. Ugh, and admit it – none of you have ever said it that way, it's pure artsy-fartsy fabrication.

"If I'm being honest, I wish you were a basketball team. It's a far more entertaining sport with more action, more scoring, more drama, and better shoes. Do any of you happen to play basketball?" She surveyed the room but saw only mystified expressions. "No? Well, okay then. For now.

"I don't have fond memories of crowding around a radio or a television to keep up with the World Series. I don't cry when I think about Lou Gehrig. In fact, I *never* think about Lou Gehrig. I don't care who gets a trophy. I don't care about the team you grew up with or what it means to you. I don't care about your motivations."

She stopped in the middle of the clubhouse and scanned each of their faces. "What I do care about is the entertainment factor, what kind of show you're putting on. This is entertainment, people," she said, raising her index finger. "Never lose sight of that. I know every one of you thinks you're special, that you have gifts that somehow make you more than the average person. But the reality is you're a bunch of gym rats with quality hand-eye coordination and an easy willingness to throw away the best years of your lives."

Charlie swallowed and waited for a response regarding this assessment, but the Coelacanths simply listened, occasionally shifting nervously. Her point was cutting, but none of them could say it wasn't at least part of the truth.

She began stalking the floor anew. "And all for some fantastical narrative you've been fed by books and magazines and newspapers and movies and television and all manner of theatrical diddle parties, wherein you can be heralded as a hero by playing well. But the reality is, you're just an entertainer. A distraction. You're not real – none of what you do is real in any sense of the word. If this is truly the national pastime, then you are what pass in-parallel with that time.

"Now, we've got a bunch of extra people today because one of you is relatively famous."

The Coelacanths turned to The Franchise, who raised his hand hesitantly. "Um, I guess–"

"I do not care, Bub," she said. "I do not care a wit. But they do. In a world of unending distractions and endless entertainments that can appear with the push of a button, they chose to come and see you. And even with that battle won, the war for their attention is not over. They've still got those options in their pockets."

She turned quickly, searching their faces. "Which one of you does the Bleating? The little one, the one who inspired that disastrous HR meeting – which one are you?"

Windy leaned out from behind Javier and raised a tentative hand.

Margaret snapped her fingers and pointed at him. "I want you recording the whole time, do you understand me?"

Windy's eyes went wide. Charlie broke in, "Mom, the rules–"

She glared at him and he halted the thought. She turned back to Windy. "Be smart. Don't get caught, do you understand me?"

Again, Windy was speechless, but this time he nodded and looked to Whalen. The skipper shrugged and pulled the recently confiscated phone from his back pocket. He weighed it in his hand a moment, then passed it back to his player.

Margaret nodded. "Good. It's utter madness to me that the only people in the building without phones are the people the building was built for. It's absurd.

"But what's *not* absurd is the fact that there are paying customers out there. Those people care. And they've paid to see something. And they will not be there much longer, so I suggest you make the most of these moments.

Charlie couldn't believe what he was hearing. "Mom, there's no need to be dire about it, we're going to win another game. Statistically speaking, it's only a matter of time–"

"I'm not talking about that," she said. "If everything was about *that,* the American League central division would have been wiped out decades ago. This goes beyond wins and losses, do you understand me? It's not a Coelacanth problem, it's a baseball problem." Her attention snapped to the manager. "Whalen, perhaps you can help me articulate this. What is it that we're producing here?"

Whalen grinned. "Why, Maggie, we're making memories."

"Very good," said Margaret, turning to the players. "More specifically, we provide a space and a point of fixation that allows us to sell the *idea* of memories to the public. We have to admit that we've not been playing particularly memorable baseball lately. My pro tip is, if you're going to lose, lose big and all the time. *That* is memorable."

"Well, we're certainly working on it, boss," said Whalen.

"Fine. Now, let's think of this as the 'equation of experience,' shall we?" Margaret crossed to the white board. She reached a hand out to Charlie, who dutifully passed her the marker. "Baseball equals desire, plus means, plus opportunity," she said, writing the words out into a formula. "Desire and means are simple enough to quantify, however, I believe opportunity can be broken down further into *fixation* – the little game you're playing out there – plus *location,* or, the place in which the fixation unfolds."

She finished writing and turned back to her players. "So, what happens when one of these factors changes? Tonight, you'll notice a series of television cameras that will be tracking the baseball goings-on of the good one..." and here, she pointed to The Franchise, "...while he slums it with us. I should also note that he brings the most value to the experience – or, *fixation* – and so he gets paid the most. Young man?"

The Franchise looked up at her in surprise. "Me?"

"Yes," said Margaret. "Please tell us what pays for the bulk of your salary? What is it that fills the coffers of your organization and allows the checks to clear?"

"Oh," he said, somewhat thrown by the question. "Well, I suppose there are lots of things that factor into it, but... yeah, I guess the TV contracts, mostly."

Margaret pointed at him and cast her steely gaze over the rest of the room. "And what does this imply?"

There was silence for a moment as the Coelacanths looked to each other for assistance.

"It means the idea of 'location' has changed," said Charlie, finally glimpsing where his mother was headed.

Margaret turned and underlined the word 'location' on the dry erase board. "Exactly." She began slowly pacing the room once more. "You see, baseball is currently operating under a broken business model that is primarily focused on what we call 'the gate.' In the old days, if you wanted to be entertained by baseball, you had to go to the baseball store and buy some. This gives us these iron and concrete monstrosities that are only fixation-fields in part and are otherwise infrastructure for supporting the customers of this baseball store.

"These are venues of escapism – places to hide from the cares of the real world. But, now the means of escape are in our customers' pockets – in *your* pockets. In my pocket." She pulled her phone from her suit coat and wagged it at them. "The interface has changed, but we're not changing with it. Yet.

"Now, allow me to prophesize on the future of what it is we do here. No longer will there be stadiums with sprawling bleachers and decks and the capacity of tens of thousands. You'll be playing in a soundstage that is only slightly larger than the field itself. Oh, no doubt there will still be some obsessives out there who will be willing to pay the exorbitant fees required to gain access. That way they can purchase expensive beers and yell at you in person, but it will largely be a boutique audience of *means...* " she underlined the word on the whiteboard, "...who will be filling the one row of seats behind home plate.

"The environment will be enclosed and controllable so there will be no more rain delays or sub-zero playoff games. The visual aesthetics won't be disturbed because the skyline over the outfield walls will be green screened to perfection. You could be playing anywhere – the forum of ancient Rome, surrounded by the temples of Jupiter and Saturn, or the Sea of Tranquility on the bright side of the moon. The soundstage itself will exist in some low-rent warehouse district that will keep the overhead of the place to a minimum, possibly in a district where other teams keep their soundstages, because, again, the location will not matter.

"The fans will make the time to watch you play at their convenience. They'll agree when to start watching and gather in the comfortable viewing rooms of their own homes, next to their own snacks and toilet systems that don't require pissing in troughs beside a line of strangers. They'll put on their glasses or goggles or visors and log into the new baseball interface platform, where they will find themselves at the immaculately rendered gates of their team's virtual ballpark. From there, they can walk a replicated concourse featuring all the interactive experiences you can find today, but with a batting cage that is never broken, and a display case you can actually open to put on your favorite legend's jersey.

"They can walk to their favorite seat – the best seat in the house – and find it is always available to them. Perhaps it will be a watchtower over the right field corner, or a glass-bottom balcony over the pitcher's mound. Maybe even a throwback to the days when baseball was one of the only entertainment options, and the fans could take a seat next to the first base coach's box. Assuming those positions survive, of course. The seat will be the perfect size and will always have an unobstructed view of the action.

"And then, they will watch you. They will *fixate* on the point of fixation, only now they will be able to pull up every statistic imaginable in whichever font they prefer, right next to you. With the slightest adjustment, they can zoom in on your face and trace the subtlest changes of expression as you choose which pitch to throw, which one to swing at. In an instant, they will be beside you in left field, watching as you pick your nose or spring into action to field a fly ball. They will pause the action moments before the ball makes contact with bat or glove and will run the result in a loop as many times as they like, at whichever speed they prefer. Umpires will vanish from the field like white rhinos on the savanna. The outrage of human error will no longer find quarter in a sport that can be broken down from every angle by every person watching it. The integrity of getting the call right will contribute to the greater integrity of the game itself and will allow your talents greater opportunity to be displayed and appreciated."

Margaret suddenly turned and pointed to Francesca. "All the while, the customers will be hearing the commentary of the announcers. No longer will the ballpark be a mute, mechanical process to be trudged through over 160 times a year. *Your* drama will now be *their* drama. The emotional core of competition will be represented through you as never before. It will be highlighted by any feed of play-by-play and color they choose, be they the home announcer's opinions, or the away announcer's opinions, or your next-door neighbor's opinions...

"Every part of what we do will be calibrated for maximum efficiency and reliability, leading to the most value as entertainment. And *that* is how the game survives. That is the bang that justifies the buck. The customer will win, the advertisers sponsoring every angle and function of the new baseball experience will win, and *we* will win as performers and administrators, even when we lose. Of course, by then, artificial intelligence might have enough learning aptitude and modeling capabilities to replace you and your salaries with three-dimensional avatars, rendering everything you do obsolete."

Margaret shrugged and Charlie watched the players jaws drop as this nightmarish reality sank in. His mom seemed to notice as well and quickly brushed the idea aside.

"But that's the future and this is still the present. I've been around long enough to know that you either have to win a lot or lose a lot in order to get people to pay attention. Now, we've always veered toward the loser-side of things, and I anticipate no difference today. If you would like to win, by all means, please feel free. But whatever you do, give them a *show*. They paid their money to see something – *show them something*. And if you show them something, they might come back. So, slip into your sailor suits and start dancing, kiddos, because you're all just a bunch of shitty Gene Kellys as far as they're concerned."

Margaret examined her players' expressions. Her words had pummeled them, leaving a landscape of puzzled, emotional craters. She sighed. "Oh, and 'Go team' and all that."

Relieved, the players exploded into a roaring "Yeah!" and stampeded from the clubhouse.

Charlie and Francesca stood frozen in awe and watched as Whalen grinned and tipped the brim of his cap at Margaret. The owner allowed the smallest of smirks to cross her face before following her team into the tunnel.

CHAPTER 15
Calibration

"THE HERBCO FIELD lights are aglow, just like the candles used when Mr. George Washington scratched out the Declaration of Independence over *one hundred years ago!*" Dip brazenly pushed his anachronistic scene setting to its limit for the coast to hear.

Francesca grimaced, but knew there was no stopping him. He was locked in, hunched over the microphone, taking no breaths. Could he possibly be receiving oxygen through his skin? Was his fedora covering secret noggin-gills?

"Ladies and gentlemen, Coelacanths and Pocket Squares, you've got Dip Lockerbie here, welcoming you to Cape Haddock and another night of this ball-we-call-base! It's a full house that's packed itself in on this fine Fourth of July evening. Meanwhile, hurricane warnings be damned, for we're watching our Dead Fish duke it out against their perennial rivals, the Splake Steelheads!"

Allowing no room, she managed to pick up a line as he dragged out the final 's' of 'Steelheads.' "That's right, Dip, and the weather report has not been looking good–"

Dip's break-in was lethal, stomping all over her take. "True enough, this Hannah storm has been causing chaos wherever she goes. And, without question, nobody feels more threatened than me, Dip Lockerbie!"

Francesca tried again. "And we will be keeping you updated as the situation unfolds, and the eastern seaboard prepares for–"

Dip's interruption was swollen with self-importance. "But, of course, the one thing that's on *everybody's* mind is the presence of ol' Number 9 at first base."

Francesca grimaced, but took the cue. She decided to throw it back to him. "And what changes will–"

"He'll be rehabbing that right hammy with the fellas during the major league All-Star break. He might be the face of the franchise, folks, but tonight he will once again join such luminaries as Scoot Monaghan, Tarp Begley, and your favorite and mine, Dip Lockerbie, in wearing the Coelacanth home whites. Yes, he'll be bringing nothing but hazy joy and emotional fireworks to the folks of the metropolitan Cape Haddock region. So, come one! Come all! It's me, Dip Lockerbie, talking loud at ya!"

Francesca closed her eyes and wondered if there had ever been a situation in which hurricanes had been preceded by asteroids.

DARK CLOUDS PROWLED the skies over the field as the business of starting baseball began. The Coelacanths fought a variety of strong winds as they ran through their fielding warmups while Whalen conferred with the umpire crew.

Charlie noted that the upper deck was now adorned with upside-down rainbows of red, white, and blue crepe paper where the traditional big-league holiday bunting would be. It all looked rather flimsy and of a patriotic child's birthday party, but Terry had done a fine job with the resources he'd been given. Charlie marveled at the unprecedented hordes of people in the stands as he meandered to the catcher's box, where J.J. was busy adjusting the straps on his mask.

"Big game tonight." Charlie offered, wondering if his recent statistical exposition on the batting order had earned him any newfound respect.

"No shit," said J.J.

Charlie nodded; at the very least he was not being ignored. "You ever play in front of max capacity?"

"Only in the other team's barn. You?"

"Not even close," said Charlie, shaking his head. "How's the warmup?"

J.J. barked a laugh. "Is that what we're doing? Because the kid hasn't put anything near the zone so far."

"That bad?"

J.J. gestured to the mound. "Just look at him!"

Charlie turned to find Hayden, staring blankly into the crowd. It was true – he looked completely lost, cast off into a different dimension.

J.J. continued, "The kid's totally spooked. He looks like he just walked through the Black Dahlia lot."

Charlie exhaled as he realized what he had to do. "I should go talk to him."

J.J. rolled his eyes. "Yeah, I'm sure that'll turn him right around."

Misreading his catcher's tone, Charlie turned to him, his eyes filled with sincerity. "Thanks, J.J. I really appreciate that."

He walked toward the mound, newly emboldened as J.J. shook his head. "Oh my god..."

Charlie slowed as he approached his pitcher. He knew he should be cautious with the volatile young man. "Heyyy, buddy..." He spoke in a tone of voice reserved for zoo-goers trying to pull fallen souvenirs out of the trench of a tiger habitat. "Big moment, huh?"

"Hey, Coach," said Hayden without looking at him.

Charlie was shocked. "Wait a minute, did you just call me *'Coach?'* Wow, this is kind of a huge moment. I guess I must be like the stepdad you've always wanted, huh?"

Hayden turned to him, confused. "What?"

Charlie waved it off. "Never mind. You feel good?"

"Hm?" Hayden's attention had drifted back to the stands. "Yep."

"You sure? Usually you're yelling at me to get out of your face right about now."

Hayden shook his head. "Sorry, it's just..." Charlie followed his gaze to the front rows of seats lining the Coelacanth dugout. "...my *dad's* here."

"He is?" Charlie spotted a middle-aged couple waving frantically at the pitcher. "Next to that lady with the bag of grapes?"

Hayden nodded. "Mom."

Charlie could certainly relate to this mom-induced level of nerves. He decided to play it cool, hoping to avoid further aggravating his ace. "Oh, well that's nice, they're here to support you–"

"Freaks me out."

"Ah. Sure. Feeling some pressure?"

Hayden dropped his eyes to the pitching rubber. He kicked at it absentmindedly. "My family's given everything for me to play ball."

Charlie nodded. "Sure they have, I get that." *Somewhat, anyway.* At least Hayden had talent to back up that level of sacrifice. "Well, uh…" He quickly scanned the field for a convenient distraction. "Well, why don't you just try not to look over there, huh?"

The pitcher frowned at him. "Don't look into our *dugout?"*

"Yeah," Charlie said, his eyes darting across the stands. "Just look over there, opposite side. See? Next to where the Network cameras for the national broadcast are."

Hayden spun to look where Charlie was pointing. His eyes bulged with panic at the sight of a headphone-wearing camera operator pointing an enormous lens right at them. He immediately started hyperventilating into his glove. Charlie put a hand on his back for support and again looked around for a potential source of relief for the inconvenient meltdown. He briefly wondered if the Steelheads would let them borrow their trainer if Hayden collapsed.

"Okay, okay, no cameras then – bad idea. Just, uh…" His eyes alit on what seemed like a perfect option. "Hey, just focus on *The Franchise,* huh?"

The Franchise was in Javier's usual position at first base, taking throws from his infielders. He looked over and noticed Charlie and Hayden ogling him. He paused, mid-throw, and squinted back in confusion.

"There he is, your *all-time favorite player,"* Charlie said with a breathless excitement that implied the big leaguer was hiding presents for the entire team in his back pocket. The excitement did not have the contagious effect he had hoped for, and Hayden stood completely frozen. Charlie decided to lay it on extra thick. "The very reason you got excited about this game in the first place, right? And now he's standing *right there.* Watching you."

Charlie waved at The Franchise, who offered a half-grin and salute in return.

"See? He's waving," said Charlie. "Go ahead and wave at your hero. Say 'Hi, Number 9, you're the greatest...'"

Hayden turned away, his glove over his mouth. "I think I'm gonna be sick."

Charlie, inwardly relieved to see Hayden move again, tried to be supportive in this, his pitcher's hour of crisis. "That's the spirit!" He grasped for an angle. "Just channel those feelings into throwing that ball, okay? You've got this!"

Charlie slapped him on the arm and trotted to the dugout without looking back. He'd done what he could. The kid would be fine.

He slowed as he reached Whalen, who was perched on the dugout's top step. The manager gazed at the teeming bleachers, admiring the packed house. "Nice crowd for it," he said. "Almost like we're playing a game that people paid to see!" He nodded toward Hayden. "What was that all about?"

"Just a case of the nerves, Skip. But don't worry about it, I was just giving him some advice."

Whalen snorted. "Oh, Jesus-pleasus..."

Charlie took his place next to the manager and crossed his arms in mimicry of the Skipper's body language. "I wouldn't worry about it, Skip. I've got him focused."

"Uh-huh," Whalen said. "Pretty confident for a man who's never seen this team win before."

The umpire swept the plate and circled around J.J. as the Steelheads' leadoff batter dug in.

"Play ball!" The order boomed across the field.

Charlie watched as Hayden stared in for the signs. He seemed fine, no different than usual. Perhaps he had finally used his years of veteran experience for the good of the team. Maybe numbers didn't work, but great advice did? He tried to remember what exactly he'd just said to the young starter but couldn't. He decided to verbalize his newfound coaching swagger instead. "I think I've got this down, Skip," he said, ignoring Whalen's unimpressed expression. "It's all about focusing that laser."

Hayden delivered the first pitch. It sailed high and outside the zone.

"Ball one," came the call.

Whalen glanced at Charlie. "I assume he wanted to throw it there?"

Charlie waved the question off like it was a mosquito. "Just gotta knock some of the rust off the ol' laser, Skip. No worries."

The second pitch gophered into the dirt before crossing the plate-region. J.J. made no effort to stop it, simply turned his masked face to watch it roll away.

"Kind of over-corrected there, huh?" said Whalen.

"Sh-sh-shh…" said Charlie. "He's just recalibrating, Skip. Just gotta recalibrate the ol' laser…"

FRANCESCA WINCED AS the wild pitch skittered into the oblivion of foul territory. "And that's ball two for Hayden Chandl–"

"You've gotta give this kid credit," came the inevitable intrusion. "The spotlight is not only on, it has *never* been brighter, coming as it does from that pair of baby blues being flashed by ol' Number 9 at first base."

Francesca looked at her partner as though he had announced himself as the new pope. It hadn't been color and it certainly wasn't much in the way of commentary. Whatever it was, there was no sign of it stopping. She braced herself as he inhaled again.

HAYDEN FELL INTO his windup. Charlie and Whalen leaned in, the bench coach muttering, "Just gotta, just gotta, just gotta–" The next pitch sailed wide.

"Ball three."

Charlie's head fell with a groan.

"Oh, I know what the issue is," said Whalen, turning to him. "I must be thinking of some *other* kind of laser, right?"

From the stands came the crowd's dull murmur of dissatisfaction.

"They're stirring, Charlie."

He jumped at the sound of his mother's voice, suddenly right beside him. He and Whalen both turned, surprised to find her mirroring their body language on the dugout steps: one leg up, arms crossed.

"These people," she said, taking in the thousands of annoyed faces. "We can't have people booing their way through the first at-bat."

Charlie didn't want to hear any more. Second-guessing? Fine. Whalen had more than earned the right. Triple-guessing? Sure. The team was not used to even *trying,* let alone trying something different. But *quadruple-guessing?* It was one wonder too far.

"He's a laser!" he huffed, as though that settled the matter.

Hayden fired his fourth pitch, a heater that drilled the batter in the ribs, sending him to the dirt. The crowd groaned as one. Charlie and Whalen winced, while his mother turned to him, unimpressed.

"He's a goddamned sniper, that's what," said Whalen.

DIP WAS LOVING every second of this, Francesca could tell. He was always enthusiastic about hearing himself do the commentary, but tonight felt especially self-obsessed. He pushed his voice across the sonic spectrum even more than usual, his metaphors and aphorisms becoming more and more obscure.

"Holey blue jeans!" he shouted as the Steelhead trainer and manager ran from the visiting dugout to tend to their leadoff batter. Francesca watched the young man rocking from side to side between the chalk lines, clutching his abdomen, before turning to her maniacal co-host. *Ugh. What is this attitude he's projecting tonight? Is it…could it be…*brio? *Gross.*

As if in response, Dip promptly topped himself. "It looks like the Steelhead lineup better strap on the ol' stove doors – Hayden Chandler has just turned this game into high noon on Mean Street!"

Francesca was certain she could feel another atom of life leave her body.

THE UMPIRE POINTED to first base as the constricted Steelhead fetus slowly unwound himself into a vaguely human shape. It was a scene that Charlie knew all too well; the panic of a projectile suddenly rifling its way directly at you at 97 miles per hour. The formerly friendly object now bearing down upon your sluggish body, red-stitched teeth exposed. The inevitable *thud* pushing the wind from your torso as though it was nothing but a leaky pool toy needing deflating. Sure, he'd live to continue the game, but the Steelhead's eventual hobble as he 'walked it off,' down the first base line, was the march of shame Charlie had lived hundreds of times over.

And yet, for the many, record-breaking times it had happened to him over his career, he'd never experienced what happened next. The umpire pointed at Hayden, then did the same to both benches. "That's a warning to both teams. Next time, you're outta here."

Charlie's jaw had barely had time to drop when Whalen vanished from beside him. The skipper rushed onto the field, fuming. Charlie was certain he'd actually heard his mother's eyes rolling beside him.

Whalen was apoplectic as he reached the batter's box. His face beamed a bright red behind his frame of whiskers as he came within inches of the umpire. "Oh, *come on!* We're four pitches into the game!'

The umpire barely nodded as he adjusted the strap on his face mask. "And your guy can't control himself. It's a warning, both sides."

"I'm sorry," Whalen said, stepping over the body of the winded Steelhead, and gesturing to the plate, "is this *not* the vicinity of where we're chucking baseballs today?"

Charlie nodded to himself in response to this reasonable question but was interrupted by a familiar sound – that of disappointment and fatigue.

"Are you going to talk to your pitcher, Charlie, or would you rather your *mommy* does it?" His mother's tone slid into something especially taunting for these last words.

He stared at her and saw that while she was definitely pushing his buttons, there was no doubt she was moments away from instigating the most embarrassing mound conference of all time. He cleared his throat, hoping the appropriate comeback would appear in his frontal lobe by way of some baseball mysticism. Of course, his wits abandoned him, and so he looked down to his spikes with a sigh, and trotted out, toward the mound.

He gave Whalen a glance, verifying that the debate was still being waged, then turned to his pitcher. A handful of infielders had encircled Hayden, Conestoga wagons surrounding a dying campfire. Windy stepped aside, allowing him entry into the meeting.

"Hey, buddy," he started, wading lightly through the waters of this borderline meltdown. "The arm good?"

Hayden didn't respond, didn't register Charlie's presence at all. Charlie examined him, then tried to follow his terrified gaze, slightly to the side, beyond his infielders. *Ah.* The pitcher was staring at The Franchise, utterly transfixed as the great man joined the mound conference.

Charlie snapped his fingers. "Hello? Hayden?"

The Franchise allowed this for a moment, then turned to the pitcher. "Hey Chief." His voice was calm, but authoritative, and Charlie immediately understood that this bout of Hayden brain-lock was probably a regular occurrence for one of the most famous athletes on the planet. "I know it's a lot of people, but don't let it distract you, okay?"

Hayden remained motionless and unblinking.

The Franchise took his silence in stride and pressed onward. "Remember, you're here for a reason. Just *breathe...* and focus."

Hayden did not respond

"Did you hear what he said, Hayden? Breathe," said Charlie.

On cue, Hayden sucked in a deep, gasping breath, his survival instincts kicking in.

"Atta boy," Charlie reached out to steady him as he staggered backward with the inhalation. He gave him a pat on the back. "There you go."

"You know the book on this guy?" said The Franchise, taking a step toward the pitcher.

Hayden reacted as though the question was a set of verbal headlights. "Th-the book?"

The Franchise nodded. "His tendencies, his trouble spots – how to miss his bat."

As the legend spoke, Charlie could not help but feel a sense of kinship with him; finally, someone who understood what he'd been saying the entire time. *Yes, Hayden,* he thought, *the same book your coach tried to tell you about earlier this week.*

It was with an odd mixture of relief and disappointment that he watched the fireballer struggle to find an answer. "Uh... uh..."

To Charlie's surprise, Hayden turned to him, his face stricken with panic.

Charlie rolled his eyes but was privately elated to finally be considered a resource. "He sits on change-ups." He glanced at the batter's box, where Whalen had begun the process of turning his torso back to the bench while continuing to argue. "Come on, guys, I think the Skipper's about had his say."

Indeed, the initial buzz of excitement the manager had sent across the stands had waned. In Charlie's experience over the past week – brief in time, yet voluminous in regard to Whalen-tantrums – this implied the skipper had surpassed the nose-to-nose lecturing and staccato hat-brim-pulling and was close to spitting his way back to his perch on the steps.

The infielders jogged back to their positions, and Charlie was surprised to see The Franchise lingering beside Hayden.

"Be sure you know the book on these guys," said the legend. Hayden was staring into the unfocused nothingness of the infield grass but seemed to hear the words. He gave a barely perceptible nod. "You might not always need it, but it'll never hurt. Especially when you get called up, right?"

The young pitcher's mouth fell open at the idea.

"Right?" The Franchise repeated glancing at Charlie with a wink.

Hayden looked up at his hero and allowed himself a smile. "Right."

The Franchise grinned back and gave him a slap on the shoulder with his glove. "Good man. Now blow 'em away."

Hayden nodded at him and gathered himself as the first baseman backed his way into position. Charlie turned to rejoin Whalen, the swell of the crowd cheering the future Hall of Famer filling his ears. Charlie had been in the system since he was a teenager and had run into every type of player one could think of. Most were either good-natured and easily washed-out, or borderline psychopaths who did all they could to climb the competitive ladder. He could not recall meeting a single man before now who was both excellent at the game and could graciously offer advice to a young player. It was, in a word, legendary.

CHAPTER 16
Force Play

"YOU KNOW, FOLKS, Manager Gray Whalen and I were talking this afternoon about ol' Number 9's early days in the league. Of course, in those days, ol' Number 9 was known as young Number 74... But if you *really* wanted to count, you could always count on the great man flashing that winning smile. A smile that says, 'Even though I'm just a mouth with teeth, I *admire* you, Dip Lockerbie.'"

This was insanity. Francesca had always entertained the notion, but as this particular tilt wore on through its – what was it? The sixth, possibly seventh inn– Dear god, were they really only *four pitches* in? – the opinion calcified in her mind as a hard fact: Dip Lockerbie had lost his mind and was bounding his way through an alternate reality. There could be no other explanation.

Francesca caught herself here, her background in journalism getting the better of her. Of course there could be another explanation. Perhaps he had taken a few hits of brown acid before donning those ridiculous suspenders and exposing her to another three hours of self-centered monologue? Perhaps. But not likely.

Only now, as the mound conference dispersed, did he begin wrapping up a rumination on a vague time he and The Franchise had crossed paths. The tale had been, in true Lockerbie fashion, long-winded and pointless. It had also walked all over what should have been a gripping back-and-forth between the two of them regarding the hit-by-pitch and warnings issued. Francesca had always tried to respect the cues borne of Dip's decades of experience, but this seemed like a gimme.

If her months with the club had taught her anything, it was that the majority of what they were charged with doing was talking about things that had either happened or could possibly happen. All while a whole lot of *nothing* happened. In a life filled with batters ducking out of the box to strip and adjust their gloves, or the pitcher taking seven years to rub down a ball before he got within a foot of the rubber, it was a gold mine for broadcasters. A series of wild pitches, culminating in the assassination Hayden had just administered, met with the rage of Gray Whalen, all before a rare sellout crowd? That should have been enough fuel to carry them through the third inning with all kinds of talking points and speculations. Of course, that was assuming such a back-and-forth existed between play-by-play and color. As it was, he had now talked over the drama, an entire three-pitch strikeout sequence and the following pitch, which was also a strike. *Goddammit,* she thought. *And now Hayden's on the comeback trail? Shut. Up.*

Dip had successfully turned the moment into a one-man show about how well he knew The Franchise. How he had shaped him as a young player with scads of advice about 'swinging through the ball' and whatnot – elements of the game that, if absent, would be cause for there to be no game whatsoever.

It was with relief that she found a gasp of space as he refilled those endless lungs of his, finally allowing her to do her job. Hayden was now bent, rolling the ball's seams across his fingertips as he stared down J.J.'s signs.

"Hey, that's a point, Dip," she said, her inflection as generous as she could muster. "Meanwhile, we've got ourselves a game as Chandler checks the runner on an 0-2 pitch...He kicks up from the stretch, and..."

"Strike two!" The call was huffed loud enough to be heard through the booth's window. The crowd roared in approval.

Not that Dip noticed. "And what *can't* be admired, when you're talking about a legendary broadcasting figure with more than his share of playing days behind him..."

Francesca turned to him again in disbelief. Was he really talking about himself right now?

"... and a shelf full of local AM radio awards at home..."

Apparently, he was.

He seemed to be speaking from another planet entirely. There was no sign of awareness that the game was quite content to continue being played before he had stopped speaking. "...A fixture in the lives of so many fans, and yet... somehow not enough?"

Francesca frowned as her partner detoured from his detouring. *Have I reached the point where I need to pull the microphone input from its jack without telling him?* She'd considered it many times over the season; the chrome 1/4-inch plug taunted her, so powerful, yet so easily within her grasp.

Hayden hurled another pitch.

"Strike three!"

The fans clapped as Francesca leaned forward, pulled by the thrill of well-played baseball. "Chandler gets him swinging, and it's now two away in the top of the–"

"And at this point, we here in the HerbCo Fishing Supply Studios would like to offer our sincerest hello from AM 1371, to our brethren in the medium of television..."

Francesca's mouth fell open in shock. She'd heard Dip's rants about the uselessness of television broadcasting multiple times since arriving. His anxiety over being replaced by photogenic anchors with flashy chyrons and pitch-tracking graphics was palpable. What was this?

"They're here with us tonight at HerbCo Field," he continued, his voice warm and needlessly pushed. "And one cannot help but notice that, despite outward appearances – of which radio has none – perhaps we are not as different as we seem."

She watched in wary confusion as he leaned toward the booth window, mic stand gripped in his wrinkled hand. She glanced down to see the game proceeding beneath them, but found his eyes were scanning the stadium itself.

"Not that there's anything wrong with AM radio and the theatre of the mind, of course," he said, his voice slowly descending into the mumble of an inner monologue. "But you have *got* to take your hat off to those bold pioneers in the 'video-game,' so to speak." He said this as though he'd finally landed upon an inevitable conclusion to a difficult question. He turned his head, taking in the entire panorama of HerbCo Field, before shaking it in dismay. "And I do *not* see them. Huh."

It was a bridge too far. What if Margaret heard this blatant selling out? Worse, what if this *was* the beginning of a precipitous slide into television broadcasting, blowing her out of the very broadcasting chair she'd only just secured? All because of the delusions of grandeur trapped inside this little man's head? *This* was how their issues were going to be resolved? She dove for the mute button.

"What are you doing?" The plea was forceful enough to grab Dip's attention away from the window. He stared at her, mouth open. His eyes flicked from her desperate face to the button she was holding down, breaking their signal. But he did not respond.

Sensing there would be no adequate explanation mid-inning like this, she released the button. Like a remote-controlled toy, he immediately fell back into his patter.

"You know folks, sometimes a ball trying to find its way out of an infield is not unlike a man trying to find his place in this world..."

Dip trailed off as his eyes continued to wander the stands and concourse. On the field, the umpire called out strike three. Francesca's eyes darted to her scorecard, which she had completely lost track of, then to the scoreboard in left field. Hayden had finally ended the inning. She sighed with relief and took a stab at reclaiming the trappings of a normal game-calling into the mic.

"So, after a wild start, it's four up and three down for Hayden Chandler and the Dead Fish. You're listening to AM 1371, the home of Cape Haddock Coelacanth baseball."

She reached across the board to start the ad break and was caught off guard by Dip vocally meandering over her outro bumper. His voice was dreamy, the mic held loosely and off-center in his hand. "Just where does that buddy, Dip... just where does *he* belong?"

Francesca's head fell as she cut to the commercials. She swiveled her chair at him and whipped her headphones off.

"Okay, Dip, you've been acting weird since we started. What the hell is up." She was borderline furious at his hijacking. He was supposed to be an industry veteran, yet here he was, muttering pure career-climbing fantasy. A thought occurred to her and she leaned toward him, her tone softened. "Hey, is this... is this one of those

'Senior Moments' I've heard about?" The idea tempered her indignation, but only slightly. "The war's over, Dip, I promise."

Dip finally tore his eyes away from the park and turned to her. "No, Frank, you dim-bulb! This isn't about some PBS documentary, it's about *the Network*. They're here, *somewhere* in the building," he said, swinging his hands wildly. The gesture gave the impression that any direction was just as likely as the next to hold double-digits' worth of cable sports personnel. He leaned toward her, his voice creaking like that of a near-dead basset hound. "And I can't find their broadcast desk for the appearance they'll want me to make!"

It seemed there would be no end to the surprises this evening. *This* was the reason for his freak-out? He'd spent the entire afternoon roaming the ballpark in search of the stupid Network crew, and still hadn't run into them?

Dip turned away from her once more, placing his hands on his boney hips, somewhere five inches below the waistline of his trousers. His fedora was cocked back on his forehead, a woolen satellite dish, swiveling left, right, then back again as he continued to examine the stands and concourse. "This is the big time we're talking about, Frank. The kind of time that can make or break a career."

"Kind of like, I don't know, calling a franchise-defining game featuring a future Hall of Famer?" Francesca's patience had nearly waned into nothingness.

"Exactly like that! Only with more bandwidth, more juice to squeeze. All in order to get those big, watery eyeballs fixed on *me*. Me! The Big Dipper! On the air like you've never seen him before!"

Seeing the obsession on his face, she was horrified to realize he absolutely believed everything he said. "Because you've never been seen before. Because you're on the radio."

Dip rubbed his chin, lost in the idea of it all. "Can you imagine the Network landing commentary from Mr. Coelacanth himself? A legend painting a portrait of another legend before a packed house of baseball-loving fanatics?" His eyes were wild, infused with the voltage of self-obsession. "That's like Picasso sketching an insane Van Gogh – at a baseball game! It'd be a ratings bonanza!"

"Dip, we already have a show where you can do that. Be your own bonanza!"

"Dammit, Frank, that show went off the air years ago! Stop talking like a crazy person!"

Francesca's eyes darted down to the board, where the digital readout counted down their final ad. "We're almost out of break. Listen, I *need* you to get a grip, okay?" It was the last drop of legitimate patience she had for him. "This could be the biggest game of our careers, and you going to the parking lot does nothing to–"

Dip grabbed her by the arms and pushed his face close to her own. She was stunned into silence. Not only was the gesture blatantly inappropriate, but it was unheard of for him to acknowledge her physical presence.

"The parking lot?" he breathed, his eyes manic, pleading. "They're in the parking lot? *Tell me!"*

The thought occurred to her that even his inside sources, the remaining vendors and maintenance people he'd worked with for years – decades in some cases – hadn't shared the information with him either. Had the scenario not been about Dip, it would have been the ultimate betrayal. And for a moment, she felt bad for him.

"Well, yeah..." she said, watching the desperation flood his face. His eyes were bulging, his mouth open. She wondered if he was going to cry. "They've got a big truck out there that becomes a stage for the broadcast–"

And like that, the moment was gone. His face slid effortlessly back into a seething mask of one who would stop at nothing to get what he felt was rightfully his. He released her from his grip, practically pushing her away as he turned back to the window and stared through to the playing field. "Frank, I can't listen to you *droning* anymore. I'm needed on set!"

He tossed his headphones aside, then grabbed his jacket and straightened the brim of his fedora with a snap of the wrist.

Francesca shot a panicked look at the board as he turned to the door. The ad was almost over, to be followed by a ten second station identification, and then... nothing? "Dip, the break–"

He spun and pointed at her. "You'd better believe the system's broken, you seat-stealing pirate! And *that's* why I'm needed in the parking lot!"

It was one of the most Lockerbie-things he'd ever proclaimed. Francesca was too flabbergasted by the stupidity of it all to respond.

His jaw fixed with determination, he spun on his heel and exited. She watched as the door closed slowly amidst the low hiss of its pneumatics, allowing her a final glimpse of him practically leaping down the staircase before it finally clicked shut.

She stood frozen for a moment, flabbergasted by this sudden turn of events. Her internal broadcasting clock, ever vigilant of the possibility of dead air, snapped her out of the daze. She turned to see the break light on the mixing board flashing. She fell into her chair and put her headphones back on as the On-Air light flashed. In the moment before her mic went live, it began to sink in that there were hundreds, if not thousands of people who were waiting to hear what happened next. Waiting for *her*.

She inhaled, gathering herself, then leaned into the mic.

"Hey there folks! We are back, and we are... talking about this baseball game." She rolled her eyes at the misstep but soldiered on.

Be compelling! Margaret Tinley's words echoed through her head.

"This is *Francesca* Moretti, and *this* is Cape Haddock Coelacanth baseball!"

CHAPTER 17
Buffering

CHARLIE WANTED TO focus – was desperate to focus. The team *needed* him to focus. He couldn't help but feel that his pushing of cold, undeniable data had possibly earned a crumb of their respect. In the big picture this was almost nothing, an ephemeral scrap. But he was hellbent on hanging onto that scrap and tending to it with the hope it might one day grow into something else.

But there could be no way for him to do that if he couldn't concentrate. And there would be no concentration while his mother remained perched beside him on the dugout steps. His eyes darted to the side at the sound of her muttering. There she stood, baseball's mindful gargoyle, cursing at her cell phone in a way usually reserved for a slow waitstaff. He considered helping her but knew this was typically the last thing she was looking for.

"Dammit all!" she finally shouted. She elbowed him in the ribs. "Charlie, I need help with my streaming."

He glanced at Whalen and saw the manager's eyes go wide before quickly falling back into a neutral concentration on the field.

Margaret held the phone out to him, sighing in exasperation.

"Mom, I told you, you have to open the app. It says 'game-stream' right on it."

She scowled at the home screen. "Good lord. I didn't pay for an 'app,' I paid for a game-stream!"

"It's the same thing, Mom. An app is an application. For the game-stream."

From the stands came the sounds of their fanbase's emotional whiplash. The crowd groaned as Windy grounded out, then reversed course into ecstatic cheering as Javier stepped from the on-deck circle and lumbered toward the batter's box.

Windy shuffled into the dugout and shelved his helmet. "Booger's throwing salt pellets today, Skip."

Whalen grunted in agreement. "Next time, I guess."

Yes, who could have predicted that a fastball pitcher would throw fastballs in the first inning, Charlie thought, shaking his head.

Beside him, Margaret was now violently shaking the phone. "This stupid piece of– oh, here it is." Charlie nodded to himself as she selected the app icon. He wondered if a small part of him was dying inside but dropped the thought at the sound of a familiar voice. His now-favorite voice.

From the phone's speaker came the tinny sound of Francesca, delivering the streaming broadcast. *"...and there's one away for Splake pitcher, Boog Altamont. And just listen to these fans as they cheer on the big man coming to the plate, Javier Coronado..."*

Charlie was impressed; one, that she was getting to say anything, and two, that she seemed to be doing it quite well.

He was surprised to note his mother frowning at the voice. She pressed the phone against her head as the crowd applauded Javier. "Moretti? Oh, what the hell is this..."

"Not bad, huh Mom?"

"Exactly – it's very good. Which means something's amiss." Margaret turned to stare up at the broadcast booth. Her eyes narrowed as she tried to make out who might be inside. Francesca's play-by-play continued to blare from the palm of her hand.

"...Coronado comes into this game hitting .386, leading the league, in fact..."

Margaret turned back to the field and seized Charlie's sleeve. "I have to check on something. Don't you even *think* about doing anything without Whalen's supervision."

She turned and stormed through the dugout door and into the tunnel. The sound of her shoes slapping against the concrete slowly faded, and he turned to find Whalen staring at him, one bushy eyebrow raised.

Charlie shook his head. "She's, ah... well, you know how she gets."

Whalen grunted but continued to eye him. It was starting to make Charlie uncomfortable.

"You know, I can do... whatever it is I wanna do," he said, flailing. "Okay?"

There was a twinkle in Whalen's eye that suggested to Charlie that maybe the skipper wasn't taking him as seriously as Charlie would like.

No sooner had the thought crossed his mind, then the old man turned back to the game. He spat and cleared his throat. "You spend a lot of time with your Ma, huh?"

It couldn't really be denied, no matter how much he wished otherwise. "Sometimes it feels like it's all the time." He turned to Whalen, suddenly suspicious. Was this some old-school mind game? A 1970s version of 'Your Mom' jokes? "Why?"

"Ah, no reason," Whalen said with a wave. "But... you are gonna get your own place here, right? Once you've settled in?"

"Oh." This was unanticipated. "Well, I hadn't really thought about it. Been kind of a crazy week. Why do you ask?"

"I don't know," Whalen shrugged, "you might like it, is all. You could stay up late... have your radio-buddy over... Make your own decisions..."

It felt a little like the manager was talking about a middle school slumber party, but Charlie couldn't be sure; he'd never had one. Yet the point was clear and not without merit. "That does sound pretty good..."

Whalen shrugged again. "Definitely worth considering. I know it's what I'd do."

MARGARET BURST INTO the booth, breathing heavily from her run up the staircase. Francesca swiveled her chair to face the door. Despite the dramatic entrance, she tried to remain focused and deliver serviceable, running commentary of the game action.

"And Altamont continues delivering a healthy diet of off-speed pitches to the middle of the Coelacanth lineup..."

Margaret stared at her and gestured to Dip's empty seat. Was that... *shock* on the unflappable Black Widow's face? Francesca shrugged in response, gave a nervous smile, and spun back to the game.

"Altamont comes set... here's the windup, and... *swing and a miss – he got him on strikes!* So, the Coelacanths threaten with a couple of walks, but do not score in the bottom of the first. It's AM 1371 and we'll be back after this."

Francesca cued the commercials and turned to Margaret as she took off her headphones. "Um... hi."

Margaret's hands again flew in the direction of Dip's vacant seat. *"Where is Lockerbie?"*

"I don't know," said Francesca, shrugging. "He kept talking about the stupid Network and ran out of here like a kid joining the circus!"

"Good lord," Margaret muttered, crossing to the booth's window and staring out at the concourse. "Well, that's the last we'll see of the Network."

Francesca waited for more of... anything. Instructions? Pity? A solid dressing-down for her probable incompetence? Not only could she not get a word in while doing a job that was wholly predicated on her getting words in, she couldn't even keep track of her co-worker. *If I was her, I'd probably fire me. Or at least demote me to the peanut stand.*

"Mrs. Tinley," she said, "what do you want me to do here?"

She was surprised when the owner waved her off with barely a glance. "You're fine, Moretti. I wouldn't have hired you if I didn't think you could do it."

Relief flooded Francesca's brain, but she was quickly drawn back into the immediacy of the situation by what came next. "It's the market share that worries me," Margaret said, her lips pursed as she mulled the situation. "Sure, you've got the young people and women, but who speaks to the Lockerbie crowd?"

Francesca nodded, trying to trace Margaret's logic. "By which you mean... the older folks who fish and are afraid of the future?"

"Exactly! They're a huge part of our audience, and they hate young, cute things like you."

Francesca checked the board and reaffixed her headphones. "We're almost out of break."

"Well, try to be old-timey!" said Margaret, looking to the mixing board with concern. "Talk about pension plans. And modesty!"

Francesca gave her a look as the feed went live. She was underqualified for most of these demands, and the jury was still out on her modesty, but she would try her damnedest to please Margaret. She leaned into the mic.

"Howdy folks." Her voice came out in an inexplicable, lazy drawl. She was already into the next sentence by the time she realized what she was doing. "This here's Francesca Moretti, and welcome back to a... a modest game of Coelacanth baseball–"

With a groan, Margaret reached over and punched the mute button. "I said 'old-timey,' not 'Western!'" she hissed.

"Westerns *are* old-timey!" Francesca hissed back, frantically waving her off the mute. Margaret rolled her eyes but leaned away from the board.

And at that moment, Francesca had a brilliant idea. Margaret wanted something compelling?

"And folks, we've got quite a treat for you, as we're joined by a very special guest..."

She could see the realization dawning on Margaret's face in her periphery.

Well, this could easily blow up in my face, Francesca considered, forging ahead. "That's right, we're here with the owner and general manager of your Cape Haddock Coelacanths: Margaret Tinley. Welcome to the show, Margaret!"

Margaret leaned over her, and slowly shook her head. She mouthed a word: *'No.'*

Oh yes. Francesca flashed her winningest smile, then nodded her boss to Dip's abandoned chair. It was a bold gambit, she knew. But she also knew that Margaret Tinley was not a woman to back away from a challenge. Francesca grabbed Dip's microphone desk stand and tossed it to Margaret, who caught it awkwardly.

"And thanks for joining us up here in the broadcast booth tonight, we certainly know how busy you must be."

Without missing a beat, Margaret sneered at her, and slipped into a radio-friendly purr. "Well, thank you for having me, Francesca. It's a real baseballer's delight to be with you here at HerbCo Field." Her words flowed effortlessly, as though she'd been addressing fans at home for years. "You know, it's the ideal place for a family outing or romantic evening for two, wouldn't you say? And who could beat the fabulous block-ticketing available for corporate outings, on-sale now at the box office or on our new interwebbing homepage."

She cocked an eyebrow at her broadcaster, and gingerly placed the second set of headphones over her ears. Then, as though it was the most natural thing in the world, she slid into Dip's seat and began adjusting her monitor levels.

Francesca grinned at her. "That's quite a bargain, Margaret, and that is *terrific* news to hear that the team is taking the bold step into the online world of the Twentieth Century!"

Margaret rolled out a perfectly timed chuckle. "Too true! It's like we're Wrigley Field, finally getting lights for night games. It's an historic moment for our team – not unlike this very broadcast."

It was a dream come true. Margaret was playing the role immaculately, better than Dip ever had or could. Good-natured. Generous. 'Our team.' And a setup Francesca could not fail to knock down.

"It's a great point, Margaret, and we would like to say a special AM 1371 hello to the people who actually matter: you folks at home, listening on the dial, and now, on your computers, tablets, and smartphones. Welcome to our first online streaming broadcast, another truly noteworthy moment for the Coelacanth franchise." Margaret smiled and mimed a small motion of applause. *Yes, this was a good idea.* "And speaking of the future of the franchise, we've heard more than our share about our future Hall of Famer tonight, but what are you seeing from Hayden Chandler?"

Margaret gazed out at the on-field action. "Now, he's the young man on the mound, correct?"

Francesca nodded, trying to mentally project encouragement her way. "He is your pitcher, that is correct, Margaret."

"Please, call me Maggie. And from what I've seen so far, it seems like Chandler is being absolutely *merciless* with the zone. He's been subtly expanding its boundaries in concert with some of catcher J.J. Pike's pitch-framing and establishing the location of his fastballs with surgical precision. All of which has been tracked as one of our primary metrics of choice for his model of power pitcher."

Francesca shot her a look of disbelief then flashed a thumbs-up.

Margaret continued. "He's been mixing his pitches favorably and has maintained a steady lead in the count, despite the scuffling start."

Francesca couldn't help herself. She muted their mics and gazed admiringly across the console. "You're *amazing!*"

The corner of Margaret's mouth twitched into a rare half-smile. "I know."

CHAPTER 18
Stringing Some Hits Together

THE CLATTER OF spikes on concrete filled the dugout as Charlie intercepted Javier on his way to the on-deck circle. With his helmet on and bat leaning up against his shoulder, the young man looked practically heroic. Despite his bulk, he moved with an ease and power that suggested he was about to knock down the walls of Troy with line drives on the field of battle.

"Hey, Coach," said Javier, giving him a curious look.

Charlie gave him a slap on the arm. "How you doing, buddy? You feel good? You know what to do?"

Javier nodded. "Sí. You want me to hit the ball a long way, right?"

Charlie gave him an embarrassed smile. "Yeah, actually, that's pretty much it." *So much for inspirational coaching – this guy should be coaching* me.

Thunder boomed overhead, drawing their attention skyward. Javier looked down at him with a mischievous grin, then strode to the batter's box. He was all confidence as he hefted his bat and dug in. The roar of the crowd reaffirmed that this giant was now in control of the game.

"AND THAT MASSIVE ovation can only mean one thing. Here's the big man, Javier Coronado, who drew a walk his first time at bat. Margaret, what can you tell us about Javi? What does he bring to the team that's so special?"

Margaret studied the explosive reaction in the stands with a small smirk of approval. "Francesca, it's very simple: he brings the *hits* to this team."

"Quite a powerhouse, isn't he?"

The owner nodded. "I mean, quite literally, there is a very low probability we would have any hits without him!"

BOOG ALTAMONT DID his best to keep a steady game face as he toed the slab and leaned in for his signs, but there was no mistaking the string of oaths and curses he had mouthed at Javier's approach. With an almost mechanical motion that suggested he just wanted to get the at-bat over with, he wound up and delivered.

Javier's swing moved the atmosphere over the batter's box like the meteor that killed the dinosaurs had once moved an ocean. The barrel of the bat meeting with the ball created the sound of a bone being snapped in two.

The crowd exploded with manic cheering and stood as one to witness the ball sailing into the upper deck behind right field. Javier began circling the bases as thunder boomed across the sky, echoing his handiwork.

"AND THERE'S A moonshot from Coronado!"

This was fantastic. Not only was Francesca living the opportunity of a lifetime, but the team was actually doing something interesting. It was a fascinating change from the routine of either losing, or having the opposing teams defeat themselves. The Coelacanths never truly 'won.' It was a side effect of some other player's fuck-up. But tonight, something felt different. Maybe it was The Franchise gracing them with his gifts and charisma, or maybe it was the full house. Hell, maybe it was having her boss not only staring over her shoulder, but actively rooting her on. Whatever it was, Javier Coronado had just electrified the yard in a way not seen since Tesla.

She turned to Margaret, who was watching the victory lap. A thin smile stole across her face. "Well! There are no doubters, and then there are *no doubters.* That was one of the longest home runs I've seen in the ballpark this season, Maggie. And by one of our own players, no less!"

Margaret shook her head in awe. "He is *absolutely* worth every last lobster."

It was an odd bit of color, but Francesca rolled with it. "I don't know what that means, but I do know the Coelacanths have taken a 1-0 lead in the top of the third. And everyone's getting a side of mashed taters down in Fish Town!"

THE DUGOUT WAS going bananas as Javier trotted down the steps to receive his high-fives. He'd rounded the bags at a leisurely pace; it may not have been Cadillacking, but he had barely broken a sweat. The fans had loved it. Likewise, Charlie had never seen the players so excited to be there. They were shouting. They were smiling. they were... doing some kind of choreographed dance? They were engaged.

Whalen looked over and grinned at the sight of Charlie shaking his head in disbelief. "You all right there, Coach?"

Charlie tilted his hat up higher on his brow. "Yeah, I just... I've never seen us actually *winning* before!"

Whalen chuckled and gave him a slap on the back. "Well, don't pop that champagne just yet, buddy. We've still got six more innings to screw it up."

As the words left his mouth, the crowd rose as one. They turned as the volume of the ballpark went from ecstatic home run aftershock murmurings, to that of jet engines being primed. Charlie and Whalen turned back to the field as The Franchise made his way to the batter's box.

"Goddamn," said Whalen, shaking his head at the din. "It's like Ringo just showed up!"

FRANCESCA STRAIGHTENED IN her seat. This was it, the big moment. A moment that should have happened in the first inning but was muted by Dip talking about a time he had played golf two parties behind The Franchise at a charity outing. The at bat had turned into a four-pitch walk, and she had been unable to call any of them. The weight of thousands of faceless people listening to her tell the tale of this second opportunity fell upon her, and she did her best to rise to the occasion.

"And here he is, folks. Worth more than the price of admission–" Margaret shot her a look of caution. "–arguably, of course. And if you can't tell by the love he is receiving from this crowd right now... well, quite simply, he *is* The Franchise."

Margaret picked up on the cue like a seasoned pro. "No question about it, Francesca. And we in the organization are so proud that he's a part of our legacy."

"The Coelacanth faithful seem to agree as the no-doubt Hall of Famer steps into the box and gives the nod to Splake pitcher, Boog Altamont."

She paused, feeling the stage was appropriately set. The ambience of the moment filtered over the airwaves and tore through the fiber optics of the northeast. Altamont delivered from the wind-up with impeccable timing, and The Franchise promptly laced it up the middle.

"And there's a base hit into center field!" Francesca called out over the roar of the stands. The Splake second baseman and shortstop converged in the awkward dance of outstretched arms as the ball bounced hard into center field. The concourse was practically shaking beneath the broadcast booth, and Francesca responded in kind. "Suddenly the Coelacanths have got something cooking on the base paths!"

"Why, this is quite novel, isn't it?" Margaret added, applauding lightly. "How marvelous."

Francesca grinned at the sight: The queen of the park, giving her nod of approval as one of the greatest to ever play the game smiled from his station at first base. If only the Network had been in their booth to catch it.

As The Franchise stripped off his batting gloves, the crowd's ovation escalated. Charlie thought he saw him laugh as he looked to the crowd. The umpire crew didn't seem to be in a hurry to take their positions, almost seemed to be waiting for something. As the home plate ump called for fresh balls, The Franchise removed his helmet and held it up in tribute to the fans for a fraction of a second. He grinned sheepishly as they ate it all up in what was probably the most exciting moment any of them could remember seeing in the recent history of HerbCo Field.

Charlie could feel the energy pulsating as this unprecedented display of consistent baseball unfolded around him. It was his first taste of what it would feel like to be a legitimate winner. The punishing drudgery of July dog-day baseball was far more compelling when your team had a chance. And as strange as it was to consider, they'd now had a couple of chances. With an opportunity for another.

The Franchise stuffed his helmet back onto his head and took a healthy lead off the bag. J.J. walked from the on-deck circle to the box, his face blank. Charlie wondered if he too was rediscovering that same feeling of competition that had allegedly died in him seasons ago.

Beside him, Whalen clapped twice. "Come on now, Pikey, make him work for it!"

"Let's keep it going, J.J.! You got this, you *got it!*" Charlie added, drawing a curious look from the skipper.

"You know he's gonna hate that, right?"

Charlie shrugged. "He doesn't listen to me anyway."

Altamont dipped into the stretch, gave his catcher a curt nod, and came set. His eyes slid to the side, eyeing The Franchise. For a moment, Charlie wondered if Altamont might make a throw to first. It would have been outrageous, but not unheard of. This flicker of tension quickly vanished as the pitcher kicked and pushed off the rubber.

Charlie could tell J.J. had a bead on it from the moment it left Altamont's hand. He had to reach for it, but the fastball sat fat at the beltline on the outside black. He connected with an easy stroke. The bench exploded as the ball sailed to the power gap in left-center.

"I can't believe it!" Charlie shouted. He found himself jumping up and down, using Whalen for leverage. "They're actually *stringing hits together!* And we might push some runs across the plate!"

Whalen shook his head at the bush league enthusiasm but couldn't disguise the smile that was slipping out beneath his mustache.

"AND THERE'S A line drive into the gap of left-center field, and this will roll all the way to the wall!" Francesca could feel the adrenaline of the moment coursing through her vocal cords. *This is so compelling,* she thought, watching as the dribbling ball was snagged and relayed back to the infield. The Franchise flew around the bases, showing no sign of slowing.

Margaret sat quietly, watching it all play out, but Francesca couldn't believe what she was seeing. *Is he trying to score from first?* He'd had a great lead, but this was going to be close. And close meant something thrilling was about to happen.

"And look who's rounding third, demanding a play at the plate!"

THE COELACANTHS SHOUTED encouragement from the dugout as The Franchise bore down on the plate. Charlie bounced with every footfall of the great man, his fist clenched around Whalen's sleeve. He was drunk on the moment. It was a rare delirium that only appeared when the cosmos aligned, and the magic of the game engaged to stamp itself into the ages.

Whalen was hollering as Charlie had never seen him before. *"Get down, 9! Get down!"*

This only ends one way, Charlie thought, his breath trapped in his chest.

The crowd was in a frenzy. The Franchise was locked in on the plate, focused on achieving this one thing.

Yes, yes, yes...

The Franchise slid feet-first as the Steelhead catcher simultaneously received the ball from the cutoff man. He turned his lower half to drop his left leg over the chalk-smeared basepath.

The impact of cleat on body armor cracked like thunder across the ballpark. It arced over the sound of the unified fan-voice, a cold slap in the face. The roar fell before the call did, a dying turbine, melting down as the shock of the collision sank into the wet concrete of reality. The two players collapsed into a heap of tangled limbs with such force that the entire ballpark seemed to recoil in horror. Charlie's jaw dropped.

"...NO."

The home plate umpire watched the scene unfold, hesitated for a fraction of a second to verify his own instincts, then jabbed downward with his fist.

"You're outta there!"

The Coelacanths' outrage was mirrored by the boos that began raining down from the crowd. Whalen exploded from the top step, shoving his face into the umpire's, his chest puffed out like a grouse on the strut. Charlie had never seen him so irate. "Are you *kidding me!?"*

"Whalen, he was out by a mile!"

Whalen waved his arms, gesturing to the Splake catcher. "And this guy might as well have pitched a tent and chopped some firewood, he was so camped-out in front of that plate! Where's my guy supposed to go, huh? Where's he supposed to go!?"

Meanwhile, The Franchise remained on the ground, clutching his ankle in agony. Charlie and the other Coelacanths rushed to his aid. The Franchise groaned as they helped him sit up.

Charlie did not like the anguish he was seeing on their star's face. "How's it feel? You think you can put any weight on it?"

The Franchise waved him off, gritting his teeth as he stretched to cradle his ankle. "Nah – I'm done, Coach."

"No way, buddy, we'll get you all patched up and you'll be back out here in no time." *Surely the team trainer left some cloth bandages around somewhere in the clubhouse,* Charlie considered. *It's not like he was packing big armfuls of medical supplies into a steamer trunk when he was let go.* Charlie wondered if he would know how much pressure to put on the wrapping but was pulled from this mental diagnosis as The Franchise grabbed him by the forearm.

"I really don't think so, Charlie. It definitely feels broken – I can tell." Charlie's insides lost cabin pressure as he absorbed the first baseman's pained expression. He was very much not a doctor, but even he knew there would be no amount of gauze to relieve the first baseman's pain for another four or five innings. "I'm out," The Franchise said, taking away any doubt. "I'm out of the game."

Charlie motioned to the other Coelacanths hovering nearby. "Windy, Javi – help him up and get him back into the clubhouse, huh?"

They righted The Franchise, balancing him on their shoulders, and hobbled off the field together while the crowd applauded. Charlie was thankful that the fans probably wouldn't hear the undoubtedly bleak diagnosis of their favorite player until after the game had wound to its conclusion. If the injury was as bad as it seemed, the shockwave would drastically rearrange the landscape of the baseball world. And he had a good idea who would take much of the blame.

AS SHE ALLOWED herself to take a breath, Francesca began sorting through this recent sequence of events. The swing in emotion from pure elation to misery had been hard, a corner taken too quickly. Only now, when The Franchise had been ushered off the field, did the harsh reality begin to settle, a slowly descending mist of despair. This was nothing short of calamitous.

She gave herself a moment to decide on an approach. It was a devastating blow; forget Cape Haddock, this was catastrophic for an entire era of baseball. She would have to get this feeling across without plunging the coastline into season-ending despair for the rest of the summer and fall.

"And there's a terrific standing ovation from this sellout crowd as the living legend is helped off the field by his new teammates." This was good – spin the bad news into something complimentary of the fans. Acknowledge, but don't wallow – that wasn't going to be good for anyone. She decided to punt to her co-host, who undoubtedly had her own thoughts on the matter. "Maggie, as the owner and general manager, this *has* to be difficult to witness, correct?"

There was no response from the seat next to her.

"Margaret?"

Francesca turned to find the owner staring blankly at the scene unfolding on the field. Her mouth was agape in a rare moment of shock. A fresh rush of adrenaline shot through Francesca at the sight of this freeze-up. This was not good.

Francesca muted their mics and leaned closer to her. "Hey, are you okay?"

Margaret's thoughts seemed to be in another dimension. Without looking at Francesca, the words fell out, slightly above a whisper: "We broke him. We *broke* The Franchise."

WHALEN WAS IN rare, explosive form. "Where's he's supposed to go, huh!? You tell me, Professor!"

It was unquestionably the most grandiose display he'd put forth during this first week of Charlie's tenure. The home plate umpire, for his part, looked more exhausted than anything else. His crew was equally disinterested, as they huddled together by second base, chatting as the impending storm whipped at their black windbreakers.

The home plate ump checked his count-indicator handset. "He's out Gray."

"He's out when I *say* he's out!" the volcanic manager fumed. It was an incoherent bit of rage, but the feeling was there.

The ump drew himself to his full height, the chest protector beneath his jacket lending him a gigantic breadth. He pointed his mask at the skipper. *"Sit down,* Whalen. Let's get this in before the sky dumps half an ocean on us."

It was almost as simple as that. The umpire was just about to pull his facemask down, when Whalen ran home the final nail into his own coffin. "Yeah, well, keep the mask up and maybe it'll wash some of the ugly off that mess you call a face."

The umpire looked back at him, his expression one of disbelief. This was short-lived. His brow became furrowed, and he threw his hand in the general direction of the locker rooms.

"You're outta here!"

And like that, it was over. The ump pulled his mask down and stomped toward the plate. The boos of the crowd swung wildly into ecstatic cheers as Whalen scowled back and gave the chalk line a proper kicking.

SEEN FROM ABOVE and removed from the immediacy of ground level, Whalen's ousting was, as always, amusing to behold. Francesca nodded as she prepared to relay the information across the airwaves and was encouraged by the familiarity of the moment. Whalen being tossed from the game was a time-honored tradition. Sure, it was usually over the top, but she admired how it always seemed to get the crowd back into things. True to form, the fans were eating it up, and it seemed as though the injury would soon be displaced by the memory of an outstanding eruption. It wasn't *just* The Franchise's ankle being shattered on a close play at the plate; things were *happening* in this ballgame.

She glanced at Margaret, who sat expressionless, staring at the face of her phone as it flashed text after text and incoming call after incoming call. The owner's eyes darted up to Francesca, then back to the device. She made no motion to answer.

The distant figure of Whalen gave one last sequence of barks over his shoulder as he crossed the third base line, cueing Francesca's commentary. "And here's hoping that Whalen got his money's worth, because he has been tossed out of this game. Drama is afoot in Cape Haddock!"

Margaret continued to eye the erupting phone, gingerly placing it on the desk in front of her as though it had recently been dusted with arsenic. "A classic Whalen-move, Francesca."

Applause and whistles came through the booth window as Whalen finally got his last words in. Francesca hoped The Network was getting plenty of close-ups. "And what an ovation for the skipper as he heads to the showers and hands the reins over to his bench coach–"

The reality of this circumstance suddenly came to life in her head as she said it. Yes, things were definitely happening in this game.

WHALEN STORMED THROUGH the dugout, toward the tunnel. He paused at the bottom of the steps to slap the lineup card into Charlie's waiting palm.

Charlie shook his head at the inevitable. "Thanks."

"Yeah, yeah..." Whalen said, waving Charlie off as he departed. He plunged into the darkness of the tunnel. Charlie watched as a lighter was sparked, briefly illuminating the skipper's silhouette, and then all was black.

Just like the sky, thought Charlie. *Just like my future.*

"AND IN THE midst of this chaos, here's a fun fact: Acting-manager-in-charge, Charlie Conroy, is actually your son, isn't he, Maggie? That must be fun for you guys!"

Francesca turned to Margaret for her breezy reply, but found the owner's headphones abandoned and seat empty. A pang of panic hit Francesca's insides as she looked behind her to find the owner pacing, phone pressed against her ear.

"You people know I can't control that – he's the catcher, he's *supposed* to stand there!" She turned and found Francesca staring at her expectantly. "Hm? Oh." She leaned over to her mic, her tone once again perfectly modulated for the broadcast. "Yes, I'm very proud, Francesca – he's a good boy and he tries hard, and he shows up on time every day, so... there you go."

She reached across the board and muted the microphones. She held up her phone. "It's the Franchise." Francesca made no attempt at disguising her confusion. Margaret lowered her voice. "I mean the GM of the *actual* Franchise."

"Oh sh–" Francesca stopped herself on the verge of breaking broadcasting's cardinal rule of never cursing in the booth. She winced at Margaret, who looked as shaken as Francesca had ever seen her. "Ouch."

"He is not happy." Margaret shook her head and straightened as she returned the phone to her ear. "Hello? Yes, our trainers will take care of it..." She shrugged as Francesca raised an eyebrow at this. "No, it's an *actual* hurricane – there are no helicopters back to the city!"

Francesca did not envy her but knew that the game would not be calling itself. She reopened the feed and adopted her most serious tone.

"And so, it looks like we'll be able to return you to normal play shortly, where the fate of the entire game now rests within the steel-trap mind... of Charlie Conroy."

CHAPTER 19
Hurricane Chandler

AS THE WIND grabbed the loose, wax paper wrappings of hot dogs gone by and hurled them across the field like flimsy missiles, Charlie considered his options. Maybe this unmitigated catastrophe was for the best? Sure, he could see his mother handing him his walking papers as a token gesture to the Big Club. Their affiliate status would have to be maintained at all costs if the Coelacanth 'business empire' was to survive. And sure, he'd never find work in the game again. Most teams would not look kindly on their best players being placed under the tutelage of a man notorious for having negative on-field talent and was destroyer of one of the all-time greats. You might as well charter the plane that took down Roberto Clemente for the next season's road trips.

Whalen would probably be removed as well; if anyone was worth two lifers losing their jobs, it was The Franchise. It couldn't just be a fall guy, it would have to be multiple fall-persons. Not only would the league call for it, but the fans would be out for blood as well. And typically, if the fans wanted something, they got it. That said, Whalen would probably be allowed to retire with full honors, so that was something. Perhaps they'd go into business together. Maybe they'd open a dive like Snooze Lagoon's.

Charlie stared out blankly at the field, detaching from his angst long enough to note that Terry Arnold's crepe paper bunting was now damp and shredded from the wind. It whipped violently against the front of the upper deck, looking like the tattered canvas sails of the

Flying Dutchman. In the outfield, the four playoff flags his father had won mirrored the repurposed party decorations, snapping and pulling against their halyards as though trying to escape the Coelacanth organization completely. Charlie couldn't blame them.

On the bright side, he would have some time to figure out what he was going to do with himself in the later innings of his life. He'd spend time on his resume, which was dangerously short, but at least his time with the Coelacanths was short enough to not even include. Otherwise, he would do his best to spin what he could into something that sounded useful. He could never give his playing stats, that was for sure, but his consistency would be hard to deny. He'd even earned a record for his attendance, much to Kurf Plunkett's chagrin. And his terrible nickname: The Starch Man. He wondered if resumes traditionally included a section for nicknames – he'd never written one.

Just as his thoughts wandered to what the maximum allowance for font size was, he was shaken from his self-loathing death spiral by an anemic ringing sound. It was startling in how ancient it sounded in a world of bleeps, bleats, and bloops. He looked for Windy, assuming the young man had found some soundbite from an old movie but found him futzing with his warmup donut in the on-deck circle.

The ring came again, and he turned to find it coming from the bullpen phone. *So, it* does *work,* he marveled as an actual, analog bell sounded from within the battered box the handset hung on. Curious, and seeing nobody else caring to answer, he did so himself.

"Uh... hello?"

"Charlie!" The voice sounded as though the call was coming from the center of a sandstorm, but the grouchy, impatient tone was unmistakably Whalen.

"Skipper?" What was this? *Does Whalen have a cell phone?* He couldn't remember ever seeing him use one, nor could he think of any reason why he'd ever need it.

"Didn't I tell you that phone was for incoming calls only?" said the manager. "Yeah, it's Whalen – go!"

"Oh." Charlie was unsure of how to proceed. "Well, you called me, so– wait, where are you calling from?" *Can smartphones order cigarettes?*

"That's the bullpen phone, poindexter – where do you think?"

As Charlie pieced this together, a roar came from the fans in the seats surrounding left field. He wheeled around to see what the commotion was about and spotted a familiar figure hanging over the bullpen wall.

"No…"

With the same sense of the miraculous that had accompanied his namesake's rediscovery off the coast of South Africa in 1938, the bulging-eyed form of Steve-O-Canth the Coelacanth stared at the home team's dugout. The bullpen phone was held against his padded cheek and Charlie swore he could see a thin trail of smoke snaking its way from the costume's mouth.

"Skip, is that *you?*"

"Yeah, the fossil record's bullshit, Conroy!" came the response as the Steve-O-Canth saluted him.

The fans in the corner were pointing, doubled over with joy at the sight of the beloved mascot sneaking around his own ballpark. Charlie thought he saw the manager waving them off, but this only sent them into further gales of cheering and laughter.

"But they ran you, Skip! If we get caught, the team's hosed!"

"Charlie, if the umps start worrying about what's going on under the dome of every team mascot, then the whole goddamned game's in trouble. This is just that 'edge' I was talking about!" Charlie nodded – this made a very Whalen-kind of sense. "Now, shut up and listen," said the manager. "You want to win this game, right?"

Charlie wondered if this was a trick question. *Why would he try to trick me like this, it doesn't make any sense. Is* that *the trick?* He shook the paranoia from his mind. "Well… well, yeah, that'd be great!"

"Uh-huh," said Whalen. "You're a numbers man, right? Do the numbers 4 and 11 mean anything to you?"

Charlie racked his brain. Every stat, every batting average of the past 100 years flew through his head as he sought what the old man was talking about. *4 and 11? But not 411? 11-4?* Was it a score? There was no time to consult his binders. "I don't think I'm following you, Skip. 4 and 11?"

Whalen chuckled. "All right, genius, listen close: According to official big league baseball rule number 4.11, a game can be called 'complete' during a rainout if the home team is ahead after four-and-a-half innings."

Charlie was baffled – what the hell was the old man talking about? He ducked his head out from beneath the dugout overhang to check the sky. "But Skipper, it's not raining yet!"

"I know that, dummy!" His disgust was palpable. "But the radar I just looked at on your Ma's computer in the clubhouse gives us about five minutes before the sky decides it's to hell with us, you read me?"

"Whoa." Charlie was taken aback by this news. "You know how a computer works?"

"Yeah, yeah, let's not make a big deal out of it."

"And here I was, thinking you didn't do email–"

"I get it, you goof, it's all very amusing." Whalen's exasperated sigh crackled down the old phone line, but there was no mistaking the deliberate calculation in his tone for what followed. "Don't forget: it's *all on the scoreboard.*"

Charlie squinted across the grass at the tiny figure behind the left field wall. There, in the distance, Whalen the Coelacanth pointed a fin at him, then jabbed it up at the scoreboard looming over his head. Charlie stared at it as the skipper's plot slowly sank in.

"It's the bottom of the fourth…"

"Yeah, and we're *winning.*"

"But you don't mean–"

"Yeah, actually I do," said Whalen. "So, listen: Snemmens is gonna strike out, Windy'll probably swing at the first pitch and bounce it right into the second baseman's glove, so you just need to talk to Javi."

Charlie frowned. Whalen was good, but this was asking for a lot of variables to line up. "You really think it'll be that easy?"

He looked over to the batter's box, where Snemmens the shortstop stood, awkward and free-swinging as Altamont blew gas right past him.

The umpire turned to gesture an emphatic, "Strike *three!*"

"Oh." Charlie watched as Snemmens passed Windy on his way to the plate. The Steelhead infield began to shift to the right side of the diamond. It was bone-chilling in its familiarity. He raised the receiver back to his mouth. "Uh, Skip, I gotta call you back."

"Yep."

The line went dead, and Charlie bashed the handset back onto the cradle. He rushed over to Javier, now poised on the top step, about to walk to the on-deck circle.

"Javi, wait!"

Javier turned to him with a grin. "It's okay, Coach, I know what to do–"

"No, no, no..." Charlie grabbed his arm as the big man took a slow-motion chop with his bat. "No, this time – this *one* time – we need you to *not* get a hit. You understand?"

Javier examined him. "No."

Charlie leaned close, trying to ask rather than beg the young slugger. "Just... trust me on this. If we can get through the next half-inning before the storm hits the field, we'll get a win by default, you see? And hey – bonus – *you'll* be the hero."

As Javier considered this, Windy took a wild swing at the first pitch and bounced it right to the Steelhead second baseman. Windy ran with all he had, but there was no beating the easy throw to first. Charlie felt like he was walking waist-deep through a recurring nightmare and looked up at his future superstar.

His request hung there for a seemingly endless moment, until finally, Javier grinned at him. "You're crazy, Coach. But I like that."

Thunder boomed anew. A light mist began to fall as the wind whipped across the field. Charlie nodded, awestruck by the sacrifice, as Javier turned to make his way to the box.

"AND HERE WE go again, folks, as Javier Coronado comes to the plate with a walk and a solo homer in his back pocket." Francesca and Margaret both leaned forward in their seats.

Javier straightened as the first pitch crossed the plate, his bat resting on his shoulder.

"Strike one!"

Francesca's baseball intuition told her something about this moment was odd. "And Coronado takes one down the middle. If you're a pitcher in this league, you've gotta know that you're not going to be getting many free ones like that when facing Javier Coronado, isn't that right, Maggie?"

Margaret rubbed her chin, the gears in her head clearly in motion. "Indeed... and you know, Francesca, the way he's not even stepping out of the batter's box suggests to me that perhaps there's something more at play here?"

Francesca wasn't sure what her new co-host was angling at. She looked down to find Javier laughing as he took another strike in similar fashion. The entire scenario was odd, but...

"You don't mean to suggest that he's striking out *on purpose?"* Could that be right? The best hitter in the league taking a pass in the biggest spot of the season's biggest game?

Margaret placed a hand on Francesca's arm as she leaned toward the microphone. "Francesca, I will say that, even though he's no longer in this game, there's a reason Gray Whalen has long managed this team." She pointed out to left field. "And this would be *classic* Whalen."

Francesca was astounded to see the presumed-dead form of Steve-O-Canth the Coelacanth lurking behind the wall. *No way.*

Meanwhile, Javier turned and began walking toward the dugout with a shrug as the third pitch sailed over the plate.

"STRIKE THREE!" CAME the call.

Charlie gave his slugger a pat on the back as he passed. Javier shrugged and threw him an easy smile as he ditched his batting gear for his hat and glove. He would be replacing the The Franchise at first base – possibly forever.

Pushing down the anxiety attached to this idea, Charlie gave the team a few supportive claps as they took the field. They ducked their heads low as the wind blew mist in their eyes. Beside him, the bullpen phone rang. He answered it on the first ring. "Well, that went well."

"I'd say so," Whalen replied, his voice wary but less stressed. "Now we just gotta let the kid do his thing and wait for the hurricane to ruin our picnic."

On the field, the Coelacanths dug into their positions. The home plate umpire pointed to Hayden and squatted down behind J.J. The rain was coming down in distinct droplets at this point, layers upon layers of them, but apparently not quite enough to arrest the game action. The stands were now a fascinating array of umbrellas and rain slickers, creating a patchwork effect that stirred like a sentient quilt made of vinyl. It was a stunning glimpse of sleeping loyalty; Franchise or not, these were Coelacanth fans, and they were here to watch this baseball game.

The call for strike one was grunted following the pop of J.J.'s glove.

Charlie adjusted the phone handset under his chin. "So, you don't feel bad wasting at-bats and playing the odds like this?"

The poncho-clad fans clapped and shouted as Hayden delivered strike two.

Whalen scoffed a distorted breath into the phone. "Charlie, if you wanna be a successful manager, you've gotta learn to take the wins when you can. Even the lousy ones."

Charlie had certainly been on the wrong end of his fair share of lousy games. But the skipper was right – if the lousy losses still counted, so too could the lousy wins.

He watched as Hayden wound up and delivered.

"STRIKE THREE!" CAME the call. It was reassuring and, oddly enough, becoming shockingly familiar.

Francesca wasted no time grabbing her cue. "Whoa-*ho,* he got him swinging! And it looks like Cape Haddock's own, Hurricane Chandler, has whipped up a maelstrom of strikes!"

Margaret pointed at her and mimed clapping. Visibly delighted, she punched the mute button.

"'Hurricane Chandler!' That's so good – you are *so good!"*

Francesca whipped off one side of her headphones and beamed. "I know, right? It just came to me!"

"It's the t-shirt idea I've been looking for!" Margaret whooped in delight, and Francesca had to sheepishly wave at her to quiet down.

A crack of thunder rattled the booth, and suddenly the door behind them was thrown open. Like a defeated movie monster back from the dead, Dip Lockerbie entered, out of breath and completely drenched. The brim of his soggy fedora drooped over his brow.

Margaret's expression morphed from one of surprise to one of disgust. "Lockerbie! Where the hell have you been?"

Dip's mouth drooped open in surprise at the icy greeting. He gestured over his shoulder. "I was in the parking lot!" He said the words as though the explanation was the most obvious thing in the world. "What'd I miss!?"

Francesca was no longer in the mood. "Pretty much everything – now shut up, we're on the air!"

Dip turned to Margaret, sputtering. She shrugged, taking her hand off the mute as he began to protest. Ever professional, he clammed up as the mics went hot.

Francesca swiveled back to the booth window, locked into the moment as though she'd never left.

"So, with two strikes and the wrath of Hurricane Hannah blasting HerbCo Field, Chandler winds up and delivers..."

"Strike three!"

"And Chandler punches him out looking!" From the corner of her eye, she thought she caught a glimpse of Margaret squeezing her hand into a fist in celebration. The batters switched out below, their grey road uniforms blurry as the sky finally unleashed the torrent it had been threatening the past three days. "And not a minute too soon as the rain begins to really come down."

She turned to see Dip make a haphazard grab at Margaret's microphone. The owner slapped his hand away and rolled her chair to block his path.

It was enjoyable to observe, but Francesca could not let herself be distracted at this critical juncture. "So, with two down and one to go, Hayden Chandler has yet to give up a hit in this outing."

"That's absolutely right, Francesca," said Margaret, as Dip paced furiously behind her. "And even an *almost*-no-hitter would surely be celebrated like V-J Day here in Cape Haddock."

Francesca could feel Dip's entire personality clench behind them. "You're not supposed to say the words!" he hissed beneath his breath, mindful of the open feed.

Margaret turned to him, clearly disgusted that he would weigh in at all. She stared him down while maintaining perfect microphone control. "Hurricane Chandler's Near No-Hitter" *does* have a pleasant ring to it, doesn't it, Francesca?"

"Sounds like a t-shirt to me, Maggie!" Francesca said with glee as Dip slapped his forehead. "But first, he needs to face the heart of the Steelhead lineup: Bart Chaney Sr."

AS THE CAPE Haddock boos fell upon the field alongside the rain, it occurred to Charlie that the worst part of baseball was the inevitability of it. Sure, there were exceptions – such as when the greatest player to ever don your team's uniform went down with a possibly career-ending injury – but most of the time, you could count on the ace of a staff giving you at least seven innings, or your third baseman making that borderline snag of a hot grounder along the line. Likewise, it was inevitable that the lineup was eventually going to roll over for both sides, and both teams would be fated into dealing with their opponent's best hitter. No matter how dire the circumstances, all it took was that batting order moving from the bottom to the top to keep the patient on the table breathing.

Perhaps he'd become inured to the feeling of dread that blossomed during such moments for the Tumbleweeds but watching it while helpless in the dugout brought the immediacy of the sensation back to the front of his mind. All he could do was watch, buried in the shadow of the dugout overhang, where hopefully no one could see him, as the season's great nemesis dug in.

"Bart Chaney Sr..."

Beside him, the dugout phone rang. He answered it immediately, his eyes riveted to the batter's box.

Whalen's tinny voice wasted no time on pleasantries as it hollered across the line. "Bart Chaney Sr.!"

Hayden's pace had been steady, the momentum just right. He wound up and threw heat. Chaney Sr. gauged the velocity but didn't swing.

"Strike one!"

Whalen's voice crackled across the line, slow and leading. "Now, if I'm not mistaken, your magic numbers say the goon can't hit soft-away, right?"

Charlie held the phone out and stared at it in shock for a moment. Was he *actually* being quoted his own statistics by the man who recently used one of his data binders as an ashtray? "Uh, yeah, that's right. Skip. I can't believe you remembered that!"

"Well, it was only last week – I'm not *that* old. Are you gonna go give our kid a reminder, or what?"

"What?" If it hadn't been for the tell-tale sound of a lighter being flicked, Charlie would have had serious doubts about who he was talking to. Was his mother having him secret-shopped by a hired soundalike? He would not put it past her. "What are you talking about, he's been cruising since the second batter. Wouldn't that be messing with his psychology or something? Crushing his vibe? Ebbing his flow?"

Hayden delivered again. Chaney Sr.'s swing was majestic, as was the shot he launched into deep left field. It soared, outpacing the very sound of it being smacked by the bat. The ball reached its apex and hung so high that there could be no guess made regarding its final landing spot… until it finally hooked back and landed in the stands, just beyond the foul line. The ballpark thrummed with anxious mutterings.

Charlie stared at the spot where the ball had landed, and without tearing his eyes from the carnage, muttered into the handset, "Skip, I gotta call you back."

"Yep."

Charlie hung up the phone and rushed to the dugout steps to signal for a time-out. The home plate umpire gave him the nod and he hustled out to the mound.

There, an anxious Hayden rolled the ball around in his hand and stared at him. His expression transmitted an annoyance Charlie had never felt before. It was as if he had stepped into the middle of an open-heart surgery wearing dirty gardening gloves.

"Hey, buddy…" Hayden frowned at this, so Charlie hurried into his counseling. "I don't want to interrupt, but I just wanted to talk about this next pitch. See, Chaney Sr. can't hit–"

"Soft-away."

Charlie was nothing less than astonished. "That's right."

"I know." Hayden stared at him as though Charlie's very existence was unnecessary. "You told me that last time. 79 and 7. I've got it."

Charlie broke into a huge grin. He nodded at the young man. "Yeah, you do. You've got it, Hayden."

Hayden shrugged. "Great. Now get the hell out of here, I wanna finish this inning."

"Fair enough!" Charlie threw him an awkward half-salute and trotted back to the dugout. He could not help but feel heartened by the entire situation; finally, he had been heard.

As if to echo this thought, the crowd rose as one, doing their best to make themselves heard over the weather.

MARGARET SHIFTED IN her seat, her jaw clenched. Francesca didn't blame her – the tension was anxiety-inducing, even in their broadcasting aerie. She did her best to relay the feeling with a measured, serious tone.

"And so, after a brief confab on the mound, Chandler comes set." The tension was ratcheted up by a hush falling over the storm-blasted crowd, coinciding with a brief window in which the wind died down to nothing.

Hayden stared into J.J.'s mitt.

"Chandler winds up... delivers..."

HAYDEN'S PITCH SPUN with a torque that could change tires and bore leads into the earth for future oil wells. It was not especially fast, and Chaney Sr. clearly had the measure of it. He grunted, throwing the maximum amount of strength into the motion, knowing it would find its target and destroy. The world fell into slow motion as Chaney Sr. muscled the barrel of the bat across the plate. It seemed to Charlie that the mass of Louisville Slugger pulled space toward it, a planet of ash with a gravity from which no pitch could escape.

Except for this one.

The final moment of execution expired, and as it did, the ball spun itself into escape velocity. As though falling off a table, it broke free of its trajectory and careened downward, to the far edge of the black. Charlie was sure that a slow-motion replay would show the pitch jumping out an inch or two as the gust of Chaney Sr.'s swing passed it. But pass it did.

"Strike three!" The umpire's fist punched through the heavy ozone.

HerbCo Field exploded, swept up in the release brought about by the vanquishing. Charlie roared with excitement in the dugout. Even Hayden punched his glove, the tendons in his neck taut as he howled a curse that was swallowed up by the din of the crowd.

Charlie gathered his composure as the Coelacanths ran into the dugout. He grabbed the nearest bat and ran up the dugout steps. J.J. was taking his time returning from the batter's box.

The catcher gave Charlie a questioning look as he approached. "It's nice to see you finally leaning into being a bat boy."

"Don't even take your pads off," said Charlie, handing him the bat. "Just stand in the batter's box and do *nothing.* "

"That's all I've ever wanted to hear."

J.J. tossed his glove and mask aside and walked back to the box as Charlie ran up to the home plate umpire. "Hey, Ump – can we get a game called here, or what? We're playing on top of a submarine!"

"Nuh-uh," said the umpire, grimacing as the raindrops splattered against the metal bars of his facemask, misting his head. "I've got strict league orders: nothing short of aliens beaming down ends this thing!"

Charlie couldn't believe it – the field was turning into marshland beneath their feet and visibility barely extended into the outfield. What good was a televised broadcast if the cameras couldn't see anything, let alone the umpires?

"Come on," he tried again, knowing this would be his last opportunity to make a plea. "Can't you at least *confer?* "

As though the machinations of the universe had decided to throw their support behind this request, thunder cracked overhead, and an empty paper cup, carried by the hurricane winds, smacked against the umpire's chest protector. The cup had clattered away harmlessly but being assaulted by refuse seemed to be all the argument needed for the umpiring crew to have a discussion. The home plate umpire blinked, his mouth a grim line betraying nothing. Finally, he turned to his fellow judges, huddled deep within their windbreakers on opposite sides of the infield and raised a hand in summons. They both began trotting in to meet with their crew chief.

J.J. stood on the first base side of the box, swinging his bat in an exaggerated golfing gesture. He looked bored. And soaked to the bone; his pants were sodden and drooped down the side of his legs, bound to him only by the straps of his shin guards.

Charlie could never be sure if aliens were involved with what happened next or not. All he knew was that while it may not have been extraterrestrial in a *technical* sense, the solution he had been seeking did in fact come from the skies.

No sooner had the umpires convened, than a bolt of lightning ignited the park, striking the enormous HerbCo fishing pole in center field in an explosion of sparks and neon tubing. The flux of electricity sprinted down the advertisement as though the prop was a 60-foot antenna built explicitly for such a purpose. The current overloaded the HerbCo Fishing Supplies signage below into further bursts of discharge that soon lit the nylon of the four playoff participation pennants ablaze. The flags were consumed in mere moments, but fortunately the rain was now so dense that the rest of the fire was quickly extinguished.

As the deafening crack of thunder that had accompanied the bolt faded away, everyone uncovered their faces to stare out at the blackened display and wall. The lightning had carried all the way to the ground, leaving nothing but twisted metal and a smoking crater. It had charred the grass of the berm in a pattern that ran down the slope and into center field, where the electric scarring spidered out in all directions.

In the awestruck silence that followed, the home plate umpire raised his fist without taking his eyes off the damage. "That's game!"

The remaining crowd cheered along with the suddenly victorious Coelacanths, who mobbed Hayden on the mound, lifting him onto their shoulders and carrying him off the field in a triumph the long-suffering Coelacanths would not soon forget.

As the field and stands began clearing out to make room for the foul weather, a brief spurt of fireworks shot out over the smoking wreckage of the fishing pole, courtesy of Terry Arnold, hot dog man and Stadium Operations Coordinator. The sparks fizzled quickly in the rain, but those present to witness the show found it to be as festive as any they had ever seen.

CHAPTER 20
Swing Away

TWENTY MINUTES LATER, the Coelacanths were still celebrating their victory. They spoke loudly and slapped each other on the back with a joy that had not been seen at their end of the tunnel for weeks. There was a dogpiling of Hayden – carefully administered in order to protect his million-dollar arm – and the young fireballer looked genuinely proud. They shook hands with The Franchise, who sat amongst them in a wheelchair that had been scrounged up from one of the utility closets. His lower leg was poorly bandaged and braced in imitation of a how-to video found on Blither, another successful medical procedure completed by Dr. Internet.

The team hooted even louder as Charlie broke through the mob and shook the hand of his temporary player. "Hey there, Number 9, how are you holding up?"

To his surprise, The Franchise grinned and gestured to the propped-up leg. "Well, it's not how I wanted to spend my holiday, but at least I didn't blow by hand off with a firecracker or anything. That's gotta count for something."

Charlie felt his stomach plunge as the gravity of the injury broke through the haze of victory. "I am so sorry this happened to you. If there's anything I can do–"

The Franchise held up a hand. "It's all right, Charlie. It was my fault for pushing like that. An old man like me oughta know better by now. Besides, if anything, I should be thanking you."

This was unexpected, and Charlie could not fathom how it could be so. He wondered if painkillers had been recently administered. "What for?"

"You know, for staying in there and taking all the big swings when you were getting your tower buzzed."

Charlie considered this, bewildered. That he was a known quantity to a future Hall of Famer was a turn he would not have expected. That he should be *thanked* for being a garbage player was not to be believed. There must have been some mistake.

The first baseman could clearly read the skepticism on the coach's face. He continued, "When I was just coming up, I always read about you and those hit-by-pitches in the paper."

The familiar hand of mortification brushed Charlie's spine. "Oh yeah. That." It had been too busy a week to reflect much on his playing legacy, but who better to quantify it than one of the all-time greats. "You know, I never hit anything with those lean-in swings."

"But you tried, didn't you?"

Charlie nodded. "Tried and failed."

The Franchise shrugged. "I suppose that depends on your measure of success. I mean, everyone always talked about your dad's talent, right? There's no accounting for that – my dad wanted it, but I was the one who got it. Who knows why it happens that way? But no matter what the numbers said, you hung in there and took a pounding for your team, grinding it out in his shadow for all those years. That changed *my* outlook anyway. I used to think, 'Man, if this guy can take that kind of abuse just to advance some runners in Single-A, I don't have much of an excuse for anything.' That showed me what real work looked like. What it would take to get where I wanted to be. So, thank you."

Charlie was speechless. His years of bruised ribs and being the target of relentless jeering suddenly seemed to ache a little less in his memory.

The Franchise leaned forward in his chair and slapped him on the arm. "And hey, you might not have had your dad's game, but you seemed just fine managing your way to a crazy W tonight, huh?" He shook his head and laughed at the thought of what had just transpired on the diamond. "You know, even though I was only down here for one game, I'm glad it was this one, Skipper. Electric stuff, man. Goddamn."

Charlie smiled in disbelief at the compliment but was relieved that the real skipper chose that moment to enter the clubhouse; it was a reality check he could appreciate.

Whalen's mascot outfit was soaked, hanging off of him like a sad, plush shroud. The Coelacanths cheered at the sight of him and the old man looked pleased with himself as he tossed them the soaked fish-head mask. Roaring in approval, the team held up the hideous, decapitated head of Steve-O-Canth the Coelacanth in triumph and began chanting, *"Skip-per! Skip-per! Skip-per!"*

Whalen chuckled and motioned for them to calm down. The gesture had almost succeeded, when Margaret walked in behind him and they erupted all over again. *"Mag-gie! Mag-gie! Mag-gie!"*

Margaret played at being embarrassed but allowed them a few rounds before raising her hands. "As much as I love the sound of you chanting my name like a squadron of baboons, we've been instructed by the Mayor to evacuate the premises before the landfall. This means you'll have to pat each other's bottoms elsewhere." The team groaned in disappointment. She ignored them and peered into their victory huddle. "Where's the one with the phone?"

Windy managed to squeeze his way out of the throng and make his way over to her. She pulled him close and in a low voice, asked, "Did you get it?"

The second baseman grinned and pulled his phone from his back pocket. Charlie and Whalen crowded around him along with the rest of the team as Windy pulled up his Blither account and pressed play on an embedded video.

The scene was brief but memorable: the players from both teams trudged to change places amidst the cloudburst, the rain caught in the glare of the ballpark lights and seen lashing every which way in the wind. There was Charlie, making his plea to the home plate umpire. There went the umpire to meet with his crew members. And then—

"Oh!" came the collective cry as the background of the tableau suddenly exploded in fluorescence and the bolt of lightning annihilated the ludicrous fishing pole advertisement. Laughter and expletives filled the locker room as Windy looped the six seconds

again and again. Charlie thought that his mother looked as happy as he had ever seen her.

"Well done!" she said, giving Windy a nod of approval. "I trust you know what to do with this?"

"Already put it everywhere, ma'am," he said, beaming with pride. "Next stop: Viral City!"

"Excellent," she said, chuckling. This important box now ticked, she then turned to the team and found Javier. She pointed at him. "Javier? My office, please." The team *Ooooohed* like petulant students as Javier smiled and dutifully followed her into Whalen's former office. Margaret poked her head out, exasperated. "Oh, stop it – you know he's the only one of you worth the shirt his name is stitched onto. Now, be good!" She closed the door in their faces.

Charlie turned to Whalen. "What's that all about, Skip?"

Whalen gave him a sad smile. "I suppose you wouldn't know what that looks like, huh?"

"What's that?"

"Getting called up."

Charlie's eyes went wide. *Of course.* "The Big Club?"

"Mmm," Whalen nodded. Though he'd always known it was bound to happen for the slugger, Charlie was left reeling by how quickly it had come about.

"The rumor is," Whalen continued, "they're gonna be needing a first baseman up there because of some bonehead trying to score from first..." He turned to The Franchise's wheelchair with a grin. "How you doing, kid?"

"Hanging in there, Skip, thanks."

Whalen shook his head and tsked. "Scoring from first – what the hell were you thinking, Number 9?"

The Franchise laughed. "You know I can't help myself, Skip. I still feel 20 years old inside."

"Well, I hope your inner child's happy, because you're out for at least the rest of the season."

"If not for keeps. EMS is bringing a wagon around now to take me to Cape Haddock General – I told them I could just get a ride, but the bosses back home insisted."

Windy joined them, throwing an arm over Charlie's shoulder. "Hey, Coach, Number 9 said we can ride with him to the hospital in the back of the ambulance – how cool is that?"

"*Is* that the best use of an ambulance during a hurricane?" said Charlie.

Windy ignored him and shouted at his teammates, "I call the flashlight if we get one!"

In the distance, the sound of a siren squawking filtered into the clubhouse and the team cheered. Windy wheeled The Franchise around in his chair, pushing him out the door as he waved goodbye.

J.J. turned to Hayden. "Hey, rookie – get our bags, huh?"

Hayden looked at him in disbelief. "But I almost threw a no-no!"

J.J. shrugged. "Yeah – *almost.* And you're still a rookie."

As the players filed out of the clubhouse, hooting with excitement, Francesca entered from the tunnel, looking after them, her portable recorder in hand. "I take it we're doing interviews tomorrow?" She spotted Charlie, who quickly joined her, leaving Whalen to observe from afar with a knowing look.

"Hi!" she said, throwing her arms around him. "Congratulations!"

Charlie felt his face go red but tried to maintain his composure as she squeezed him. "Thank you, thank you," he said. "Really, the hurricane did most of the work."

"Get out of here!" she said, looking up at him with what he considered to be the loveliest smile to ever float in his direction. "That was all you, calling shots like a big wheel, confabbing Hayden into that last strikeout – you did great!"

Charlie's eyes darted over to Whalen, who quickly looked away, suddenly interested in the acoustic ceiling tiles. He turned back to her. "Yeah, well, sometimes you just play the numbers the right way, I guess. How was the show?"

Her eyes went wide. "You have no idea – it was *insane.*"

"Yeah?" He looked around the room. "Hey, where's Dip anyway?"

"Dip-who?" she said, laughing. "I think that guy's circling a storm drain somewhere in the parking lot."

Charlie had no idea what she was talking about. "Is that broadcast slang?"

She laughed and looked over his shoulder at the sight of Javier exiting Whalen's office, chatting with Margaret. "I'll tell you all about it when I'm off duty, okay?"

"Deal," he said. "Hey–" She looked at him as he struggled to find the right words. "Uh… do you maybe…"

"…want to find a cozy basement for two and ride this thing out together until FEMA gets here?"

"Oh!" he said, surprised to find that she could read minds. "Well… yeah. What do you think?"

She smiled at him. "We should do that – if you want to, of course."

"That sounds nice," he said, nodding.

"If the generator at my building is still working, we can stream *Murder, She Wrotes* all night long," she said, shooting him a devilish look.

From behind them came the familiar sound of Margaret's phone. She patted Javier on the arm and moved to a corner to take the call.

Whalen shook Javier's hand. "Congrats, kid, I knew it'd only be a matter of time."

Javier beamed a winning smile at the manager. "Gracias, Skipper. I am very happy I get to play. And you made me better, so I thank you." He leaned over and gave the old man a crushing bear hug.

Whalen laughed, somewhat embarrassed about being so easily manhandled. "It's no trouble, kid. It's why I'm here." He patted the giant on the stomach. "You just lay off the lobsters, huh? No more than two a day, right?"

"Okay, Skipper, I'll be good." Javier turned to Charlie, who held his arms open, ready for an embrace. Javier gave him a look, and then laughed, slapping him on the back. "You're a good man, Coach."

Charlie looked up at him in awe. "You really mean that, Javi? You think I'm a good baseball coach?"

Javier tilted his head. "I said what I said, Coach."

"Oh. Well, wh–"

"No English, Coach." Javier winked at him.

Whalen slapped the first baseman on the back. "Hey buddy, if you hurry, you can still make the ambulance with the other fellas – maybe get yourself an I.V. bag to snack on, huh?" He turned and gestured to Francesca, whose digital recorder was poised for action.

"Oh, and you should tell the radio lady your good news on the way out, huh? I hear she's looking for a scoop."

Javier grinned and made his way toward the door, his head bent low to hear her familiar broadcaster's voice pummel him with questions. Charlie watched them both with admiration. He had never been around so many people who were receiving the good things they deserved.

Whalen slapped him on the back, shaking him from his thoughts. He turned to find the skipper grinning at him beneath his mustache. "Hey, way to get yourself run out of the game, again, Skipper. Trying to rally the team, huh?"

"Huh?" Whalen ran a hand over his whiskers, his expression cagey. "Oh yeah, I guess that'd be a classic me-move, wouldn't it."

"You did it because The Network was here, huh?"

The old man smiled. "Now Charlie, you know I would never admit to such a thing even if it was true."

"Uh-huh."

"But, I gotta admit, it's a lot nicer watching some other guy be on the hook for everything." He placed a hand on Charlie's shoulder. "You did a good job tonight, Charlie. Jackie would've been proud."

Charlie thought he couldn't possibly feel more satisfied, until a voice came from behind them. "I agree."

They turned to find Margaret tucking her phone into her pocket. She approached Charlie, her eyes alive with something he had rarely seen. Was it… pride?

"Congratulations, my boy," she said, placing a hand on the side of his face. "You're a *winner.*"

Charlie smiled as she embraced him – in itself, a stunning turn of events. "Thanks, Mom."

Francesca appeared, beside them, waving the recorder. "You'll never believe the story I just got – Maggie, it's incredible!"

"Oh, I know," Margaret said, waving her off. *"I'm* quite a gal, Javier's about to become a star, the Coelacanths are playing winning baseball – everyone's talking about it." She turned to Charlie. "But now the bad news. For tacky egomaniacs, I mean."

"Oh?"

"That was the harbor master calling. Apparently, the yacht is no more."

Charlie's eyes went wide. "What? Really?"

Margaret shrugged. "Apparently ludicrous displays of misspent wealth and hurricanes don't mix. Who knew?"

"You didn't have it taken out of here before the landfall?" Charlie's mind flashed to his Starting Lineup action figures, now most likely bobbing along the surface of international waters.

"Who's got time to move a boat around?" Margaret scoffed. "Besides, it's insured, so good riddance to bad wreckage. But I'm afraid it means we'll have to hole up in the fishing supply factory and sleep on the minnow buckets tonight."

"Oh, um... actually, Mom, we were thinking..." Charlie gestured to Francesca.

Margaret raised an eyebrow. *"Yes...?"*

"Well, we were thinking we might... seek shelter. Together. You know, uh... shelter for two?"

"I see," Margaret sighed. "And so, it begins, eh?"

Francesca smiled. "Safety first, Margaret."

"Mmm. Of course, dear."

Whalen cleared his throat. "Uh, Maggie, why don't you come back to our place? The basement's finished, and Iris has about nine years' worth of canned preserves down there, so we'll be all right."

Margaret gave each of them a calculating look. She sighed, apparently satisfied that there were no shenanigans at work. "Well, I... I suppose, if you wouldn't mind–"

"Not at all," said Whalen. "I can think of nothing better than locking myself in a cellar with my boss and my wife... and my kids... and my grandkids..." He sighed, suddenly looking very tired. He lit a cigarette and began shrugging into his raincoat.

Charlie patted him on the shoulder. "Stay alive, Skipper – we're off the skid now! And we need our mascot."

Whalen gave him a pointed look. "I'm sure I have no idea what you're talking about. You two be safe out there."

There were state of emergency hugs exchanged and hoods and slickers snapped into place. As Charlie and Francesca passed through the clubhouse door to face the storm outside, Charlie heard his mother and Whalen speaking in the way old friends do.

"Fair enough," she said. "I guess we all need to swing wild sometimes."

"Nah," said Whalen, his words slipping through the door as it was about to click shut. "That's the heart of the plate right there, Maggie. The heart of the plate."

EPILOGUE
Home Opener

HOPE TRAINS IN spring eternal, but eventually the winds change and the snow sticks to the ground no more. The bleachers fill with the buzzing of the faithful, eager to witness the beginning stages of what just might be the season they've been waiting for. Tentative first steps are taken with an eye toward extra steps in the fall and a chance for the fretting and feting of a rollercoaster summer's worth of games to climax in victory and celebration.

Opening Day in Cape Haddock saw the shoots of such hopes spring forth from the small houses, bars, and restaurants of the harbor. Hats were donned and barbeques lit in a tribal ceremony as sacred as any in the world. They came from all over the county to spend a day watching the future unfold in their small stadium, the newly renamed Coelacanth Park. It was just as welcoming and lovely as ever, minus one large advertisement for a company that now existed only in memory. A press release over the winter had stated that the Tinley Estate would be paying for repairs and that the four immolated playoff appearance flags would not be replaced until an actual postseason series had been won.

Margaret Conroy had arrived at dawn to oversee the final preparations for what was projected to be a strong season from the Dead Fish. Refreshed from a March spent at the seaside cottage she now occupied, she made a few mental notes for her forthcoming broadcast with the new Voice of the Coelacanths, Francesca Moretti, who had arrived moments later with her son.

The couple's apartment was within walking distance, and the chill of the ocean air had invigorated each step taken, pushing them along their path. Charlie Conroy had talked the entire way, anxious to confer with the team's new coaches over the recent scouting reports, and soon bid Francesca a tender farewell before darting across the street to catch up with Gray Whalen. The manager, now entering what was rumored to be his final year at the helm, could be heard grunting a salutation as his jaw ground away at a piece of gum that may or may not be laced with nicotine.

The sherbet light of dawn crept over the upper deck of Coelacanth Park as they all passed through the stately Courtyard of Champions just beyond the turnstiles. There, each offered a glance of tribute at the recently unveiled, larger-than-life statue of Coelacanth legend, Jackie Conroy. The figure had been cut from a piece of the finest white, Italian marble, procured from a mysterious domestic source at next to no cost.

And in a game in which no outcome is guaranteed, all of them could not help but wonder if this might be their year.

Acknowledgments

MY THANKS FOR the feedback and support of the following class acts: Michael McKeogh, Meghan Keedy, Francis Michael Keedy, Rick Kunzi, Carmen Molina, Marsha Harman, Matthew Isler, Jose Garcia, Matt Fletcher, Paul Edward Pasulka, Michael Johnson, the McCartan family, Erla Erlingsdóttir, Tryggvi Edwald, the Naoroz family, Dad, Mom, Ed, Sis, my grandfathers, and Elín Edwald.